一次戰勝新制多益

TOEIC

必考聽力

答案＋解析

SINAGONG 多益專門小組、趙康壽、金廷根（Julia Kim）／著

林芳如／譯

要學就學必考的！

NEW TOEIC LISTENING

答案＋解析

類型分析 1　以人為主的照片
Unit 01　出現單人的照片

Step 3　實戰演練

1. (A) He is reaching for a file.（正確答案）

▶ 這是出現單人上半身的照片，所以主詞都一樣。聆聽時要以動詞和名詞為主。這是為了拿資料夾而伸手的動作，動詞（reach）的動作和名詞（file）都跟照片描述一致，所以是正確答案。

(B) He is opening a cabinet.（錯誤答案）

▶ 照片中沒有出現動詞的動作（open）和名詞（cabinet），所以是錯誤答案。

(C) He is sealing an envelope.（錯誤答案）

▶ 照片中沒有出現動詞（seal）和名詞（envelope），所以是錯誤答案。

(D) He is drawing a picture.（錯誤答案）

▶ 照片中沒有出現動詞（draw）和名詞（picture），所以是錯誤答案。

翻譯
(A) 他伸手拿資料夾。
(B) 他正在開櫃子。
(C) 他正在封信封。
(D) 他正在畫畫。

單字　reach for 伸手拿～　open 打開　seal 密封　envelope 信封　draw 畫畫

解答　(A)

2. (A) The bicycle is leaning against the railing.（錯誤答案）

▶ 照片中沒有出現動詞（lean against）的動作和名（railing），所以是錯誤答案。

(B) The bicycle is being pulled by the woman.（正確答案）

▶ 這是單人照片，所以聆聽時要專注於人物的行為。腳踏車正被女子牽著走，所以是正確答案。

(C) A woman is resting on a beach.（錯誤答案）

▶ 照片中沒有出現動詞的動作（rest），所以是錯誤答案。

(D) A woman is chaining a bicycle to a tree.（錯誤答案）

▶ 照片中沒有出現動詞（chain）的動作，也沒有出現名詞（tree），所以是錯誤答案。

翻譯
(A) 腳踏車靠在欄杆上。
(B) 腳踏車正被女子牽著走。
(C) 女子正在海邊休息。
(D) 女子正在用鎖鏈把腳踏車綁在樹上。

單字　lean against 倚靠～　railing 欄杆　pull 拉，牽　rest 休息　beach 海邊　chain 鎖鏈

解答　(B)

Unit 02　出現雙人的照片

Step 3　實戰演練

1. (A) They are sitting next to a brick wall.（錯誤答案）

▶ 照片中人物的相同動作表達錯誤的錯誤答案。

(B) They are entering a building.（錯誤答案）

▶ 共同動作（enter）的描述有誤，照片中沒有出現名詞（building），所以是錯誤答案。

(C) They are working on a construction project.（正確答案）

▶ 主詞是複數，所以這題問的是照片中的人物的共同動作。兩名人物的共同動作是工作，所以是正確答案。

(D) They are lifting a ladder.（錯誤答案）

▶ 共同動作（lift）的描寫有誤，照片中沒有出現名詞（ladder），所以是錯誤答案。

翻譯
(A) 他們正坐在磚牆的旁邊。
(B) 他們正在進入大樓。
(C) 他們正在施工。
(D) 他們正在舉梯子。

單字　next to 在～旁邊　brick wall 磚牆　enter 進入～　lift 舉起～　ladder 梯子

解答　(C)

2. (A) A man is putting on his glasses.（錯誤答案）

▶ 男子的動作（put on）描寫有誤，照片中沒有出現名詞（glasses），所以是錯誤答案。

(B) Customers are buying books.（錯誤答案）

▶ 客人的共同動作（buy）描寫有誤，照片中沒有出現名詞（books），所以是錯誤答案。

(C) A salesperson is assisting a customer.（正確答案）

▶ 主詞是一名店員，所以要專心聆聽店員的動作。店員正在協助客人，收下信用卡幫忙結帳，所以是正確答案。

(D) A woman is handing a business card to the man.（錯誤答案）

▶ 照片中沒有出現名詞（business card），所以是錯

誤答案。business card 意即名片，並非結帳用的信用卡，請勿搞混。

翻譯
(A) 男子正在戴眼鏡。
(B) 客人正在買書。
(C) 店員正在協助客人。
(D) 女子正在遞名片給男子。

單字　put on 穿戴～　glasses 眼鏡　salesperson 店員　assist 協助　hand 傳遞～　business card 名片

解答　(C)

Review Test

1. 出現單人的照片

(A) She is writing on a notepad. （錯誤答案）
▶ 照片中沒有出現動詞（write）和名詞（notepad），所以是錯誤答案。

(B) She is pushing a file cabinet. （錯誤答案）
▶ 動詞（push）的描述不恰當，所以是錯誤答案。

(C) She is turning off a light. （錯誤答案）
▶ 照片中沒有出現動詞（turn off）和名詞（light），所以是錯誤答案。

(D) She is typing on a keyboard. （正確答案）
▶ 看到只有露出上半身的單人照片時，要專心聆聽動詞和名詞。照片中的女子正在用鍵盤打字，所以是正確答案。

翻譯
(A) 她正在寫記事本。
(B) 她正在推檔案櫃。
(C) 她正在關燈。
(D) 她正在用鍵盤打字。

單字　notepad 記事本，筆記本　push 推　file cabinet 檔案櫃　turn off 關　light 燈　type 打字

解答　(D)

2. 出現單人的照片

(A) She is washing her hands. （正確答案）
▶ 畫面是女子正在洗手，動詞和名詞的描述都跟照片一致，所以是正確答案。

(B) She is serving a meal. （錯誤答案）
▶ 照片中沒有出現動詞（serve）和名詞（meal），所以是錯誤答案。

(C) She is sweeping the floor. （錯誤答案）
▶ 照片中沒有出現動詞（sweep）和名詞（floor），

所以是錯誤答案。

(D) She is cleaning the counter. （錯誤答案）
▶ 照片中沒有出現動詞（clean）和名詞（counter），所以是錯誤答案。

翻譯
(A) 她正在洗手。
(B) 她正在上菜。
(C) 她正在掃地。
(D) 她正在清理櫃臺。

單字　wash 洗滌　serve 上菜　meal 餐點　sweep 打掃　clean 清理

解答　(A)

3. 出現雙人的照片

(A) They are photocopying a document. （錯誤答案）
▶ 照片中沒有出現動詞（photocopy）和名詞（document），所以是錯誤答案。

(B) They are pointing at the board. （錯誤答案）
▶ 照片中沒有出現名詞（board），所以是錯誤答案。

(C) They are looking at a computer monitor. （正確答案）
▶ 主詞是 they，所以要專心聆聽共同動作和名詞。照片中兩人的共同動作是看螢幕，所以是正確答案。

(D) They are sitting at the table. （錯誤答案）
▶ 只有男子坐著，這不是共同的動作，所以是錯誤答案。

翻譯
(A) 他們正在影印文件。
(B) 他們正指著黑板。
(C) 他們正在看電腦螢幕。
(D) 他們坐在桌子前。

單字　photocopy 影印　document 文件　point 指　board 黑板　look at 看～

解答　(C)

4. 出現雙人以上的照片

(A) Some people are holding a meeting. （錯誤答案）
▶ 照片中沒有開會的場面（hold a meeting），所以是錯誤答案。

(B) Technicians are working in a laboratory. （正確答案）
▶ 主詞是複數，所以要專心聆聽共同的動作。照片中人物的共通點是都在工作，所以是正確答案。

(C) Microscopes are being removed from the room. （錯誤答案）

▶ 照片中沒有動詞的動作（are being removed），所以是錯誤答案。

(D) Supplies are being unloaded from a cart.（錯誤答案）

▶ 動詞的動作（are being unloaded）描寫有誤，照片中沒有出現名詞（cart），所以是錯誤答案。

翻譯
(A) 某些人正在開會。
(B) 技術人員正在實驗室工作。
(C) 顯微鏡正被移到房外。
(D) 物品正從推車上被卸下來。

單字　hold a meeting 開會　technician 技術人員　laboratory 實驗室　microscope 顯微鏡　remove 移除　supply 物品　unload 卸下

解答　**(B)**

聽寫訓練

Unit 1 出現單人的照片

1. (A) He is reaching for a file.
(B) He is opening a cabinet.
(C) He is sealing an envelope.
(D) He is drawing a picture.

2. (A) The bicycle is leaning against the railing.
(B) The bicycle is being pulled by the woman.
(C) A woman is resting on a beach.
(D) A woman is chaining a bicycle to a tree.

Unit 2 出現雙人以上的照片

1. (A) They are sitting next to a brick wall.
(B) They are entering a building.
(C) They are working on a construction project.
(D) They are lifting a ladder.

2. (A) A man is putting on his glasses.
(B) Customers are buying books.
(C) A salesperson is assisting a customer.
(D) A woman is handing a business card to the man.

Review Test

1. (A) She is writing on a notepad.
(B) She is pushing a file cabinet.
(C) She is turning off a light.
(D) She is typing on a keyboard.

2. (A) She is washing her hands.
(B) She is serving a meal.
(C) She is sweeping the floor.
(D) She is cleaning the counter.

3. (A) They are photocopying a document.
(B) They are pointing at the board.
(C) They are looking at a computer monitor.
(D) They are sitting at the table.

4. (A) Some people are holding a meeting.
(B) Technicians are working in a laboratory.
(C) Microscopes are being removed from the room.
(D) Supplies are being unloaded from a cart.

類型分析2　以事物、風景與人物、背景為主的照片
Unit 03　事物、風景照片

Step 3 實戰演練

1. (A) All of the balcony doors have been left open.（錯誤答案）

▶ 聽到 all、both 的選項大部分都是錯誤答案。

(B) There are stairs in the building's entrance.（錯誤答案）

▶ 聽到照片中沒有的名詞（stairs）的選項是錯誤答案。

(C) The house is covered with flowers.（錯誤答案）

▶ 聽到照片中沒有的名詞（flowers）的選項是錯誤答案。

(D) There are different styles of railings on the balcony.（正確答案）

▶ 每層的欄杆外觀都不一樣，所以是正確答案。

翻譯
(A) 所有陽臺的門都是開著的。
(B) 大樓入口有階梯。
(C) 房子被花朵所覆蓋。
(D) 陽臺欄杆的樣式不一樣。

單字　entrance 入口　stair 階梯　be covered with 以～覆蓋的　railing 欄杆

解答　**(D)**

2. (A) Boats are sailing along the shoreline.（錯誤答案）

▶ 動詞的動作（sail）描寫有誤，出現了照片中沒有的名詞（shoreline），所以是錯誤答案。

(B) Buildings overlook a harbor.（正確答案）

▶ 照片畫面是建築群俯瞰著港口，所以是正確答案。

(C) Rocks have been piled along the shore. （錯誤答案）

▶ 出現了照片中沒有的名詞（rock），所以是錯誤答案。

(D) A bridge extends across the water. （錯誤答案）

▶ 出現了照片中沒有的名詞（bridge），所以是錯誤答案。

翻譯
(A) 船隻沿著海岸線航行。
(B) 建築群俯瞰著港口。
(C) 石頭沿著海岸堆積。
(D) 橋梁橫跨水面。

單字 shoreline 海岸線 harbor 港口 be piled 堆積 extend 延伸

解答 **(B)**

Unit 04　人物、背景照片

Step 3 實戰演練

1. (A) They are boarding up the windows of a house. （錯誤答案）

▶ 聽到照片中沒有的動詞（board）和名詞（window）的選項是錯誤答案。

(B) One of the men is painting a balcony. （錯誤答案）

▶ 聽到照片中沒有的動詞（paint）和名詞（balcony）的選項是錯誤答案。

(C) Ladders of different heights are propped against the wall. （正確答案）

▶ 兩個高度不一樣的梯子靠在牆上，所以是正確答案。

(D) There is a patio between the buildings. （錯誤答案）

▶ 聽到照片中沒有的名詞（patio）的選項是錯誤答案。

翻譯
(A) 他們正在用木板封住屋子的窗戶。
(B) 其中一個男子正在油漆陽臺。
(C) 高度不同的梯子靠在牆上。
(D) 建築物之間有個露臺。

單字 board up 用木板封住 height 高度 prop 倚靠，支撐 patio 露臺，天井

解答 **(C)**

2. (A) A sail is being raised above a boat. （錯誤答案）

▶ 聽到照片中沒有的名詞（sail），是錯誤答案。

(B) A passenger is waving a flag in the air. （錯誤答案）

▶ 聽到照片中沒有的動詞（wave）和名詞（flag），是錯誤答案。

(C) Some people are riding on boats. （正確答案）

▶ 某些人正在坐船，所以是正確答案。

(D) Water is splashing onto a boat deck. （錯誤答案）

▶ 這是無法從照片得知答案的抽象句子，是錯誤答案。

翻譯
(A) 船帆正升到船隻上方。
(B) 乘客正在空中揮旗。
(C) 某些人正在坐船。
(D) 水花正濺到船的甲板上。

單字 sail 帆 raise 上升 wave 搖動 flag 旗子 in the air 在空中 splash 濺 boat deck 船隻甲板

解答 **(C)**

Review Test

1. 事物、風景照片

(A) Rugs have been rolled up against the wall. （錯誤答案）

▶ 地毯的位置（wall）有誤。

(B) A sofa is next to a cabinet. （錯誤答案）

▶ 聽到照片中沒有的名詞（cabinet）的選項是錯誤答案。

(C) The blinds are drawn. （錯誤答案）

▶ 聽到照片中沒有的名詞（blinds）的選項是錯誤答案。

(D) The lamps have been turned on. （正確答案）

▶ 這是描寫事物和背景的題目，所以要先確認事物的中心，再確認周遭環境。後方牆面上的兩盞燈開著，所以是正確答案。

翻譯
(A) 地毯被捲起來靠在牆上。
(B) 沙發在櫃子的旁邊。
(C) 百葉窗拉起來了。
(D) 燈開著。

單字 rug 地毯 roll up 捲起 blind 百葉窗 draw 拉（窗簾） lamp 燈 turn on 開

解答 **(D)**

2. 人物、背景照片

(A) A man is being handed a piece of artwork. （錯誤答案）

▶ 若聽到照片中沒有的動詞（hand），便是錯誤答案。「hand」當動詞時意即「傳遞」。

(B) Pottery has been arranged on the shelf. （正確答案）

▶ 陶器被陳列在架上，所以是正確答案。若聽到東西被陳列、擺出來的照片描述有display、lay out、arrange等詞彙的話，便是正確答案。

(C) A man is walking into a workshop.（錯誤答案）

▶ 若聽到照片中沒有的動詞（walk），便是錯誤答案。

(D) A picture has been hung on the wall.（錯誤答案）

▶ 聽到照片中沒有的名詞（picture）的選項是錯誤答案。

翻譯
(A) 男子正在收下一件藝術品。
(B) 陶器被陳列在架上。
(C) 男子正走進工作坊。
(D) 畫像被掛在牆上。

單字　hand 傳遞　artwork 藝術品　pottery 陶器　arrange 整理，布置　workshop 工作坊　hang 掛

解答　**(B)**

3. 人物、背景照片

(A) People have gathered for an outdoor event.（錯誤答案）

▶ 這是無法從照片得知答案的抽象句子，是錯誤答案。我們無法得知人們是不是為了活動而聚集。

(B) Workers are installing glass doors.（錯誤答案）

▶ 聽到照片中沒有的動詞（install），是錯誤答案。

(C) There are tools in the middle of the hallway.（錯誤答案）

▶ 聽到照片中沒有的名詞（tools），是錯誤答案。

(D) Windows extend from the floor to the ceiling.（正確答案）

▶ 須一邊聆聽，一邊確認人們的共同動作和周遭事物。窗戶從地板延伸到天花板，所以是正確答案。

翻譯
(A) 大家為了戶外活動聚在一起。
(B) 工人正在安裝玻璃門。
(C) 走廊中央有些工具。
(D) 窗戶從地板延伸到天花板。

單字　gather 聚集　outdoor event 戶外活動　install 安裝　glass 玻璃　tool 工具　hallway 走廊　extend 延伸　ceiling 天花板

解答　**(D)**

4. 事物、風景照片

(A) Chairs are arranged on either side of a sofa.（錯誤答案）

▶ 椅子不在沙發兩邊，而是在桌子的兩邊。東西的位置描述錯誤。

(B) Some cups are being removed from a table.（錯誤答案）

▶ 如果聽到照片中沒有的名詞（cups），便是錯誤答案。而且，這是沒有人物的照片，所以這裡的被動句是錯誤答案。

(C) There are many books on the table.（錯誤答案）

▶ 書不在桌子上，而是在書櫃中，所以是錯誤答案。

(D) Light fixtures are suspended above the table.（正確答案）

▶ 看到事物和風景照片時，要先確認事物的中央，再確認周遭環境。燈具被掛在桌子上方的天花板，所以是正確答案。

翻譯
(A) 椅子被擺放在沙發的兩邊。
(B) 有些杯子正從桌上被清掉。
(C) 桌上有很多本書。
(D) 燈具被掛在桌子上方。

單字　arrange 布置　on either side of 在～的兩邊　remove 移除　light fixture 燈具　suspend 懸掛

解答　**(D)**

聽寫訓練

Unit 3　事物、風景照片

1. (A) All of the balcony doors have been left open.

(B) There are stairs in the building's entrance.

(C) The house is covered with flowers.

(D) There are different styles of railings on the balcony.

2. (A) Boats are sailing along the shoreline.

(B) Buildings overlook a harbor.

(C) Rocks have been piled along the shore.

(D) A bridge extends across the water.

Unit 4　人物、背景照片

1. (A) They are boarding up the windows of a house.

(B) One of the men is painting a balcony.

(C) Ladders of different heights are propped against the wall.

(D) There is a patio between the buildings.

2. (A) A sail is being raised above a boat.

(B) A passenger is waving a flag in the air.

(C) Some people are riding on boats.

(D) Water is splashing onto a boat deck.

Review Test

1. (A) Rugs have been rolled up against the wall.

(B) A sofa is next to a cabinet.

(C) The blinds are drawn.

(D) The lamps have been turned on.

2. (A) A man is being handed a piece of artwork.

(B) Pottery has been arranged on the shelf.

(C) A man is walking into a workshop.

(D) A picture has been hung on the wall.

3. (A) People have gathered for an outdoor event.

(B) Workers are installing glass doors.

(C) There are tools in the middle of the hallway.

(D) Windows extend from the floor to the ceiling.

4. (A) Chairs are arranged on either side of a sofa.

(B) Some cups are being removed from a table.

(C) There are many books on the table.

(D) Light fixtures are suspended above the table.

PART 1 FINAL TEST - 1

1. 出現單人的照片

(A) He is wearing a wristwatch.（錯誤答案）

▶ 聽到照片中沒有的動詞（wear）和名詞（wristwatch）的選項是錯誤答案。

(B) He is carrying some boxes.（正確答案）

▶ 描述搬東西的畫面時，這句可以用來當作正確答案。男子正在搬箱子，所以是正確答案。

(C) He is fixing a printer.（錯誤答案）

▶ 聽到照片中沒有的動詞（fix）和名詞（printer）的選項是錯誤答案。

(D) He is working at a desk.（錯誤答案）

▶ 只聽到動詞（work）的話，可能會誤以為這句是答案，但是這裡的地點／位置描述有誤。

翻譯

(A) 他正在戴手錶。

(B) 他正在搬箱子。

(C) 他正在修印表機。

(D) 他正在桌前工作。

單字 wristwatch 手錶 carry 搬運，運送 fix 修理

解答 **(B)**

2. 出現雙人以上的照片

(A) Some flower arrangements are being delivered.（錯誤答案）

▶ 照片中沒有出現動詞（deliver）的動作，所以是錯誤答案。

(B) A woman is resting her chin on her hand.（錯誤答案）

▶ 照片中沒有出現女子的動作（rest her chin），所以是錯誤答案。

(C) Sofas are positioned in the lobby.（正確答案）

▶ 沙發被放在大廳，所以是正確答案。

(D) A man is reading a newspaper.（錯誤答案）

▶ 照片中沒有出現男子的動作（read），所以是錯誤答案。

翻譯

(A) 某些插花正在被運送。

(B) 女子正在用手托下巴。

(C) 沙發被放在大廳。

(D) 男子正在看報紙。

單字 flower arrangement 插花 deliver 寄送 rest one's chin 托下巴 position 把～放在～

解答 **(C)**

3. 背景照片

(A) The plant is on the table.（錯誤答案）

▶ 植物被擺在角落，而不是桌上。

(B) The picture is hanging on the wall.（正確答案）

▶ 牆上掛了一幅畫，所以是正確答案。

(C) The pottery is situated in the corner.（錯誤答案）

▶ 聽到照片中沒有的名詞（pottery），是錯誤答案。

(D) The sofas are facing the same directions.（錯誤答案）

▶ 沙發面向的方向不一樣（different directions），所以是錯誤答案。

翻譯

(A) 植物在桌上。

(B) 畫像被掛在牆上。

(C) 陶器位於角落。

(D) 沙發都面向同一個方向。

單字 plant 植物 hang 掛 pottery 陶器 situate 使位於～ corner 角落 direction 方向

解答 **(B)**

4. 出現單人的照片

(A) She is walking through a doorway.（錯誤答案）

▶ 動詞的動作（walk）描寫有誤，照片中沒有出現名詞（doorway），所以是錯誤答案。

(B) She is getting into a vehicle.（正確答案）

▶ 女子正在上車，所以是正確答案。若聽到搭乘交通運輸工具的照片描述有boarding、getting on、getting into、stepping into / onto等詞彙的話，便是正確答案。

(C) She is riding on a bus.（錯誤答案）

▶ 聽到照片中沒有出現的名詞（bus），是錯誤答案。

(D) She is pushing a cart.（錯誤答案）

▶ 動詞的動作（push）描寫有誤，出現了照片中沒有的名詞（cart），所以是錯誤答案。

翻譯
(A) 她正在走過門口。
(B) 她正在上車。
(C) 她正在搭公車。
(D) 她正在推推車。

單字　doorway 門口　vehicle 車輛　ride 搭乘～　push 推

解答　**(B)**

5. 人物、背景照片

(A) A man is sweeping a balcony.（錯誤答案）

▶ 聽到照片中沒有出現的名詞（balcony），是錯誤答案。

(B) A man is leaning against the tree.（錯誤答案）

▶ 男子的動作（lean）和照片上的不一樣。

(C) Some leaves are being gathered into a pile.（正確答案）

▶ 被掃在一起的樹葉變成一堆（pile），所以是正確答案。leaves、gathered、pile是正確答案的關鍵字，該句的意思和「A man is gathering some leaves into a pile.（男子正在將樹葉掃成一堆。）」一樣。

(D) The plants are beside the entrance.（錯誤答案）

▶ 出現了照片中沒有的名詞（entrance），所以是錯誤答案。

翻譯
(A) 男子正在掃陽臺。
(B) 男子正靠在樹上。
(C) 有些樹葉被掃成一堆。
(D) 植物在入口的旁邊。

單字　sweep 清掃　lean against 倚靠～　leaf 樹葉　gather 聚集　pile 堆　beside 在～旁邊

解答　**(C)**

6. 事物、風景照片

(A) The wall is being painted.（錯誤答案）

▶ 照片中沒有人物，所以這裡使用被動句是錯的。而且，動詞的動作（paint）描述也有誤。

(B) Vegetables are piled on the chair.（錯誤答案）

▶ 聽到照片中沒有出現的名詞（vegetables），是錯誤答案。

(C) The table is set with fruit.（錯誤答案）

▶ 出現了照片中沒有的名詞（fruit），所以是錯誤答案。

(D) There is a plant on the table.（正確答案）

▶ 桌上有一個放了花的花瓶，所以是正確答案。

翻譯
(A) 牆正在被油漆。
(B) 蔬菜被堆在椅子上。
(C) 桌上擺了水果。
(D) 桌上有一盆植物。

單字　wall 牆　paint 油漆　vegetable 蔬菜　pile 堆疊

解答　**(D)**

PART 1 FINAL TEST - 2

1. 出現單人的照片

(A) He is opening a door .（錯誤答案）

▶ 照片中沒有出現動詞的動作（open），所以是錯誤答案。

(B) He is working in the garden.（錯誤答案）

▶ 出現了照片中沒有的名詞（garden），所以是錯誤答案。

(C) A door is being repaired by a worker.（正確答案）

▶ 這是出現單人的照片，所以要專心聆聽人物的行為。男子正在修門，所以是正確答案。

(D) The door is being closed by the wind.（錯誤答案）

▶ 只看照片時無法確認是否屬實的句子，不會是正確答案。

翻譯
(A) 他正在開門。
(B) 他正在花園裡工作。
(C) 門正在被工人修理。
(D) 門因為風的緣故關上了。

單字　garden 花園　repair 修理　close 關閉

解答　**(C)**

2. 人物、背景照片

(A) The woman is taking a book from the cabinet.（錯誤答案）

▶ 聽到照片中沒有出現的名詞（cabinet），是錯誤答案。女子是從書櫃中取出書，而不是從櫥櫃中取出。

(B) Books have been organized on a table. （錯誤答案）

▶ 聽到照片中沒有出現的名詞（table），是錯誤答案。

(C) The woman is packing a book into a box. （錯誤答案）

▶ 聽到照片中沒有出現的動詞（pack）的動作和名詞（box），所以是錯誤答案。

(D) The shelves are full of books. （正確答案）

▶ 架子上都是書，所以是正確答案。

翻譯
(A) 女子正從櫥櫃中取出一本書。
(B) 書本被整理好放在桌上。
(C) 女子正在把書放到箱子裡。
(D) 架上都是書。

單字　take 拿　organize 整理　be full of 充滿

解答　(D)

3. 事物、風景照片

(A) A boat is passing under a bridge. （錯誤答案）

▶ 聽到照片中沒有出現的名詞（boat），是錯誤答案。

(B) The scenery is reflected on the surface of the water. （正確答案）

▶ 若是水、鏡子映照出某物的照片描述包含reflect的話，便是正確答案。

(C) The bridge is being constructed out of stone. （錯誤答案）

▶ 沒有正在建設的人，所以這裡的被動句是錯誤答案。

(D) Some trees are being planted along the riverbank. （錯誤答案）

▶ 沒有正在種樹的人，所以是錯誤答案。

翻譯
(A) 船正經過橋下。
(B) 風景映照在水面上。
(C) 正在用石頭造橋。
(D) 正沿著河堤種樹。

單字　pass 經過　bridge 橋　scenery 風景　surface 表面　plant 種植　riverbank 河堤

解答　(B)

4. 出現雙人的照片

(A) He is pouring water into a glass. （正確答案）

▶ 男子正往杯子裡倒水，所以是正確答案。

(B) She is setting a bowl on a table. （錯誤答案）

▶ 動詞的動作（set）描述有誤。

(C) He is putting away some plates. （錯誤答案）

▶ 動詞的動作（put away）描述有誤。

(D) She is drinking from a cup. （錯誤答案）

▶ 動詞的動作（drink）描述有誤。

翻譯
(A) 他正往杯子裡倒水。
(B) 她正在桌子上擺碗。
(C) 他正在收一些盤子。
(D) 她正在用杯子喝東西。

單字　pour 倒，灌　bowl 碗　put away 收好　plate 盤子

解答　(A)

5. 人物、背景照片

(A) A man is unloading a box. （錯誤答案）

▶ 動詞的動作（unload）描述有誤，改成load才對。

(B) There's a fence around a car. （錯誤答案）

▶ 出現了照片中沒有的名詞（fence），是錯誤答案。

(C) A man is climbing up the steps. （錯誤答案）

▶ 聽到照片中沒有出現的名詞（steps），是錯誤答案。

(D) The back of the truck is open. （正確答案）

▶ 這是出現單人的照片，所以要多注意人物的行為和周遭事物。卡車的後門開著，所以是正確答案。

翻譯
(A) 男子正在卸下箱子。
(B) 車子周遭有柵欄。
(C) 男子正在爬樓梯。
(D) 卡車的後門開著。

單字　unload 卸下　fence 柵欄　climb 攀爬　step 樓梯　open 打開的

解答　(D)

6. 事物、風景照片

(A) They are standing on the road. （錯誤答案）

▶ 照片中沒有人物，所以是錯誤答案。

(B) Some people are buying bicycles on the street. （錯誤答案）

▶ 出現了照片中沒有的動詞（buy），所以是錯誤答案。

(C) Some bicycles are parked near trees. （正確答案）

▶ 腳踏車停在樹前，所以是正確答案。

(D) There are some bicycles on display in the window. （錯誤答案）

▶ 聽到照片中沒有出現的名詞（window），是錯誤答案。腳踏車是被停在那裡，而不是在櫥窗裡展示。

翻譯
(A) 他們站在路上。
(B) 有些人在街上買腳踏車。
(C) 有些腳踏車被停在樹的附近。
(D) 櫥窗裡展示了一些腳踏車。

單字　buy 買　on display 展示中

解答　**(C)**

PART 2

類型分析 3　疑問詞問句①
Unit 05　Who問句

Step 3 實戰演練

1. Who is the director's new secretary?
(A) Betty Rodman. （正確答案）
▶ 提到人名的正確答案。

(B) Sending an email. （錯誤答案）
▶ 這是適合回覆What問句的錯誤答案。

(C) On the table. （錯誤答案）
▶ 這是適合回覆Where問句的錯誤答案。

翻譯
經理的新祕書是誰？
(A) 貝蒂・羅德曼。
(B) 寄電子郵件。
(C) 在桌上。

單字　director 董事，主任，經理　secretary 祕書

解答　**(A)**

2. Who's coming to the staff meeting tomorrow?
(A) In the museum. （錯誤答案）
▶ 這是適合回覆Where問句的錯誤答案。

(B) The design team. （正確答案）
▶ 在Who問句的答覆中聽到「部門名稱」的話，便是正確答案。

(C) Yes, 2 o'clock. （錯誤答案）
▶ 在疑問詞問句的答覆中，Yes選項是錯誤答案。

翻譯
誰明天會來員工會議？
(A) 在博物館。
(B) 設計組。
(C) 對，兩點。

單字　staff 員工　meeting 會議　museum 博物館

解答　**(B)**

3. Who decorated the restaurant?
(A) The supervisor. （正確答案）
▶ 在Who問句的答覆中聽到「職責名稱」的話，便是正確答案。

(B) No, she didn't.（錯誤答案）
▶ 在疑問詞問句的答覆中，No選項是錯誤答案。

(C) In red.（錯誤答案）
▶ 這是適合回覆「Which color~?」的錯誤答案。

翻譯
誰裝飾了餐廳？
(A) 上司。
(B) 不，她沒有。
(C) 用紅色。

單字　decorate 裝飾，布置　supervisor 上司，管理者

解答　(A)

4. Who should I call to reserve a meeting room?
(A) It's in the cinema.（錯誤答案）
▶ 這是適合回覆Where問句的錯誤答案。

(B) Ask Andy to do it.（正確答案）
▶ 叫對方找別人的迴避型正確答案。

(C) For dinner.（錯誤答案）
▶ 這是適合回覆Why問句的錯誤答案。

翻譯
我應該打給誰預約會議室？
(A) 在電影院裡。
(B) 叫安迪去做。
(C) 為了晚餐。

單字　reserve 預約　meeting room 會議室　cinema 電影院

解答　(B)

Unit 06　When、Where問句

Step 3　實戰演練

1. When's the concert?
(A) A singer.（錯誤答案）
▶ 這是適合回覆Who問句的錯誤答案。

(B) On Friday.（正確答案）
▶ 提到星期的正確答案。

(C) Five tickets.（錯誤答案）
▶ 跟題目中的單字有直接關聯的（concert - tickets）選項幾乎都是錯誤答案。

翻譯
演唱會在什麼時候？
(A) 一個歌手。
(B) 在星期五。
(C) 五張票。

單字　concert 演唱會　ticket 門票

解答　(B)

2. Where should I send this package?
(A) By international mail.（錯誤答案）
▶ 這是適合回覆How問句的錯誤答案。

(B) After 5 p.m.（錯誤答案）
▶ 這是適合回覆When問句的錯誤答案。

(C) To the new office.（正確答案）
▶ 出現「介系詞＋地點」的正確答案。

翻譯
我應該要把這個包裹寄到哪？
(A) 用國際郵件。
(B) 下午五點之後。
(C) 寄到新辦公室。

單字　package 包裹　international mail 國際郵件

解答　(C)

3. When was Mr. Erickson supposed to arrive?
(A) Near the park.（錯誤答案）
▶ 這是適合回覆Where問句的錯誤答案。

(B) Yes, she drove.（錯誤答案）
▶ 在疑問詞問句的答覆中，Yes選項是錯誤答案。

(C) At one o'clock.（正確答案）
▶ 出現「介系詞＋時間點」的正確答案。

翻譯
艾瑞克森先生本來預計在幾點到？
(A) 在公園附近。
(B) 對，她開車。
(C) 一點整。

單字　be supposed to 預計～，應該～

解答　(C)

4. Where should I file the report?
(A) Anytime before you leave.（錯誤答案）
▶ 這是適合回覆When問句的錯誤答案。

(B) On the second bookshelf.（正確答案）
▶ 出現「介系詞＋地點」的正確答案。

(C) I heard from him.（錯誤答案）
▶ 與題目中的單字有關聯的（report - heard）選項是造成混淆的錯誤答案。

翻譯
我應該將報告歸檔到哪裡？
(A) 在你離開前隨時都可以。
(B) 第二個書櫃。
(C) 我從他那裡聽說了。

單字　file（整理文件之後）把～歸檔　bookshelf 書櫃

解答　**(B)**

Review Test

1. When 問句

When will the merger take place?
(A) Many companies.（錯誤答案）
▶ 與題目中的單字有關聯的（merger - companies）
　選項是造成混淆的錯誤答案。

(B) Sometime in November.（正確答案）
▶ 出現「in＋月份」的正確答案。

(C) No, not yet.（錯誤答案）
▶ 在疑問詞問句的答覆中，Yes、No選項是錯誤答案。

翻譯
什麼時候會合併？
(A) 很多公司。
(B) 十一月的時候。
(C) 不，還沒。

單字　merger 合併　take place 發生，舉行　sometime 某個時候

解答　**(B)**

2. Who 問句

Who's designing the new office building?
(A) The Merch architectural firm.（正確答案）
▶ 提及公司名稱的正確答案。

(B) In the storage area.（錯誤答案）
▶ 這是適合回覆Where問句的錯誤答案。

(C) A new design.（錯誤答案）
▶ 聽到相似單字（designing - design）的錯誤答案。

翻譯
誰在設計新辦公大樓？
(A) 墨奇建築公司。
(B) 在儲藏區。
(C) 新設計。

單字　design 設計　architectural firm 建築公司　storage area 儲藏區

解答　**(A)**

3. Where 問句

Where did Nelson leave the agenda?
(A) By two o'clock.（錯誤答案）
▶ 這是適合回覆When問句的錯誤答案。

(B) On the desk.（正確答案）
▶ 出現「on＋地點」的正確答案。

(C) From Chicago.（錯誤答案）
▶ 這是適合表示出身地的選項，為錯誤答案。

翻譯
奈爾森把議程放在哪裡？
(A) 到兩點為止。
(B) 在桌上。
(C) 來自芝加哥。

單字　leave 留下，丟下　agenda 議程

解答　**(B)**

4. Who 問句

Who will be giving the presentation?
(A) In the meeting room.（錯誤答案）
▶ 這是適合回覆Where問句的錯誤答案。

(B) Ms. Miranda.（正確答案）
▶ 提到人名的正確答案。

(C) In December.（錯誤答案）
▶ 這是適合回覆When問句的錯誤答案。

翻譯
誰會做簡報？
(A) 在會議室。
(B) 米蘭達女士。
(C) 十二月。

單字　give a presentation 做簡報

解答　**(B)**

5. Where 問句

Where did you put my book?
(A) A bestseller.（錯誤答案）
▶ 與題目中的單字有關聯的（book - bestseller）選項是造成混淆的錯誤答案。

(B) Isn't it on the chair?（正確答案）
▶ 反問句型是正確答案。

(C) I will leave soon. （錯誤答案）
▶ 這是適合回覆When問句的錯誤答案。

翻譯
你把我的書放到哪了？
(A) 暢銷書。
(B) 不是在椅子上嗎？
(C) 我就快離開了。

單字 put 放，擺 bestseller 暢銷書

解答 (B)

6. When 問句

When do we get reimbursed for travel expenses?
(A) One thousand dollars. （錯誤答案）
▶ 這是適合回覆How much問句的錯誤答案。

(B) The prices are fixed. （錯誤答案）
▶ 用有關聯的詞彙（expense - price）誘導考生選為正確答案的錯誤答案。

(C) After the form's been approved.（正確答案）
▶ 出現「after＋主詞＋動詞」時間副詞子句的正確答案。

翻譯
我們何時可以拿回出差的報銷款項？
(A) 一千美元。
(B) 價格是固定的。
(C) 等表格經過批准後。

單字 get reimbursed 報銷，得到補償 travel expense 出差費 approve 批准

解答 (C)

7. Who 問句

Who's in charge of the order?
(A) We only need an invoice. （錯誤答案）
▶ 用有關聯的詞彙（charge - invoice）誘導考生選為正確答案的錯誤答案。

(B) Mr. Park is.（正確答案）
▶ 提到人名的正確答案。

(C) It's too expensive. （錯誤答案）
▶ 用有關聯的詞彙（charge - expensive）誘導考生選為正確答案的錯誤答案。

翻譯
誰負責訂購？
(A) 我們只需要一張發票。
(B) 帕克先生。

(C) 太貴了。

單字 be in charge of 負責～ order 訂購，訂單 invoice 發票，發貨單

解答 (B)

8. Where 問句

Where should I put those bills?
(A) He isn't. （錯誤答案）
▶ 提到第三人稱的錯誤答案。

(B) Not until tomorrow. （錯誤答案）
▶ 這是適合回覆When問句的錯誤答案。

(C) Ask the accountant. （正確答案）
▶ 回覆「不知道」，迴避型的選項是正確答案。

翻譯
我應該把這些帳單放到哪裡？
(A) 他沒有。
(B) 明天之前不行。
(C) 去問會計。

單字 bill 帳單，請款單 accountant 會計師

解答 (C)

9. Who 問句

Who's responsible for this department?
(A) Julie is.（正確答案）
▶ 提到人名的正確答案。

(B) This apartment is too small. （錯誤答案）
▶ 聽到相似單字（department - apartment）的錯誤答案。

(C) He responded to it. （錯誤答案）
▶ 聽到相似單字（responsible - responded）的錯誤答案。

翻譯
誰負責這個部門？
(A) 茱莉。
(B) 這間公寓太小了。
(C) 他回覆了那個。

單字 responsible 負責的，有責任感的 department 部門

解答 (A)

10. When 問句

When does the new manager begin the project?
(A) For a week. （錯誤答案）
▶ 這是適合回覆How long問句的錯誤答案。

(B) In the meeting room.（錯誤答案）

▶ 這是適合回覆Where問句的錯誤答案。

(C) On August 30.（正確答案）

▶ 出現「on＋日期」的正確答案。

翻譯

新經理是何時開始進行這個案子的？
(A) 一個禮拜。
(B) 在會議室。
(C) 在八月三十日。

單字　begin 開始，著手　meeting room 會議室

解答　(C)

聽寫訓練

Unit 5　Who 問句

1. Who is the director's new secretary?
(A) Betty Rodman.
(B) Sending an email.
(C) On the table.

2. Who's coming to the staff meeting tomorrow?
(A) In the museum.
(B) The design team.
(C) Yes, 2 o'clock.

3. Who decorated the restaurant?
(A) The supervisor.
(B) No, she didn't.
(C) In red.

4. Who should I call to reserve a meeting room?
(A) It's in the cinema.
(B) Ask Andy to do it.
(C) For dinner.

Unit 6　When、Where 問句

1. When's the concert?
(A) A singer.
(B) On Friday.
(C) Five tickets.

2. Where should I send this package?
(A) By international mail.

(B) After 5 p.m.
(C) To the new office.

3. When was Mr. Erickson supposed to arrive?
(A) Near the park.
(B) Yes, she drove.
(C) At one o'clock.

4. Where should I file the report?
(A) Anytime before you leave.
(B) On the second bookshelf.
(C) I heard from him.

Review Test

1. When will the merger take place?
(A) Many companies.
(B) Sometime in November.
(C) No, not yet.

2. Who's designing the new office building?
(A) The Merch architectural firm.
(B) In the storage area.
(C) A new design.

3. Where did Nelson leave the agenda?
(A) By two o'clock.
(B) On the desk.
(C) From Chicago.

4. Who will be giving the presentation?
(A) In the meeting room.
(B) Ms. Miranda.
(C) In December.

5. Where did you put my book?
(A) A bestseller.
(B) Isn't it on the chair?
(C) I will leave soon.

6. When do we get reimbursed for travel expenses?
(A) One thousand dollars.
(B) The prices are fixed.
(C) After the form's been approved.

7. Who's in charge of the order?

(A) We only need an invoice.

(B) Mr. Park is.

(C) It's too expensive.

8. Where should I put those bills?

(A) He isn't.

(B) Not until tomorrow.

(C) Ask the accountant.

9. Who's responsible for this department?

(A) Julie is.

(B) This apartment is too small.

(C) He responded to it.

10. When does the new manager begin the project?

(A) For a week.

(B) In the meeting room.

(C) On August 30.

類型分析 4　疑問詞問句②
Unit 07　What、Which問句

Step 3 實戰演練

1. What's the registration deadline?

(A) It's a week from today.（正確答案）

▶ 用時間點回覆「What~ deadline?」的正確答案。

(B) One of the staff members finished it.（錯誤答案）

▶ 與題目中的單字有關聯的（deadline - finished）選項是可能會造成混淆的錯誤答案。

(C) On the corner of Bull Street.（錯誤答案）

▶ 這是適合回覆Where問句的錯誤答案。

翻譯

報名截止日是何時？

(A) 今天起一個禮拜後。

(B) 其中一個員工完成了。

(C) 在公牛街的轉角。

單字　**registration** 報名，登記　**deadline** 期限，截止時間　**corner** 角落，街角

解答　**(A)**

2. Which copier should I use?

(A) Only a hundred copies.（錯誤答案）

▶ 聽到相似單字的（copier - copies）的選項是錯誤答案。

(B) The manager has arrived.（錯誤答案）

▶ 提到第三者的錯誤答案。

(C) The one next to the door.（正確答案）

▶ 在「Which＋名詞」問句的答覆中，包含the one詞彙的選項是正確答案。

翻譯

我應該使用哪台影印機？

(A) 只有一百份複本。

(B) 經理到了。

(C) 門旁邊那一台。

單字　**copier** 影印機　**copy** 影印　**next to** 在～的旁邊

解答　**(C)**

3. What's the registration fee?

(A) By next Monday.（錯誤答案）

▶ 這是適合回覆When問句的錯誤答案。

(B) Cash will be better.（錯誤答案）

▶ 與題目中的單字有關聯的（fee - cash）選項幾乎都是錯誤答案。

(C) It's $20.（正確答案）

▶ 可以將「What's~ fee?」理解為How much問句，所以聽到金額的選項即為正確答案。

翻譯

報名費多少？

(A) 到下個星期一為止。

(B) 現金比較好。

(C) 二十美元。

單字　**registration fee** 報名費　**cash** 現金

解答　**(C)**

4. What are the papers in the meeting room?

(A) In the first hall beside the stairs.（錯誤答案）

▶ 這是適合回覆Where問句的錯誤答案。

(B) A report I'm writing.（正確答案）

▶ 準確告知是什麼東西的正確答案。

(C) I will bring it later.（錯誤答案）

▶ 這是適合回覆When問句的錯誤答案。

翻譯

會議室裡的文件是什麼？

(A) 在樓梯旁的第一條走廊。

(B) 我正在寫的報告。

(C) 我等一下會帶去。

單字　paper 紙張，文件　hall 大廳，走廊　stair 樓梯

解答　**(B)**

Unit 08　How、Why問句

Step 3 實戰演練

1. How long will it take us to get downtown?
(A) I'm leaving town.（錯誤答案）
▶ 聽到相似單字（downtown - town）的錯誤答案。

(B) It starts at seven p.m.（錯誤答案）
▶ 這是適合回覆When問句的錯誤答案。

(C) About an hour.（正確答案）
▶ 提到所需時間的正確答案。

翻譯
我們到市中心要多久？
(A) 我要出城。
(B) 晚上七點開始。
(C) 大概一個小時。

單字　downtown 市區，往市區　leave 離開

解答　**(C)**

2. Why is there a billing delay?
(A) The computer system is down.（正確答案）
▶ 提到問題點的正確答案（省略了because）。

(B) I just saw it today.（錯誤答案）
▶ 與題目中的單字有關聯的（delay - today）錯誤答案。

(C) Yes, I guess so.（錯誤答案）
▶ 在疑問詞問句的答覆中，Yes選項是錯誤答案。

翻譯
為什麼帳單有延誤？
(A) 電腦系統故障了。
(B) 我今天才看到。
(C) 對，我想是吧。

單字　delay 延誤，耽擱　be down 故障的

解答　**(A)**

3. How can I make sure Bruce gets this form?
(A) I will pay for it.（錯誤答案）
▶ 這是適合回覆Who問句的錯誤答案。

(B) Put it in his mailbox.（正確答案）
▶ 用命令句給予指示的正確答案。

(C) He is in New York now.（錯誤答案）
▶ 這是適合回覆Where問句的錯誤答案。

翻譯
我該怎麼確保布魯斯會收到這個表格？
(A) 我會付錢。
(B) 放到他的信箱裡。
(C) 他現在在紐約。

單字　form 表格　pay 付款，結帳　mailbox 信箱

解答　**(B)**

4. Why is the J&J office closing?
(A) Because they're remodeling.（正確答案）
▶ 提到原因的正確答案。

(B) The restaurant is open.（錯誤答案）
▶ 聽到相反詞（closing - open）的選項幾乎都是錯誤答案。

(C) The new staff.（錯誤答案）
▶ 這是適合回覆Who問句的錯誤答案。

翻譯
為什麼J&J辦公室關了？
(A) 因為他們正在翻修。
(B) 餐廳開業了。
(C) 新員工。

單字　close 關門　remodel 翻修，改造

解答　**(A)**

Review Test

1. What 問句

What kind of experience do you have in sales?
(A) I sold furniture for five years.（正確答案）
▶ 提到工作經歷期間的正確答案。

(B) The sale will begin next weekend.（錯誤答案）
▶ 與題目中的單字有關聯（sales - sale）的錯誤答案。

(C) It will be a good experience.（錯誤答案）
▶ 聽到同個單字（experience）的選項幾乎都是錯誤答案。

翻譯
你有什麼種類的銷售經驗？
(A) 我賣了五年的家具。
(B) 折扣將在下週末開始。
(C) 這將會是很好的經驗。

單字　furniture 家具　begin 開始　experience 經驗，經歷

解答　(A)

2. Why 問句

Why was the seminar rescheduled?
(A) On Tuesday.（錯誤答案）
▶ 這是適合回覆When問句的錯誤答案。

(B) Whenever you like.（錯誤答案）
▶ 這是適合回覆When問句的錯誤答案。

(C) Because the manager hasn't arrived yet.（正確答案）
▶ 提到because的正確答案。

翻譯
為什麼研討會的日程改了？
(A) 在星期二。
(B) 任何你有空的時間。
(C) 因為經理還沒抵達。

單字　reschedule 變更日程　whenever 無論何時

解答　(C)

3. What 問句

What's your manager's name?
(A) For three years now.（錯誤答案）
▶ 這是適合回覆How long問句的錯誤答案。

(B) Yes, it was him.（錯誤答案）
▶ 在疑問詞問句的答覆中，Yes選項是錯誤答案。

(C) It's Monica Ben.（正確答案）
▶ 可以將「What~ name?」理解為Who問句，所以這是提到名字的正確答案。

翻譯
您的經理叫什麼名字？
(A) 目前三年了。
(B) 對，是他。
(C) 莫妮卡・本。

單字　manager 經理，管理人

解答　(C)

4. Which 問句

Which cafe has the fastest service?
(A) From here to the bank.（錯誤答案）
▶ 這是適合回覆How far問句的錯誤答案。

(B) French Coffee House.（正確答案）
▶ 提到咖啡廳名稱，與名詞（cafe）同樣屬於「咖啡廳」的正確答案。

(C) A variety of cakes.（錯誤答案）
▶ 與題目中的單字有關聯的（cafe - cake）錯誤答案。

翻譯
哪間咖啡廳的服務最快？
(A) 從這裡到銀行。
(B) 法蘭奇咖啡廳。
(C) 各式各樣的蛋糕。

單字　fast 快速的　variety 多種，多樣化

解答　(B)

5. How 問句

How do I call the front desk?
(A) It's only for guests.（錯誤答案）
▶ 這是適合回覆Who問句的錯誤答案。

(B) Just dial 0.（正確答案）
▶ 用命令句給予指示的正確答案。

(C) Yes, it's at the front desk.（錯誤答案）
▶ 在疑問詞問句的答覆中，Yes選項是錯誤答案。

翻譯
我該怎麼打電話給服務台？
(A) 這個只給客人用。
(B) 按0就可以了。
(C) 對，在服務台。

單字　front desk 服務台，前台　guest 客人，顧客　dial 撥號，打電話

解答　(B)

6. 建議句

Why don't you ask Mr. Roy if you can leave early tomorrow?
(A) A scheduled meeting.（錯誤答案）
▶ 這是適合回覆What問句的錯誤答案。

(B) No, it isn't.（錯誤答案）
▶ 這是適合回覆一般問句的錯誤答案。

(C) Yes, we'd like that.（正確答案）
▶ 用「Yes, we'd like that.」正面回覆建議問句的正確答案。

翻譯
你們何不問問羅伊先生你們明天能不能提早走？
(A) 安排好的會議。
(B) 不，不是。
(C) 好，那應該不錯。

單字　leave 離開　schedule 日程，安排日程

解答　(C)

7. Which 問句

Which switch turns off the heater?

(A) I sent him yesterday.（錯誤答案）

▶ 這是適合回覆When問句的錯誤答案。

(B) The one on the right.（正確答案）

▶ 在「Which＋名詞」問句的回答中，包含the one一詞的選項是正確答案。

(C) No, I won't be there.（錯誤答案）

▶ 在疑問詞問句的答覆中，No選項是錯誤答案。

翻譯
哪個開關可以關掉暖氣機？
(A) 我昨天寄給他了。
(B) 右邊那個。
(C) 不，我不會在那裡。

單字　turn off 關閉　heater 暖氣機

解答　(B)

8. Why 問句

Why did you decide to move to Moil Village?

(A) Yes, very decisive.（錯誤答案）

▶ 在疑問詞問句的答覆中，Yes選項是錯誤答案。

(B) It's closer to my office.（正確答案）

▶ 具體告知搬家原因的正確答案（省略了because）。

(C) Since last month.（錯誤答案）

▶ 這是適合回覆When問句的錯誤答案。

翻譯
你為什麼決定搬到摩伊村？
(A) 對，很果斷。
(B) 離我的辦公室比較近。
(C) 從上個月開始。

單字　move 移動，搬　since 自從～，自～以後

解答　(B)

9. What 問句

What are the advantages of using a membership card?

(A) Yes, it's expired.（錯誤答案）

▶ 在疑問詞問句的答覆中，Yes選項是錯誤答案。

(B) You can receive special discounts.（正確答案）

▶ 表示會員卡的優點是可以享有折扣的正確答案。

(C) You have to pay here.（錯誤答案）

▶ 與題目中的單字有關聯的（card - pay）選項幾乎都是錯誤答案。

翻譯
使用會員卡的優點是什麼？
(A) 對，過期了。
(B) 您可以獲得特別折扣。
(C) 您必須在這裡付款。

單字　advantage 優點，好處　membership 會員　expire 到期，結束

解答　(B)

10. How 問句

How do I clean the computer screen?

(A) If you want to come.（錯誤答案）

▶ 聽到相似單字的（computer - come）錯誤答案。

(B) I like your keyboard.（錯誤答案）

▶ 與題目中的單字有關聯的（computer - keyboard）錯誤答案。

(C) With a dry cloth.（正確答案）

▶ 回答詢問方法的題目時，通常會使用by、through、with等介系詞。

翻譯
我該怎麼清潔電腦螢幕？
(A) 如果你想來的話。
(B) 我喜歡你的鍵盤。
(C) 用乾布。

單字　screen 螢幕　clean 清潔　cloth 布

解答　(C)

聽寫訓練

Unit 7　What、Which 問句

1. What's the registration deadline?

(A) It's a week from today.

(B) One of the staff members finished it.

(C) On the corner of Bull Street.

2. Which copier should I use?

(A) Only a hundred copies.

(B) The manager has arrived.

(C) The one next to the door.

3. What's the registration fee?

(A) By next Monday.

(B) Cash will be better.

(C) It's $20.

4. What are the papers in the meeting room?

(A) In the first hall beside the stairs.

(B) A report I'm writing.

(C) I will bring it later.

Unit 8 How、Why 問句

1. How long will it take us to get downtown?

(A) I'm leaving town.

(B) It starts at seven p.m.

(C) About an hour.

2. Why is there a billing delay?

(A) The computer system is down.

(B) I just saw it today.

(C) Yes, I guess so.

3. How can I make sure Bruce gets this form?

(A) I will pay for it.

(B) Put it in his mailbox.

(C) He is in New York now.

4. Why is the J&J office closing?

(A) Because they're remodeling.

(B) The restaurant is open.

(C) The new staff.

Review Test

1. What kind of experience do you have in sales?

(A) I sold furniture for five years.

(B) The sale will begin next weekend.

(C) It will be a good experience.

2. Why was the seminar rescheduled?

(A) On Tuesday.

(B) Whenever you like.

(C) Because the manager hasn't arrived yet.

3. What's your manager's name?

(A) For three years now.

(B) Yes, it was him.

(C) It's Monica Ben.

4. Which cafe has the fastest service?

(A) From here to the bank.

(B) French Coffee House.

(C) A variety of cakes.

5. How do I call the front desk?

(A) It's only for guests.

(B) Just dial 0.

(C) Yes, it's at the front desk.

6. Why don't you ask Mr. Roy if you can leave early tomorrow?

(A) A scheduled meeting.

(B) No, it isn't.

(C) Yes, we'd like that.

7. Which switch turns off the heater?

(A) I sent him yesterday.

(B) The one on the right.

(C) No, I won't be there.

8. Why did you decide to move to Moil Village?

(A) Yes, very decisive.

(B) It's closer to my office.

(C) Since last month.

9. What are the advantages of using a membership card?

(A) Yes, it's expired.

(B) You can receive special discounts.

(C) You have to pay here.

10. How do I clean the computer screen?

(A) If you want to come.

(B) I like your keyboard.

(C) With a dry cloth.

類型分析 5　一般問句＆選擇疑問句
Unit 09　一般問句

Step 3 實戰演練

1. Have you found an apartment to rent?
(A) Yes, I just have to sign the contract.（正確答案）
▶ 表示已經找到而且要簽約的正確答案。

(B) It's in the Sales Department.（錯誤答案）
▶ 聽到相似單字（apartment - department）的選項幾乎都是錯誤答案。

(C) He asked me yesterday（錯誤答案）
▶ 提到第三人稱的錯誤答案。

翻譯
你找到要租的公寓了嗎？
(A) 嗯，我只需要簽約就行了。
(B) 在銷售部門。
(C) 他昨天問過我。

單字　rent 租賃　sign a contract 簽約　Sales Department 銷售部門

解答　(A)

2. Isn't Paul going to the train station?
(A) No, it's not raining.（錯誤答案）
▶ 聽到相似單字（train - raining）的選項幾乎都是錯誤答案。

(B) Attend the training session.（錯誤答案）
▶ 這是適合回覆How問句的錯誤答案。

(C) He was planning to go.（正確答案）
▶ 提到行為的主體（He）的正確答案。

翻譯
保羅不是要去火車站嗎？
(A) 不，沒有下雨。
(B) 出席培訓課程。
(C) 他本來打算去的。

單字　train station 火車站　attend 出席　training session 培訓課程

解答　(C)

3. Didn't Mr. Smith send the papers to us yesterday?
(A) Anywhere around here.（錯誤答案）
▶ 這是適合回覆Where問句的錯誤答案。

(B) From a newspaper article.（錯誤答案）
▶ 這是適合回覆Where問句的錯誤答案。

(C) Yes, they're right here.（正確答案）
▶ 表示已經抵達這裡，迂迴型表達的正確答案。

翻譯
史密斯先生昨天沒有寄文件給我們嗎？
(A) 在附近的任何一個地方。
(B) 從一篇新聞報導。
(C) 有，就在這裡。

單字　paper 紙張，文件　anywhere 任何地方

解答　(C)

4. Will the weather be nice today?
(A) I hope so.（正確答案）
▶ 表示「但願如此」，迂迴型表達的正確答案。

(B) Whenever you can.（錯誤答案）
▶ 這是適合回覆When問句的錯誤答案。

(C) I'm sorry.（錯誤答案）
▶ 這是適合回覆建議問句的錯誤答案。

翻譯
今天會是好天氣嗎？
(A) 但願如此。
(B) 任何你可以的時候。
(C) 我很抱歉。

單字　weather 天氣　whenever 無論何時

解答　(A)

Unit 10　選擇疑問句

Step 3 實戰演練

1. Do you want my home or work address?
(A) Yes, I will be there.（錯誤答案）
▶ 在選擇疑問句的答覆中，Yes選項是錯誤答案。

(B) He will leave the office soon.（錯誤答案）
▶ 以第三人稱回覆的錯誤答案。

(C) Could I have both?（正確答案）
▶ 在選擇疑問句的答覆中聽到both的話，一定是正確答案。

翻譯
您想要我家的地址，還是公司地址？
(A) 對，我會在那裡。
(B) 他快下班了。
(C) 可以兩個都給我嗎？

單字　address 地址　both 兩者都

解答　(C)

2. Are you buying a house or renting?
(A) 110 Main Street.（錯誤答案）
▶ 這是適合回覆Where問句的錯誤答案。

(B) We're renting for two years.（正確答案）
▶ 選了renting的正確答案。

(C) No, it is.（錯誤答案）
▶ 在選擇疑問句的答覆中，No選項是錯誤答案。

翻譯

你要買房子，還是租房子？
(A) 主街一一〇號。
(B) 我們預計要租兩年。
(C) 不，沒錯。

單字　buy 購買　rent 租賃

解答　**(B)**

3. Would you like dessert or coffee?
(A) He sent it yesterday.（錯誤答案）
▶ 以第三人稱回覆的錯誤答案。

(B) She will like it.（錯誤答案）
▶ 以第三人稱回覆的錯誤答案。

(C) I'll have coffee.（正確答案）
▶ 選擇兩者之一的正確答案。

翻譯

您想吃甜點，還是喝咖啡？
(A) 他昨天寄了。
(B) 她會喜歡的。
(C) 我要咖啡。

單字　dessert 甜點　send 寄送

解答　**(C)**

4. Are the best seats in front or in the balcony?
(A) At the ticket counter.（錯誤答案）
▶ 這是適合回覆Where問句的錯誤答案。

(B) I'll send them back later.（錯誤答案）
▶ 用有關聯的詞彙（front - back）誘導考生選為正確答案的錯誤答案。

(C) You can see better from the balcony.（正確答案）
▶ 選擇兩者之一的正確答案。

翻譯

最好的位置是前面的座位，還是包廂的座位？
(A) 在售票櫃檯。
(B) 我稍後會寄回去。
(C) 從包廂看，視野更好。

單字　seat 座位　ticket counter 售票櫃檯

解答　**(C)**

1. 一般問句

Have you hired a receptionist yet?
(A) Yes. He'll start next month.（正確答案）
▶ 給予正面答覆後，再補充說明的正確答案。

(B) I will call you later.（錯誤答案）
▶ 用有關聯的詞彙（receptionist - call）造成混淆的錯誤答案。

(C) It is the newest one.（錯誤答案）
▶ 代名詞不對，所以是錯誤答案。

翻譯

你已經僱用接待員了嗎？
(A) 對，他從下個月開始工作。
(B) 我之後再打給你。
(C) 這是最新的。

單字　hire 僱用　receptionist 接待員

解答　**(A)**

2. 一般問句

Does this building have more storage space?
(A) Yes, there's more on the top floor.（正確答案）
▶ 提到儲藏空間的位置的正確答案。

(B) I bought a new wardrobe.（錯誤答案）
▶ 用有關聯的詞彙（storage - wardrobe）造成混淆的錯誤答案。

(C) He will send an email.（錯誤答案）
▶ 主詞不對，所以是錯誤答案。

翻譯

這棟大樓有更多的儲藏空間嗎？
(A) 對，頂樓有更多的空間。
(B) 我買了新衣櫥。
(C) 他會寄電子郵件。

單字　storage 倉庫，儲藏　space 空間　on the top 在頂部，在最上面　wardrobe 衣櫥

解答　**(A)**

3. 選擇疑問句

Is this a full-time or part-time position?
(A) About three years ago.（錯誤答案）
▶ 這是適合回覆When問句的錯誤答案。

(B) We're hoping to hire someone full-time.（正確答案）
▶ 選擇兩者之一的正確答案。

(C) James is the general manager. （錯誤答案）

▶ 與題目中的單字有關聯的（position - manager）錯誤答案。

翻譯

這是全職還是兼職的職位？
(A) 大概三年前。
(B) 我們想僱用做全職的人。
(C) 詹姆士是總經理。

單字　full-time 正職　part-time 兼職　position 職位，位置
general manager 總經理

解答　**(B)**

4. 一般問句

Don't we have an appointment tomorrow?
(A) Once a day. （錯誤答案）

▶ 這是適合回覆How often問句的錯誤答案。

(B) Sorry, I have to cancel.（正確答案）

▶ 以cancel（取消）回覆詢問約會的題目，是正確答案。

(C) Mary was appointed president. （錯誤答案）

▶ 單字相似的（appointment - appointed）錯誤答案。

翻譯

我們明天不是有約嗎？
(A) 一天一次。
(B) 抱歉，我必須取消了。
(C) 瑪莉被任命為總裁。

單字　appointment 約會　appoint 任命，指名

解答　**(B)**

5. 一般問句

Did you pay for the order in advance?
(A) Yes, here's the receipt.（正確答案）

▶ 給予正面答覆後出示證據的正確答案。

(B) No, there is no advantage. （錯誤答案）

▶ 單字相似的（advance - advantage）選項幾乎都是錯誤答案。

(C) She didn't make an order. （錯誤答案）

▶ 以第三人稱回覆的錯誤答案。

翻譯

你事先付完訂單的錢了？
(A) 對，收據在這裡。
(B) 不，沒有好處。
(C) 她沒有下訂單。

單字　order 訂單　in advance 事先，提前　receipt 收據
advantage 優點，好處

解答　**(A)**

6. 選擇疑問句

Which would you prefer, soup or salad?
(A) I hope so. （錯誤答案）

▶ 這是適合回覆陳述句的錯誤答案。

(B) In the office. （錯誤答案）

▶ 這是適合回覆Where問句的錯誤答案。

(C) Neither, thank you.（正確答案）

▶ 在選擇疑問句的答覆中聽到either、whichever、whatever、it doesn't matter、both、each、neither 的話，該選項一定是正確答案。

翻譯

您比較喜歡哪一個，湯品還是沙拉？
(A) 但願如此。
(B) 在辦公室。
(C) 都不喜歡，謝謝。

單字　prefer 偏好～　neither 兩者都不

解答　**(C)**

7. 一般問句

Do you have the secretary's phone number?
(A) Ten copies of a document. （錯誤答案）

▶ 這是適合回覆How many問句的錯誤答案。

(B) Check the directory.（正確答案）

▶ 表示「不知道、跟別人（其他來源）確認看看」的句型一定是正確答案。

(C) Nobody is here. （錯誤答案）

▶ 這是適合回覆Where問句的錯誤答案。

翻譯

你有祕書的電話號碼嗎？
(A) 十份文件複本。
(B) 確認一下電話簿。
(C) 沒人在這裡。

單字　secretary 祕書　directory 電話簿

解答　**(B)**

8. 一般問句

Did you know that the concert will be outdoors?
(A) I hope it doesn't rain.（正確答案）

▶ 省略Yes並補充說明的正確答案。通常提到I hope、I think，表示「希望」的選項會是正確答案。

(B) No, I have never heard that song. （錯誤答案）
▶ 用有關聯的詞彙（concert - song）造成混淆的錯誤答案。

(C) I will leave for a business trip. （錯誤答案）
▶ 這是適合回覆Where問句的錯誤答案。

翻譯
你知道演唱會將會辦在戶外嗎？
(A) 希望不會下雨。
(B) 不，我從來沒聽過那首歌。
(C) 我會去出差。

單字　outdoor 戶外的，室外的　business trip 出差

解答　(A)

9. 一般問句

Have you already booked a room?
(A) Yes, there is. （錯誤答案）
▶ 代名詞不對，所以是錯誤答案。

(B) No, not yet. （正確答案）
▶ 用not yet回覆是否預約的提問，為正確答案。

(C) I'll read it. （錯誤答案）
▶ 用有關聯的詞彙（book - read）造成混淆的錯誤答案。

翻譯
你已經訂房了嗎？
(A) 對，有。
(B) 不，還沒有。
(C) 我會看的。

單字　book 預約　already 已經，早就

解答　(B)

10. 選擇疑問句

Is the chairperson arriving this week or next?
(A) Oh, the new staff member. （錯誤答案）
▶ 這是適合回覆Who問句的錯誤答案。

(B) He'll be here on the 25th. （正確答案）
▶ 沒有選擇其中之一，而是提出第三種選項的正確答案。

(C) Yes, all of these chairs. （錯誤答案）
▶ 在選擇疑問句的答覆中，Yes選項是錯誤答案。

翻譯
主席是這個禮拜來，還是下個禮拜？
(A) 噢，是新員工。

(B) 他會在二十五號來這裡。
(C) 對，所有椅子。

單字　chairperson 主席　staff 員工

解答　(B)

聽寫訓練

Unit 9 一般問句

1. Have you found an apartment to rent?
(A) Yes, I just have to sign the contract.
(B) It's in the Sales Department.
(C) He asked me yesterday.

2. Isn't Paul going to the train station?
(A) No, it's not raining.
(B) Attend the training session.
(C) He was planning to go.

3. Didn't Mr. Smith send the papers to us yesterday?
(A) Anywhere around here.
(B) From a newspaper article.
(C) Yes, they're right here.

4. Will the weather be nice today?
(A) I hope so.
(B) Whenever you can.
(C) I'm sorry.

Unit 10 選擇疑問句

1. Do you want my home or work address?
(A) Yes, I will be there.
(B) He will leave the office soon.
(C) Could I have both?

2. Are you buying a house or renting?
(A) 110 Main Street.
(B) We're renting for two years.
(C) No, it is.

3. Would you like dessert or coffee?
(A) He sent it yesterday.
(B) She will like it.
(C) I'll have coffee.

4. Are the best seats in front or in the balcony?

(A) At the ticket counter.

(B) I'll send them back later.

(C) You can see better from the balcony.

1. Have you hired a receptionist yet?

(A) Yes. He'll start next month.

(B) I will call you later.

(C) It is the newest one.

2. Does this building have more storage space?

(A) Yes, there's more on the top floor.

(B) I bought a new wardrobe.

(C) He will send an email.

3. Is this a full-time or part-time position?

(A) About three years ago.

(B) We're hoping to hire someone full-time.

(C) James is the general manager.

4. Don't we have an appointment tomorrow?

(A) Once a day.

(B) Sorry, I have to cancel.

(C) Mary was appointed president.

5. Did you pay for the order in advance?

(A) Yes, here's the receipt.

(B) No, there is no advantage.

(C) She didn't make an order.

6. Which would you prefer, soup or salad?

(A) I hope so.

(B) In the office.

(C) Neither, thank you.

7. Do you have the secretary's phone number?

(A) Ten copies of a document.

(B) Check the directory.

(C) Nobody is here.

8. Did you know that the concert will be outdoors?

(A) I hope it doesn't rain.

(B) No, I have never heard that song.

(C) I will leave for a business trip.

9. Have you already booked a room?

(A) Yes, there is.

(B) No, not yet.

(C) I'll read it.

10. Is the chairperson arriving this week or next?

(A) Oh, the new staff member.

(B) He'll be here on the 25th.

(C) Yes, all of these chairs.

類型分析 6　建議（請求）句、陳述句
Unit 11　建議（請求）句

Step 3 實戰演練

1. Would you like to see our latest catalog?
(A) I'll bring it. （錯誤答案）
▶ 這是適合回覆Who問句的錯誤答案。

(B) In five categories. （錯誤答案）
▶ 聽到相似單字（catalog - categories）的選項幾乎都是錯誤答案。

(C) Do you have a copy? （正確答案）
▶ 利用反問句，委婉地表示「想看」的正確答案。

翻譯
您要看看我們最新的目錄嗎？
(A) 我會帶去。
(B) 五個種類。
(C) 你有一本嗎？

單字　**catalog** 目錄　**category** 種類

解答　**(C)**

2. May I suggest an idea for a new product?
(A) It's for you. （錯誤答案）
▶ 這是適合回覆Who問句的錯誤答案。

(B) I have an idea for you. （錯誤答案）
▶ 用相同的單字（idea）造成混淆的錯誤答案。

(C) I'd be glad to consider your ideas. （正確答案）
▶ 使用了表示同意的「I'd be glad to」句型的正確答案。

翻譯
我可以提議一個關於新產品的點子嗎？
(A) 這是給你的。
(B) 我有個主意要給你。
(C) 我很樂意考慮看看你的點子。

單字　**suggest** 建議，提議　**consider** 考慮

解答　**(C)**

3. Why don't we travel together?
(A) At the bus station.（錯誤答案）
▶ 這是適合回覆Where問句的錯誤答案。

(B) When are you leaving?（正確答案）
▶ 聽到一起旅遊的提議後，反問對方何時動身的正確答案。

(C) I don't want to call him.（錯誤答案）
▶ 這是適合回覆Why問句的錯誤答案。

翻譯
我們何不一起旅遊呢？
(A) 在公車站。
(B) 你什麼時候要動身？
(C) 我不想打電話給他。

單字　**bus station** 公車站

解答　**(B)**

4. Can you give me a hand with this project?
(A) Sure, I'll be right there.（正確答案）
▶ 使用了sure的正面型正確答案。

(B) We handed him a document.（錯誤答案）
▶ 用有關聯的詞彙（hand - handed）造成混淆的錯誤答案。

(C) I don't remember.（錯誤答案）
▶ 無關的錯誤答案，請不要誤以為是拒絕對方的句型。

翻譯
這個案子你可以協助我嗎？
(A) 沒問題，我現在過去。
(B) 我們給了他文件。
(C) 我不記得了。

單字　**give a hand** 幫忙　**hand** 傳遞，給

解答　**(A)**

Unit 12 陳述句

Step 3 實戰演練

1. Today's meeting shouldn't take too long.
(A) I have some.（錯誤答案）
▶ 這是適合回覆建議句的錯誤答案。

(B) What will we be talking about?（正確答案）
▶ 反問的選項大部分都是正確答案。

(C) This is the longest river.（錯誤答案）
▶ 用有關聯的詞彙（long - longest）造成混淆的錯誤答案。

翻譯
今天的會議應該不會開太久。
(A) 我有一些。
(B) 我們要討論什麼？
(C) 這是最長的河流。

單字　**meeting** 會議　**river** 河流

解答　**(B)**

2. The copy machine is making loud noises.
(A) I waited for you.（錯誤答案）
▶ 代名詞不對，所以是錯誤答案。

(B) You have to come.（錯誤答案）
▶ 代名詞不對，所以是錯誤答案。

(C) I think it's broken.（正確答案）
▶ 使用I think來代替Yes表達想法的正確答案。

翻譯
影印機很吵。
(A) 我剛才在等你。
(B) 你一定要來。
(C) 我覺得它故障了。

單字　**copy machine** 影印機　**make noise** 發出噪音，吵鬧

解答　**(C)**

3. Maybe we should extend the deadline.
(A) It's in the office.（錯誤答案）
▶ 這是適合回覆Where問句的錯誤答案。

(B) Okay, let's do that.（正確答案）
▶ 表示同意的「Okay, let's~」句型大部分都是正確答案。

(C) No, I don't want to attend.（錯誤答案）
▶ 用有關聯的詞彙（extend - attend）造成混淆的錯誤答案。

翻譯
也許我們應該延長截止日期。
(A) 在辦公室裡。
(B) 好，我們那樣做吧。
(C) 不，我不想出席。

單字　**extend** 延長　**deadline** 截止日期，期限　**attend** 出席

解答　**(B)**

4. I can't open this window latch.

(A) They close around 7 p.m. (錯誤答案)

▶ 聽到相反詞 （open - close）的選項是錯誤答案。

(B) I sent it with an attachment. (錯誤答案)

▶ 用有關聯的詞彙 （open this window - attachment） 造成混淆的錯誤答案。

(C) Let me take a look. (正確答案)

▶ 提議說「要看看」的正確答案。

翻譯

我打不開這個窗門。

(A) 他們晚上七點左右關門。

(B) 跟附件檔案一起寄出了。

(C) 讓我看看。

單字　latch 門閂，窗閂，彈簧鎖　attachment 附件檔案

解答　**(C)**

Review Test

1. 陳述句

The directory is in the filing cabinet.

(A) In the top drawer? (正確答案)

▶ 反問的選項大部分都是正確答案。

(B) The files are missing. (錯誤答案)

▶ 聽到相似單字的 （filing - files）錯誤答案。

(C) No, the director left the office. (錯誤答案)

▶ 聽到相似單字的 （directory - director）錯誤答案。

翻譯

電話簿在檔案櫃中。

(A) 在最上面的抽屜裡嗎？

(B) 檔案不見了。

(C) 不，主任離開辦公室了。

單字　directory 電話簿　filing cabinet 檔案櫃　top drawer 頂層抽屜　director 董事，主任

解答　**(A)**

2. 建議句

Could you put together an inventory of our merchandise?

(A) I'll buy it. (錯誤答案)

▶ 聽到聯想單字的 （merchandise - buy）錯誤答案。

(B) Sure, I have some time. (正確答案)

▶ 使用了sure的正面型正確答案。

(C) The new inventory will arrive. (錯誤答案)

▶ 使用相同單字 （inventory - inventory）當作陷阱的 錯誤答案。

翻譯

你可以就我們的產品做一份清單嗎？

(A) 我會買。

(B) 沒問題，我有一點時間。

(C) 新的清單貨品要抵達了。

單字　inventory 清單貨品，庫存　merchandise 商品，物品

解答　**(B)**

3. 陳述句

I need ten copies of this document by this afternoon.

(A) Where should I leave them for you? (正確答案)

▶ 回覆反問句的正確答案。

(B) He is the leader of that club. (錯誤答案)

▶ 這是適合回覆Who問句的錯誤答案。

(C) No, I have it already. (錯誤答案)

▶ 否認之後的補充說明內容不適合這個題目，所以是 錯誤答案。

翻譯

我在下午之前需要這個文件的十份影本。

(A) 我要把它們放到哪裡給你？

(B) 他是那個俱樂部的領袖。

(C) 不，我已經有了。

單字　copy 影本　leader 領袖，帶領者　club 俱樂部，會所

解答　**(A)**

4. 建議句

Can I fax my job application to you?

(A) No, there is no tax on education. (錯誤答案)

▶ 聽到相似單字的 （fax - tax）錯誤答案。

(B) Yes, that would be fine. (正確答案)

▶ 表示同意，用來回覆提議問句的正確答案。

(C) The interview will start soon. (錯誤答案)

▶ 聽到聯想單字的 （job - interview）錯誤答案。

翻譯

我可以把我的應徵信傳真給您嗎？

(A) 不，不會對教育課稅。

(B) 可以，那樣很好。

(C) 面試即將開始。

單字　job application 應徵信　tax 稅金　education 教育 interview 面試

解答　**(B)**

5. 陳述句

I'll introduce you to the new cashier.

(A) No, we paid with cash.（錯誤答案）

▶ 聽到相似單字的（cashier - cash）錯誤答案。

(B) It's the old one I have.（錯誤答案）

▶ 聽到相反詞（new - old）的錯誤答案。

(C) Thanks, but we've already met.（正確答案）

▶ 表示已經見過面，鄭重地拒絕介紹的正確答案。

翻譯

我會把您介紹給新的收銀員。

(A) 不，我們付現了。

(B) 我有的是舊的那個。

(C) 謝謝，但我們已經見過面了。

單字　introduce 介紹　cashier 收銀員

解答　**(C)**

6. 建議句

Would you like a copy of our newsletter?

(A) I'm feeling better.（錯誤答案）

▶ 這是適合回覆How問句的錯誤答案。

(B) That would be nice.（正確答案）

▶ 表示接受，用來回覆提議問句的正確答案。

(C) In the newspaper.（錯誤答案）

▶ 這是適合回覆Where問句的錯誤答案。

翻譯

您想要一份我們的時事通訊嗎？

(A) 我覺得好多了。

(B) 那太好了。

(C) 在報紙中。

單字　newsletter 時事通訊　newspaper 報紙

解答　**(B)**

7. 建議句

Could you give me the blueprints for the Liael Project?

(A) It is one of our branches.（錯誤答案）

▶ 這是適合回覆What問句的錯誤答案。

(B) Those come from here.（錯誤答案）

▶ 這是適合回覆Where問句的錯誤答案。

(C) I think Bob has them.（正確答案）

▶ 表示東西在第三者那邊的正確答案。

翻譯

你可以給我賴埃爾工程的藍圖嗎？

(A) 這是我們的分公司之一。

(B) 那些來自這裡。

(C) 我想在鮑伯那邊。

單字　blueprint 藍圖，計畫　branch 分公司

解答　**(C)**

8. 陳述句

I think we should hire Mr. Davidson.

(A) About an hour later.（錯誤答案）

▶ 這是適合回覆When問句的錯誤答案。

(B) Our profits need to be higher.（錯誤答案）

▶ 聽到相似單字的（hire - higher）錯誤答案。

(C) Unfortunately, he withdrew his application.（正確答案）

▶ 否定後說明理由的正確答案。

翻譯

我覺得我們應該僱用大衛森先生。

(A) 大概一個小時後。

(B) 我們的利潤應該再高一點。

(C) 很可惜，他撤回申請了。

單字　hire 僱用　withdraw 取消，撤回　application 申請，申請書

解答　**(C)**

9. 建議句

Could you make me a copy of this receipt?

(A) Yes, I received a good job offer.（錯誤答案）

▶ 聽到相似單字的（receipt - receive）錯誤答案。

(B) I have to take the bus.（錯誤答案）

▶ 聽到相似單字的（make - take）錯誤答案。

(C) I'm afraid the copy machine is broken.（正確答案）

▶ 鄭重拒絕提議後，說明理由的正確答案。

翻譯

你可以替我影印一份這個收據嗎？

(A) 對，我得到了很好的工作機會。

(B) 我必須搭公車。

(C) 我擔心影印機好像壞了。

單字　receipt 收據　take the bus 搭公車

解答　**(C)**

10. 陳述句

I'd like to see last year's sales figures.

(A) I have to go to the bookstore.（錯誤答案）

▶ 聽到聯想單字的（sales - bookstore）錯誤答案。

(B) Would you like me to print you a copy? （正確答案）

▶ 針對陳述句提出建議的正確答案。

(C) It's too expensive. （錯誤答案）

▶ 聽到聯想單字的（sales - expensive）錯誤答案。

翻譯
我想看去年的銷售額。
(A) 我得去書店。
(B) 要我替你列印一份嗎？
(C) 太貴了。

單字　**figure** 數值，數字　**print** 列印

解答　**(B)**

聽寫訓練

Unit 11 建議（請求）句

1. Would you like to see our latest catalog?
(A) I'll bring it.
(B) In five categories.
(C) Do you have a copy?

2. May I suggest an idea for a new product?
(A) It's for you.
(B) I have an idea for you.
(C) I'd be glad to consider your ideas.

3. Why don't we travel together?
(A) At the bus station.
(B) When are you leaving?
(C) I don't want to call him.

4. Can you give me a hand with this project?
(A) Sure, I'll be right there.
(B) We handed him a document.
(C) I don't remember.

Unit 12 陳述句

1. Today's meeting shouldn't take too long.
(A) I have some.
(B) What will we be talking about?
(C) This is the longest river.

2. The copy machine is making loud noises.
(A) I waited for you.
(B) You have to come.
(C) I think it's broken.

3. Maybe we should extend the deadline.
(A) It's in the office.
(B) Okay, let's do that.
(C) No, I don't want to attend.

4. I can't open this window latch.
(A) They close around 7 p.m.
(B) I sent it with an attachment.
(C) Let me take a look.

Review Test

1. The directory is in the filing cabinet.
(A) In the top drawer?
(B) The files are missing.
(C) No, the director left the office.

2. Could you put together an inventory of our merchandise?
(A) I'll buy it.
(B) Sure, I have some time.
(C) The new inventory will arrive.

3. I need ten copies of this document by this afternoon.
(A) Where should I leave them for you?
(B) He is the leader of that club.
(C) No, I have it already.

4. Can I fax my job application to you?
(A) No, there is no tax on education.
(B) Yes, that would be fine.
(C) The interview will start soon.

5. I'll introduce you to the new cashier.
(A) No, we paid with cash.
(B) It's the old one I have.
(C) Thanks, but we've already met.

6. Would you like a copy of our newsletter?
(A) I'm feeling better.
(B) That would be nice.
(C) In the newspaper.

7. Could you give me the blueprints for the Liael Project?
(A) It is one of our branches.
(B) Those come from here.
(C) I think Bob has them.

8. I think we should hire Mr. Davidson.
(A) About an hour later.
(B) Our profits need to be higher.
(C) Unfortunately, he withdrew his application.

9. Could you make me a copy of this receipt?
(A) Yes, I received a good job offer.
(B) I have to take the bus.
(C) I'm afraid the copy machine is broken.

10. I'd like to see last year's sales figures.
(A) I have to go to the bookstore.
(B) Would you like me to print you a copy?
(C) It's too expensive.

PART 2 FINAL TEST - 1

7. Where 問句

Where are the instructions for the new computers?
(A) They're still in the boxes.（正確答案）
▶ 出現「in＋地點」的正確答案。

(B) It's a new computer system.（錯誤答案）
▶ 使用相同單字（computer），造成混淆的錯誤答案。

(C) No, I won't attend it.（錯誤答案）
▶ 在疑問詞問句的答覆中，No選項是錯誤答案。

翻譯
新電腦的說明書在哪裡？
(A) 還在箱子裡。
(B) 這是新的電腦系統。
(C) 不，我不會出席。

單字　instruction 說明書，指示　still 仍然，還　attend 出席

解答　(A)

8. How 問句

How did the Sales Department do last quarter?
(A) Better than expected.（正確答案）
▶ 提到正面形容詞的正確答案。

(B) A long time ago.（錯誤答案）
▶ 這是適合回覆When問句的錯誤答案。

(C) Of course, he will be.（錯誤答案）
▶ 使用了代替Yes的詞彙（Of course）的錯誤答案。

翻譯
銷售部門上一季表現得怎樣？

(A) 比預期中的好。
(B) 很久以前。
(C) 當然，他會的。

單字　Sales Department 銷售部門　quarter 季度　expect 預期，期待

解答　(A)

9. 一般問句

Are you going to the concert tonight, or do you have other plans?
(A) Yes, that's impossible.（錯誤答案）
▶ 在選擇疑問句的答覆中，Yes選項是錯誤答案。

(B) Yes, I was there.（錯誤答案）
▶ 在選擇疑問句的答覆中，Yes選項是錯誤答案。

(C) Actually, I'm going to the theater.（正確答案）
▶ 出現actually的選項幾乎都是正確答案，而這句是提出第三種選擇的正確答案。

翻譯
你今晚會去演唱會嗎？還是你有其他的計畫？
(A) 對，那不可能。
(B) 對，我曾在那裡。
(C) 其實，我要去電影院。

單字　concert 音樂會，演唱會　impossible 不可能的　theater 電影院

解答　(C)

10. 一般問句

Can you help me with a safety demonstration?
(A) It wasn't safe.（錯誤答案）
▶ 使用相似的單字（safety - safe），造成混淆的錯誤答案。

(B) Sure. Just let me get my materials.（正確答案）
▶ 使用了sure來回覆提議問句的正確答案。

(C) I don't think I need any help.（錯誤答案）
▶ 使用相同的單字（help），造成混淆的錯誤答案。

翻譯
你可以協助我做安全示範嗎？
(A) 這不安全。
(B) 沒問題，讓我拿一下教材。
(C) 我覺得我不需要任何幫助。

單字　safety demonstration 安全示範　material 材料，教材

解答　(B)

11. 選擇疑問句

Do you already know Mr. Jackson, or should I introduce you to him?

(A) We've worked together before. （正確答案）

▶ 說「一起工作過」的意思是迂迴地表示自己已經認識對方了，這句是正確答案。

(B) We are ready to begin.（錯誤答案）

▶ 使用相似的單字（already - ready），造成混淆的錯誤答案。

(C) Yes, it will reduce the cost.（錯誤答案）

▶ 在選擇疑問句的答覆中，Yes選項是錯誤答案。

翻譯
你已經認識傑克遜先生了嗎？還是需要我把你介紹給他嗎？
(A) 我們以前一起工作過。
(B) 我們準備好要開始了。
(C) 對，這會降低成本。

單字　already 已經　introduce 介紹　reduce 減少

解答　**(A)**

12. 建議句

Why don't we ask how much this jacket costs?

(A) On the top shelf.（錯誤答案）

▶ 這是適合回覆Where問句的錯誤答案。

(B) That's a good idea.（正確答案）

▶ 表示同意的正確答案。

(C) I was in the office.（錯誤答案）

▶ 這是適合回覆Where問句的錯誤答案。

翻譯
我們何不問問這件夾克多少錢呢？
(A) 在最上面的架子。
(B) 這是個好主意。
(C) 我在辦公室。

單字　cost 費用，價格　shelf 架子，書架

解答　**(B)**

13. When 問句

When does the art exhibit open?

(A) Hasn't it been canceled?（正確答案）

▶ 反問並迂迴地表示展覽已取消的正確答案。

(B) I can't find the exits.（錯誤答案）

▶ 使用相似的單字（exhibit - exits），造成混淆的錯誤答案。

(C) No, it never closes.（錯誤答案）

▶ 在疑問詞問句的答覆中，No選項是錯誤答案。

翻譯
藝術展何時開幕？
(A) 那不是取消了嗎？
(B) 我找不到出口。
(C) 不，那裡從來不關門。

單字　exhibit 展示品，展示　exit 出口

解答　**(A)**

14. 一般問句

Don't you have a dental appointment today?

(A) I could offer you more.（錯誤答案）

▶ 這是適合回覆How問句的錯誤答案。

(B) Yes, I'd better go to it.（正確答案）

▶ 回覆Yes後補充說明的正確答案。

(C) I'm sorry about that.（錯誤答案）

▶ 跟題目完全無關的錯誤答案。

翻譯
你今天不是有預約牙醫嗎？
(A) 我可以給你更多。
(B) 對，我最好該走了。
(C) 我對此感到很遺憾。

單字　dental 牙科的，牙齒的　offer 提議，提供

解答　**(B)**

15.Who 問句

Who coordinated the fundraiser last year?

(A) My supervisor.（正確答案）

▶ 提到職責的正確答案。

(B) No, but it was fun.（錯誤答案）

▶ 在疑問詞問句的答覆中，No選項是錯誤答案。

(C) Around two thousand dollars.（錯誤答案）

▶ 使用聯想單字（fundraiser - two thousand dollars）的錯誤答案。

翻譯
誰協調了去年的募款活動？
(A) 我的上司。
(B) 不，但是很好玩。
(C) 大概兩千美元。

單字　coordinate 協調，調節　fundraiser 募款活動

解答　**(A)**

16. Where 問句

Where can I find our office supplies?

(A) We close at 6 o'clock. (錯誤答案)

▶ 這是適合回覆When問句的錯誤答案。

(B) In that cabinet by the door. (正確答案)

▶ 出現「in＋地點」的正確答案。

(C) No, I haven't been there. (錯誤答案)

▶ 在疑問詞問句的答覆中，No選項是錯誤答案。

翻譯

我可以在哪裡找到我們的辦公用品？

(A) 我們六點整關門。

(B) 在門旁邊的那個櫃子裡。

(C) 不，我沒去過那裡。

單字　office supply 辦公用品　cabinet 櫃子

解答　(B)

17. Why 問句

Why is Mr. Baker being transferred to another branch office?

(A) In Buenos Aires. (錯誤答案)

▶ 是適合回覆Where問句的錯誤答案。

(B) Why don't you ask the personnel director? (正確答案)

▶ 要對方問別人的迴避型正確答案。

(C) Because we're understaffed. (錯誤答案)

▶ 雖然以because開頭很適合回覆Why問句，但是後面的內容意思不對，所以是錯誤答案。把「we're」改成「they're」的話，就能變成「他們人力不足」的正確答案。

翻譯

為什麼貝克先生要被調到另一個分部？

(A) 在布宜諾斯艾利斯。

(B) 你何不問問人事主任？

(C) 因為我們人力不足。

單字　be transferred to 被調到～　branch office 分部 personnel director 人事主任　be understaffed 人力不足

解答　(B)

18. How 問句

How may I help you?

(A) I'm looking for the mailroom. (正確答案)

▶ 請對方幫忙找收發室的正確答案。

(B) Oh, you're welcome. (錯誤答案)

▶ 這是適合回覆Thank you的錯誤答案。

(C) It will be helpful for you. (錯誤答案)

▶ 聽到相似單字的（help - helpful）錯誤答案。

翻譯

有什麼我能為您效勞的嗎？

(A) 我正在找收發室。

(B) 哦，不客氣。

(C) 這會對你有幫助。

單字　mailroom 收發室　helpful 有幫助的

解答　(A)

19. When 問句

When will the office supplies be delivered?

(A) Within three days. (正確答案)

▶ 提到期間的正確答案。

(B) The professor asked them. (錯誤答案)

▶ 這是適合回覆Who問句的錯誤答案。

(C) To my home address. (錯誤答案)

▶ 這是適合回覆Where問句的錯誤答案。

翻譯

辦公用品何時送達？

(A) 三天內。

(B) 教授問過他們了。

(C) 寄到我家的地址。

單字　delivery 寄送，運送　home address 住家地址

解答　(A)

20. 附加問句

This computer comes with a one-year warranty period, doesn't it?

(A) Sure. It covers parts for one year. (正確答案)

▶ 給予正面答覆後，補充說明的正確答案。

(B) Yes, every day except Saturday. (錯誤答案)

▶ 雖然Yes是恰當的回覆，但是補充說明不對，所以是錯誤答案。

(C) Sorry. It doesn't come in that size. (錯誤答案)

▶ 題目並非詢問電腦的大小，所以是錯誤答案。

翻譯

這台電腦有一年的保固期，不是嗎？

(A) 當然，包含一年的零件保固。

(B) 對，每天除了星期六。

(C) 抱歉，沒有那個尺寸。

單字　come with 附帶～　warranty period 保固期間　cover 包含，涵蓋

解答　(A)

21. 一般問句

Has Mr. Hong already gone to the airport?
(A) He's from Washington.（錯誤答案）
▶ 這是適合回覆Where問句的錯誤答案。

(B) I have to finish the report.（錯誤答案）
▶ 用有關聯的詞彙（airport - report）造成混淆的錯誤答案。

(C) Yes, he just left.（正確答案）
▶ 出現Yes後，補充説明的正確答案。

翻譯
洪先生已經去機場了嗎？
(A) 他來自華盛頓。
(B) 我必須完成報告。
(C) 對，他剛離開。

單字　already 已經　report 報告

解答　(C)

22. 陳述句

You can pick up your order at the service desk.
(A) After he left.（錯誤答案）
▶ 這是適合回覆When問句的錯誤答案。

(B) Not at all.（錯誤答案）
▶ 這是適合回覆Thank you的錯誤答案。

(C) Is it ready now?（正確答案）
▶ 反問的正確答案。

翻譯
您可以在服務台領取您訂購的物品。
(A) 在他離開之後。
(B) 不客氣。
(C) 現在已經準備好了嗎？

單字　pick up 領取，獲得～

解答　(C)

23. Who 問句

Who wants to organize the company picnic this year?
(A) We picked the same thing.（錯誤答案）
▶ 用有關聯的詞彙（picnic - picked）造成混淆的錯誤答案。

(B) I'd be happy to.（正確答案）
▶ 使用第一人稱代名詞的正確答案。

(C) I won't attend.（錯誤答案）
▶ 聽到聯想單字的（picnic - attend）選項是錯誤答案。

翻譯
誰想籌備今年的公司野餐？
(A) 我們選了一樣的東西。
(B) 我很樂意。
(C) 我不會出席。

單字　organize 籌備，組織　company picnic 公司野餐
pick 選擇　attend 出席

解答　(B)

24. 選擇疑問句

Did you email the evaluation or fax it?
(A) I haven't sent it yet.（正確答案）
▶ 沒有選擇其中一個選項，而是給了其他答覆的正確答案。

(B) I lost an envelope.（錯誤答案）
▶ 用相似的單字（email - envelope）造成混淆的錯誤答案。

(C) It will be fine.（錯誤答案）
▶ 這是適合回覆「How is the weather?（天氣如何？）」的錯誤答案。

翻譯
你是用電子郵件寄出評估報告，還是用傳真的？
(A) 我還沒寄。
(B) 我弄丟信封了。
(C) 會很好的。

單字　evaluation 評估，評估報告　envelope 信封

解答　(A)

25. 建議句

Could you make the delivery a day earlier?
(A) Yes, I think I can.（正確答案）
▶ 正面回覆提議的正確答案。

(B) I was late for the meeting.（錯誤答案）
▶ 這是適合回覆Why問句的錯誤答案。

(C) No, it's a document.（錯誤答案）
▶ 代名詞不對，所以是錯誤答案。

翻譯
你可以提早一天寄達嗎？
(A) 好，我想應該可以。
(B) 我開會遲到了。
(C) 不，這是文件。

單字 **delivery** 寄送 **document** 文件

解答 **(A)**

26. 陳述句

I'm sorry, but the replacement parts are out of stock.
(A) Can you order them for me?（正確答案）
▶ 反問是否能幫忙訂缺貨的零件的正確答案。

(B) We shipped it on Tuesday.（錯誤答案）
▶ 這不是索取零件的人會說的話，而是接受訂單的人會說的話，所以是錯誤答案。

(C) Our stock price is rising now.（錯誤答案）
▶ 內容不僅跟零件沒關係，還重複使用了題目中的stock來誘導應答者選錯答案。

翻譯
抱歉，替換零件目前缺貨。
(A) 你可以幫我訂嗎？
(B) 我們星期二寄出了。
(C) 我們的股價目前正在上升。

單字 **replacement part** 替換零件 **be out of stock** 缺貨 **ship** 船，寄送 **stock price** 股價

解答 **(A)**

27. Which 問句

Which route did you take to the library?
(A) Thirteen kilometers.（錯誤答案）
▶ 這是適合回覆How far問句的錯誤答案。

(B) I hope I can do it.（錯誤答案）
▶ 這是適合回覆Who問句的錯誤答案。

(C) I went through town.（正確答案）
▶ 用go through表示經過地點的正確答案。

翻譯
你走哪條路去圖書館？
(A) 十三公里。
(B) 希望我能做到。
(C) 我穿過市區。

單字 **route** 路，路徑 **through** 穿過～

解答 **(C)**

28. 建議句

Would you be able to get me a couple of file folders?
(A) I can't find the document.（錯誤答案）
▶ 用聯想單字（file folder - document）造成混淆的錯誤答案。

(B) No problem. What color do you want?（正確答案）
▶ 透過「No problem.」可以知道聽者會幫忙拿文件夾，而且還反問要什麼顏色的，詢問更多的資訊。

(C) Yes, there is a new office supply store.（錯誤答案）
▶ 作答時可能會因為題目的file folders而聯想到office supply store，這是利用聯想單字誘導答錯的錯誤答案。

翻譯
你可以替我拿一些文件夾嗎？
(A) 我找不到文件。
(B) 沒問題。你要什麼顏色的？
(C) 對，有一間新的辦公用品店。

單字 **file folder** 文件夾 **document** 文件 **office supply** 辦公用品

解答 **(B)**

29. What 問句

What supplies are we going to need for this project?
(A) It won't be available anymore.（錯誤答案）
▶ 這是適合回覆建議問句的錯誤答案。

(B) We have to start the project now.（錯誤答案）
▶ 聽到同個單字（project）的錯誤答案。

(C) Some poster boards and marking pens.（正確答案）
▶ 使用了適合回覆「What＋名詞」問句的名詞（pens、poster board）的正確答案。

翻譯
這個案子我們會需要什麼補給品？
(A) 不會再提供了。
(B) 我們必須現在開始進行案子。
(C) 一些海報看板和麥克筆。

單字 **supply** 補給品 **poster board** 海報看板

解答 **(C)**

30. 陳述句

I have an appointment this afternoon.
(A) Let's appoint a director.（錯誤答案）
▶ 聽到相似單字的（appointment - appoint）錯誤答案。

(B) After 2 o'clock.（錯誤答案）
▶ 這是適合回覆When問句的錯誤答案。

(C) When will you be back?（正確答案）
▶ 反問對方的正確答案。

翻譯
我今天下午有個約會。

(A) 我們來任命董事吧。

(B) 兩點過後。

(C) 你什麼時候會回來？

單字　appointment 約會　appoint 任命，指名

解答　**(C)**

31. 一般問句

Do you want to purchase a three-year extended warranty?

(A) Cash or charge?（錯誤答案）

▶ 此回答跟付款方式有關，是跟題目沒關係的錯誤答案。

(B) No, this one looks good.（錯誤答案）

▶ 拒絕購買的否定回覆，跟表示「看起來很好」的正面補充說明彼此矛盾，所以是內容有誤的錯誤答案。

(C) That depends. How much does it cost?（正確答案）

▶ 反問價格，正面表示會根據價格決定是否購買的正確答案。

翻譯

您想購買延展三年的保固嗎？

(A) 付現還是刷卡？

(B) 不，這個看起來很好。

(C) 看情況。那要多少錢？

單字　extended warranty 延長的保固　charge 賒購　that / it depends 看情況而定

解答　**(C)**

PART 2 FINAL TEST - 2

7. 建議句

Would you like some tea?

(A) Yes, with milk, please.（正確答案）

▶ 正面答覆建議問句的正確答案。

(B) It's in the cupboard.（錯誤答案）

▶ 聽到聯想單字的（tea - cupboard）選項是錯誤答案。

(C) Of course, you may.（錯誤答案）

▶ 主詞不對，所以是錯誤答案。

翻譯

您要喝茶嗎？

(A) 好，加牛奶，謝謝。

(B) 在櫥櫃裡。

(C) 當然可以。

單字　cupboard 櫥櫃　of course 當然

解答　**(A)**

8. Where 問句

Where are you taking our clients after the seminar?

(A) To a Chinese restaurant.（正確答案）

▶ 出現「to＋地點」的正確答案。

(B) About equipment instructions.（錯誤答案）

▶ 這是適合回覆What問句的錯誤答案。

(C) I'll show you a demonstration.（錯誤答案）

▶ 聽到聯想單字的（seminar - demonstration）錯誤答案。

翻譯

研討會之後，你要帶我們的客戶去哪裡？

(A) 去一間中式餐廳。

(B) 關於裝備說明。

(C) 我會示範給你看。

單字　client 客戶　equipment 裝備　instruction 說明　demonstration 示範說明，實地示範

解答　**(A)**

9. When 問句

When should I submit the travel expense report?

(A) Yes, be sure to do it as soon as possible.（錯誤答案）

▶ 在疑問詞問句的答覆中，Yes／No選項是錯誤答案。

(B) Before leaving the office today.（正確答案）

▶ 說要在下班前繳交，提出具體繳交期限的正確答案。

(C) I'm going on a business trip next Monday.（錯誤答案）

▶ 雖然提到了下週一這個時間點，但這不是繳交報告的時間點，而是出差的日子，所以是錯誤答案。

翻譯

我應該在何時繳交出差經費報告？

(A) 對，請務必盡快做。

(B) 今天下班之前。

(C) 我下週一要出差。

單字　submit 繳交　travel expense report 出差經費報告　be sure to do 務必做～　as soon as possible 盡快　leave the office 下班　go on a business trip 出差

解答　**(B)**

10. 陳述句

I'm looking for someone to organize the business trip.

(A) Yes, he did.（錯誤答案）

▶ 無法得知he是誰的錯誤答案。

(B) A farm organization.（錯誤答案）

▶ 聽到相似單字的（organize - organization）錯誤答案。

(C) I will help with that. （正確答案）

▶ 在命令句的答覆中，用「I will~」表示自己會做什麼事的選項是最常見的正確答案。

翻譯
我正在找人籌備出差的事。
(A) 對，他做了。
(B) 農業組織。
(C) 我會幫忙。

單字　organize 籌備，組織　business trip 商務旅行　organization 組織，機構

解答　(C)

11. 一般問句

Didn't Ben study science at his university?

(A) I'll send it to you. （錯誤答案）

▶ 主詞不對的錯誤答案。

(B) He studied chemistry. （正確答案）

▶ 省略Yes／No並補充說明的正確答案。

(C) Another laboratory. （錯誤答案）

▶ 聽到聯想單字的（science - laboratory）錯誤答案。

翻譯
班恩在大學不是念科學的嗎？
(A) 我會寄給你。
(B) 他念化學。
(C) 另一個實驗室。

單字　science 科學　university 大學　chemistry 化學　laboratory 實驗室

解答　(B)

12. 陳述句

I heard the entire staff is getting a raise.

(A) Really? I haven't heard that. （正確答案）

▶ 表示「不知道」的正確答案。

(B) We will leave the company this year. （錯誤答案）

▶ 用聯想單字（get a raise - company）造成混淆的錯誤答案。

(C) No, I have never been there. （錯誤答案）

▶ 這是適合回覆一般問句（have p.p.）的錯誤答案。

翻譯
我聽說全體員工都會加薪。
(A) 真的嗎？我沒聽說。
(B) 我們今年會離開公司。
(C) 不，我從未去過那裡。

單字　get a raise 加薪
解答　(A)

13. Why 問句

Why did you throw away that calendar?

(A) Yes, I'm planning to go to the meeting. （錯誤答案）

▶ 在疑問詞問句的答覆中，Yes選項是錯誤答案。

(B) It was outdated. （正確答案）

▶ 恰當地說明原因的正確答案。

(C) Once a month, I think. （錯誤答案）

▶ 這是適合回覆How often問句的錯誤答案。

翻譯
你為什麼扔掉月曆了？
(A) 對，我打算參加會議。
(B) 過時了。
(C) 我覺得一個月一次。

單字　outdated 過時的

解答　(B)

14. 陳述句

The shopping district is always very crowded on weekends.

(A) He manages the staff with strict rules. （錯誤答案）

▶ 聽到相似單字的（district - strict）錯誤答案。

(B) Two skirts and a jacket. （錯誤答案）

▶ 聽到聯想單字的（shopping - skirts and a jacket）錯誤答案。

(C) Yes, but the prices are good. （正確答案）

▶ 表示同意後，恰當地補充說明的正確答案。

翻譯
購物區在週末時總是人潮擁擠。
(A) 他用嚴格的規定管理員工。
(B) 兩件裙子和一件夾克。
(C) 對，不過價格很好。

單字　district 地區，區域　crowded 擁擠的　strict 嚴格的　rule 規定

解答　(C)

15. 一般問句

Won't it take too long to revise that report?

(A) It starts next week. （錯誤答案）

▶ 是適合回覆When問句的錯誤答案。

(B) Mr. Brown will do it. （錯誤答案）

▶ 這是適合回覆Who問句的錯誤答案。

(C) You can ask Michael about that.（正確答案）
▶ 要對方問別人，表示「不知道」的正確答案。

翻譯
修改那份報告不會花很久時間嗎？
(A) 下個禮拜開始。
(B) 布朗先生會做這件事。
(C) 你可以問問邁可。

單字　revise 變更，修改

解答　**(C)**

16. Who 問句

Who gave the presentation?
(A) Yes, just now.（錯誤答案）
▶ 在疑問詞問句的答覆中，Yes選項是錯誤答案。

(B) Very interesting.（錯誤答案）
▶ 這是適合回覆How問句的錯誤答案。

(C) The sales team.（正確答案）
▶ 提到部門的正確答案。

翻譯
誰做了簡報？
(A) 對，剛才。
(B) 非常有趣。
(C) 銷售組。

單字　give the presentation 做簡報　sales team 銷售組

解答　**(C)**

17. Why 問句

Why did you leave the office early yesterday?
(A) I had another meeting.（正確答案）
▶ 恰當地提出理由的正確答案。

(B) I lost it this morning.（錯誤答案）
▶ 聽到聯想單字的（yesterday - this morning）錯誤答案。

(C) Just before the end.（錯誤答案）
▶ 這是適合回覆When問句的錯誤答案。

翻譯
你昨天為什麼提早下班？
(A) 我有另一個會議。
(B) 我今天早上弄丟了。
(C) 在結束之前。

單字　meeting 會議　leave the office 下班

解答　**(A)**

18. When 問句

When's your next trip to New York?
(A) I'll go on a business trip.（錯誤答案）
▶ 用同個單字（trip - trip）當陷阱，誘導考生答錯的錯誤答案。

(B) We'll meet him in New York.（錯誤答案）
▶ 用同個單字（New York）造成混淆的錯誤答案。

(C) Later this month.（正確答案）
▶ 提到時間點的正確答案。

翻譯
你下次什麼時候去紐約？
(A) 我要出差。
(B) 我們會在紐約跟他見面。
(C) 本月稍晚。

單字　business trip 商務旅行　meet 見面

解答　**(C)**

19. 一般問句

Do you want to talk about the new project today?
(A) Let's discuss that on Friday instead of today.（正確答案）
▶ 針對提議又提出另一個建議的正確答案。

(B) In the meeting this morning.（錯誤答案）
▶ 這是適合回覆When問句的錯誤答案。

(C) It is an urgent project.（錯誤答案）
▶ 用同個單字（project）造成混淆的錯誤答案。

翻譯
你想在今天談新案子的事嗎？
(A) 不要今天，我們禮拜五再討論吧。
(B) 在今天早上的會議。
(C) 這是緊急的案子。

單字　discuss 討論　instead 代替　urgent 緊急的

解答　**(A)**

20. How long 問句

How long will it take to process my order?
(A) Only one day.（正確答案）
▶ 提到所需時間的正確答案。

(B) No, it already arrived.（錯誤答案）
▶ 在疑問詞問句的答覆中，No選項是錯誤答案。

(C) Yes, more than I expected.（錯誤答案）
▶ 在疑問詞問句的答覆中，Yes選項是錯誤答案。

我的訂單要處理多久？
(A) 只要一天。
(B) 不，已經抵達了。
(C) 對，超乎我的期待。

單字　process 處理　arrive 抵達　expect 期待，預期

解答　**(A)**

21. 一般問句

Have you decided on the color for the new carpet?
(A) In an hour.（錯誤答案）
▶ 這是適合回覆When問句的錯誤答案。

(B) Yes, I thought so.（錯誤答案）
▶ 這是適合回覆陳述句的錯誤答案。

(C) Either blue or gray.（正確答案）
▶ 提到顏色的正確答案。

翻譯
你決定好新地毯的顏色了嗎？
(A) 一個小時內。
(B) 對，我也那樣覺得。
(C) 不是藍色，就是灰色。

單字　decide 決定，決心　either 兩者之中任一的

解答　**(C)**

22. How 問句

How was the lecture?
(A) Very interesting.（正確答案）
▶ 在How is問句的答覆中，聽到跟感覺有關的形容
　 詞，便是正確答案。

(B) On television.（錯誤答案）
▶ 這是適合回覆Where問句的錯誤答案。

(C) In the seminar hall.（錯誤答案）
▶ 用聯想單字（lecture - hall）造成混淆的錯誤答案。

翻譯
演講怎麼樣？
(A) 非常有趣。
(B) 在電視上。
(C) 在研討會大廳裡。

單字　lecture 演講　interesting 有趣的，引起興趣的

解答　**(A)**

23. 陳述句

The forklift will be repaired tomorrow.
(A) Is there another one available?（正確答案）
▶ 反問的正確答案，詢問有沒有其他堆高機可以代替
　 故障的那台。

(B) Some electronic equipment.（錯誤答案）
▶ 用聯想單字（forklift - equipment）造成混淆的錯誤
　 答案。

(C) Yes, I am prepared for the construction project.（錯誤
答案）
▶ 用聯想單字（forklift - construction）造成混淆的錯
　 誤答案。

翻譯
堆高機會在明天修理。
(A) 有其他可以用的嗎？
(B) 某些電子設備。
(C) 是的，我為建設工程做好準備了。

單字　forklift 堆高車　electronic 電子的　construction 建設

解答　**(A)**

24. 建議句

Why don't you try the office supply store across the street?
(A) It's in the supply closet.（錯誤答案）
▶ 這是適合回覆Where問句的錯誤答案。

(B) To get there faster.（錯誤答案）
▶ To不定詞片語適合回覆Why問句（詢問理由時），
　 所以是錯誤答案。

(C) That's okay with me.（正確答案）
▶ 接受對方的勸說的正確答案。

翻譯
你何不去看看街上對面的辦公用品店？
(A) 在儲藏室裡。
(B) 為了快一點到那裡。
(C) 我覺得沒關係。

單字　supply closet 儲藏室　try 嘗試　office supply 辦公用品

解答　**(C)**

25.Which 問句

Which position did you apply to?
(A) The one for the assistant manager.（正確答案）
▶ 在「Which＋名詞」問句的答覆中，包含The one一
　 詞的選項是正確答案。

(B) Until next Friday.（錯誤答案）

► 這是適合回覆When問句的錯誤答案。

(C) It starts next month.（錯誤答案）

► 這是適合回覆When問句的錯誤答案。

翻譯
你申請了哪個職位？
(A) 協理的職位。
(B) 直到下週五。
(C) 下個月開始。

單字　apply to 申請　assistant manager 協理

解答　**(A)**

26. What 問句

What's the new mailing address?
(A) By overnight mail.（錯誤答案）

► 「By mail / ship / car / train / air」是適合回覆
「How to send~」題目的錯誤答案。

(B) Of course, I knew it.（錯誤答案）

► 「Of course（當然）」表示「同意、接受、強調」
對方的話，無法用來回覆疑問詞問句。

(C) 154 Lamar Road.（正確答案）

► 恰當地回覆地址的正確答案。

翻譯
新的郵件地址是什麼？
(A) 用隔夜寄達的郵件。
(B) 當然，我知道。
(C) 拉瑪路一五四號。

單字　overnight mail 隔夜寄達的郵件

解答　**(C)**

27. 建議句

Would you care to join us for coffee after this seminar?
(A) Yes, I'd like that.（正確答案）

► 「Yes / Sure, I'd like that.」是常見的提議、邀請句
的答覆，在這裡是正確答案。

(B) There'll only be four of us.（錯誤答案）

► 用發音相似的單字（for - four）造成混淆的錯誤答案。

(C) You need to lift it carefully.（錯誤答案）

► 跟題目無關的錯誤答案。

翻譯
這個研討會結束之後，你要跟我們一起喝咖啡嗎？
(A) 好，我很樂意。
(B) 只會有我們四個人。
(C) 你要小心地拿起來。

單字　carefully 小心地

解答　**(A)**

28. 選擇疑問句

Can you meet our subcontractors, or do I need to ask Marie to do that?
(A) We're trying to negotiate.（錯誤答案）

► 跟題目無關的錯誤答案。

(B) They received a subsidy.（錯誤答案）

► 用相似的單字（subcontractor – subsidy）造成混
淆的錯誤答案。

(C) What time do you need me?（正確答案）

► 選擇前者並反問的正確答案。

翻譯
你可以去見我們的外包廠商嗎？還是我需要叫瑪麗去？
(A) 我們正試著協商。
(B) 他們收到了補助。
(C) 你需要我什麼時候去？

單字　subcontractor 外包廠商　negotiate 協商　subsidy
補助

解答　**(C)**

29.How many 問句

How many suitcases would you like to check?
(A) 20 dollars will do.（錯誤答案）

► 價錢適合用來回覆How much問句，是錯誤答案。

(B) Two, thanks.（正確答案）

► 提到要託運的手提箱數量為兩個的正確答案。

(C) I'll check in at the hotel.（錯誤答案）

► 不僅跟託運數量無關，還聽到題目出現過的單字
（check）的錯誤答案。

翻譯
您要託運幾個手提箱？
(A) 二十美元就可以了。
(B) 兩個，謝謝。
(C) 我會在飯店辦理入住手續。

單字　check 託運　will do ～就可以了，～就夠了　check
in 辦理入住手續

解答　**(B)**

30. 陳述句

I've noticed some mistakes on the menu.
(A) Can you show me where they are?（正確答案）

▶ 大部分的反問句都是正確答案。

(B) I'll have the homemade soup, please.（錯誤答案）
▶ 這是適合回覆What問句的錯誤答案。

(C) The restaurant serves wonderful meals.（錯誤答案）
▶ 聽到聯想單字的（menu - restaurant）錯誤答案。

翻譯
我發現菜單上有些錯誤。
(A) 可以讓我看看在哪裡嗎？
(B) 請給我自製濃湯。
(C) 那家餐廳提供很棒的餐點。

單字　notice 發現，意識到～　mistake 錯誤，失誤　meal 餐點

解答　(A)

---

31. 選擇疑問句

Are we having the accounting seminar in the conference room or the convention center?

(A) No, I'll meet them there.（錯誤答案）
▶ 在選擇疑問句的答覆中，Yes／No選項是錯誤答案。

(B) I'm still thinking about it.（正確答案）
▶ 表示不知道兩者之中該選哪一個的正確答案。

(C) There's plenty of room.（錯誤答案）
▶ 跟題目無關的答覆，而且是使用了題目出現過的單字（room）的錯誤答案。

翻譯
我們會在會議室還是大會中心舉辦會計研討會？
(A) 不，我會在那裡見他們。
(B) 我還在思考。
(C) 空間很充足。

單字　accounting seminar 會計研討會　conference room 會議室　plenty of （數量）很多的　room 房間，空間

解答　(B)

PART 3

類型分析 7　各大題型攻略
Unit 13　詢問主題、目的的題目

Step 3 實戰演練

Question 1 refers to the following conversation.
第 1 題請參照以下的對話。

> M : [1] How are you doing with the computer program you use to enter customer data?
> ▶ 這是詢問主題的題目，所以要仔細聆聽第一句話。透過男子的發言，可以知道對話內容跟「電腦程式的使用」有關，所以 (A) 為正確答案。
>
> W : I'm quite familiar with it. I did the same kind of data entry at my last job.
> M : That sounds really great! If you have any problems, don't hesitate to call me.
>
> ---
>
> 男：用來輸入顧客資料的電腦程式妳用得怎麼樣？
> 女：我還滿熟悉的。我在上一份工作中做過一樣的資料輸入作業。
> 男：聽起來很棒！如果妳有任何問題，不用猶豫，儘管打給我。

單字　enter 輸入　be familiar with 對～感到熟悉　hesitate 猶豫

1. 對話跟什麼有關？
(A) 使用電腦程式
(B) 購買新電腦
(C) 邀請顧客
(D) 聘僱條件

解答　(A)

Question 2 refers to the following conversation.
第 2 題請參照以下的對話。

> W : [2] Hello. I bought a refrigerator at your store this morning, and I heard from the store that you'll be delivering my new refrigerator today.
> ▶ 這是詢問目的的題目，所以要仔細聆聽第一句話。透過女子的發言，可以知道對話內容跟「確認寄送」有關，所以 (D) 為正確答案。
>
> M : Yes, we will. You are Mrs. Jackson, right?
> W : Yes, I am. Can you take away my old refrigerator as well?

M : Sure. There will be an additional cost for that service, though.

女：嗨，我今天早上在你們店裡買了一台冰箱，我聽店裡說你們今天會運送我的新冰箱。

男：對，我們會的。您是傑克遜女士，對吧？

女：對，我是。你們可以也拿走我的舊冰箱嗎？

男：當然。不過，那項服務要另外加錢。

單字　**refrigerator** 冰箱　**delivery** 寄送　**as well** ～也　**additional** 追加的，附加的

2. 女子打電話的目的是什麼？

(A) 為了下單
(B) 為了要求修理
(C) 為了買新的冰箱
(D) 為了確認寄送

解答　(D)

Unit 14　詢問職業／對話地點的題目

Step 3 實戰演練

Question 1 refers to the following conversation.
第 1 題請參照以下的對話。

W : Excuse me. I'd like to go to the Central Shopping Mall. Will your bus take me there?

▶ 這題問的是男子的職業，所以要仔細聆聽第一句話。女子詢問「公車是否會到中央購物中心」，由此可知男子是公車司機。(B) 為正確答案。

M : No, it won't. You'll have to take the number 50 bus. It will bring you there.
W : Thank you. Does the bus stop at this station? I totally have no idea about taking the bus.
M : You have to go across the road. You can see the bus station with the yellow roof.

女：不好意思，我想去中央購物中心。這台公車會到嗎？

男：不，不會。妳要搭 50 號公車。那台會到。

女：謝謝。公車會在這一站停車嗎？我對搭公車一竅不通。

男：妳要過馬路。妳會看到黃色屋頂的公車站。

單字　**totally** 完全地　**have no idea** 不知道　**go across the road** 過馬路　**bus station** 公車站

1. 男子最有可能是誰？

(A) 路人
(B) 公車司機
(C) 銷售員
(D) 觀光導遊

解答　(B)

Question 2 refers to the following conversation.
第2題請參照以下的對話。

M : Hi. This is Kim from Daily Plumbing. We got a call from the restaurant manager saying that there is a problem with the toilet.

▶ 這題問的是對話地點，所以要仔細聆聽第一句。從第一句話中可以得知男子的職業是「配管工人」，「接到餐廳經理的電話說馬桶有問題」。由此可知對話地點是「餐廳」，所以 (C) 為正確答案。

W : Oh, thanks for coming so quickly. I was cleaning the restroom and noticed that the water in the toilet had overflowed.
M : Okay. I just have to get some equipment from my truck. I'll be back in a minute.

男：您好，我是每日配管系統的金。我們接到餐廳經理的電話說馬桶有問題。

女：噢，謝謝您這麼快就過來。我那時正在打掃洗手間，然後發現馬桶的水溢出來了。

男：好，我得從卡車上拿一些裝備。我等一下就回來。

單字　**plumbing** 配管，配管系統　**toilet** 馬桶　**quickly** 快速地　**restroom** 洗手間　**notice** 發現～　**overflow** 溢出

2. 對話地點最有可能是哪裡？

(A) 配管工程辦公室
(B) 電腦店
(C) 餐廳
(D) 飯店

解答　(C)

Unit 15　詢問說話者的建議的題目

Step 3 實戰演練

Questions 1-2 refer to the following conversation.
第1-2題請參照以下的對話。

W : I was almost late again this morning. ¹I got stuck in a terrible traffic jam.

▶ 問題點會在前半段出現。女子的問題是塞車，所以 (A) 為正確答案。

M : Really? It's even worse than taking the subway.
W : I wish I could take the subway, too, but my house is quite far from the subway station.
M : Maybe someone who lives near you would like to carpool to the station. ²Why don't you talk with our colleagues?

42

▶ 這是詢問建議（suggest）內容的題目，所以要仔細聆聽句子 Why don't~。男子表示說不定會有人想要一起搭車到地鐵站，建議女子跟同事說說看，所以 (C) 為正確答案。

女：我今天早上又差點遲到了。我被可怕的塞車給困住了。
男：真的嗎？那比搭地鐵還糟糕。
女：我也希望我能搭地鐵，但是我家離地鐵站很遠。
男：說不定住在妳家附近的人會想一起搭車到地鐵站。跟妳的同事說說看吧？

單字　**get stuck** 被堵住，被困住　**traffic jam** 交通擁擠　**quite** 相當，很　**carpool** 共乘汽車　**colleague** 同事

1. 說話者正在討論什麼問題？
　(A) 交通擁擠
　(B) 新員工
　(C) 培訓課程
　(D) 新系統

解答　(A)

2. 男子建議女子做什麼？
　(A) 買車
　(B) 搭地鐵
　(C) 跟同事說
　(D) 走路上下班

解答　(C)

Unit 16　詢問接下來會做什麼事的題目

Step 3 實戰演練

Questions 1-2 refer to the following conversation.
第1-2題請參照以下的對話。

M : Doris, [1] did you know that the post office on Park Avenue has relocated? Now, a restaurant is being built in its place.
▶ 主題會在前半段出現。兩人正在討論郵局搬遷的事，所以 (D) 為正確答案。

W : Yes. The post office just moved to a new location on Main Street two weeks ago.
M : Oh, really? Do you know the address? I have to send this parcel today.
W : No, I don't, but [2] I can make you a rough map.
▶ 這是 next 題型，詢問接下來會做什麼事，所以要專心聆聽最後一句話。男子「想去郵局，所以問了地址」，而女子回答「可以替他畫個大概的地圖」。由此可知，(D) 為正確答案。

男：朵莉絲，妳知道公園大道上的郵局搬走了嗎？那個地方現在正在蓋餐廳。
女：嗯，郵局兩個禮拜前剛搬到主街的新地點。
男：哦，真的嗎？妳知道地址嗎？我今天得寄出這個包裹。
女：不，我不知道，但我可以畫一個大概的地圖給你。

單字　**rough map** 草圖

1. 說話者主要在討論什麼？
　(A) 主街上的餐廳
　(B) 城市導覽地圖
　(C) 新的辦公大樓
　(D) 郵局的位置

解答　(D)

2. 女子接下來可能會做什麼？
　(A) 給男子地址
　(B) 展示城市地圖
　(C) 帶男子到郵局
　(D) 畫大概的地圖

解答　(D)

Unit 17　詢問細節的題目

Step 3 實戰演練

Questions 1-3 refer to the following conversation.
第1-3題請參照以下的對話。

M : Hello there. I moved in to the apartment complex last month. [1] I'd like to register for the fitness center.
▶ 第一題問的是男子想做什麼，所以要透過前半段的男子發言來確認線索。男子說想報名健身中心，所以 (C) 為正確答案。

W : No problem. [2] I'll need a copy of your lease or a utility bill, anything that proves you are currently living in your apartment.
▶ 詢問細節的出題順序為第二題，所以答題線索會在女子中間的發言出現。女子要求男子出示目前住在這個公寓的證據。正確答案為 (A)。

M : Unfortunately, I didn't bring anything with me. Can I come back after work?
W : Of course. We close early on Wednesdays, though, so try to make it by 7 o'clock. [3] This information brochure lists our gym hours and the office hours.
▶ 這題問的是男子從女子那裡獲得了什麼，屬於詢問細節的題目。出題順序為第三題，所以要從女子後半段的發言中確認她給男子什麼東西。女子拿手冊給男子看，告訴他上面寫了健身房的營業時間和辦公時

concert?

間。對話中的 information brochure 在選項中被改述成
schedule information。正確答案為 (C)。

男：妳好，我上個月搬進這個公寓社區。我想報名健
　　身中心。
女：沒問題。我需要一份您的租約或水電費帳單等任
　　何可以證明您目前住在公寓裡的東西。
男：很可惜，我沒帶任何東西。我可以下班之後再來
　　嗎？
女：當然。我們星期三較早關門，所以請盡量在七點
　　之前來。這份資訊手冊列有我們健身房的營業時
　　間和辦公時間。

單字　apartment complex 公寓社區　register for 報名
fitness center 健身中心　lease 租約　utility bill 水電費帳
單　prove 證明，證實　currently 目前　make a copy 影
印　information brochure 資訊手冊　gym 健身房，體育館
office hours 營業時間，辦公時間

1. 男子想做什麼？
(A) 簽訂租約
(B) 找公寓
(C) 加入健身房
(D) 影印

解答　(C)

2. 女子索取什麼東西？
(A) 居住證明
(B) 保證金
(C) 延遲報名的費用
(D) 一些運動器材

解答　(A)

3. 男子從女子那裡收到什麼？
(A) 簽好名的租約
(B) 報名表
(C) 日程資訊
(D) 水電費帳單

解答　(C)

Unit 18　掌握句子意圖的題目

Step 3　實戰演練

Questions 1-2 refer to the following conversation with three speakers.
第1-2題請參照以下三人的對話。

M1 : [1]Did you hear the radio yesterday about the blue jazz

▶ 詢問主題的題目答題線索通常會在前半段出現。
三人正在討論 concert，將對話中的 concert 改成
performance 的 (A) 為正確答案。

W : Yes, I did. I thought the show would definitely sell out.
[2]How shocking!

▶ 女子以為門票已經賣完，說了「How shocking」。
只聽到這邊的話，無法確定「How shocking」的意思。

M2 : [2]I know. Everyone was so excited about the concert.
Who would've imagined that so few people would attend?

▶ 另一個男子同意女子的發言，說沒想到人會這麼
少。由此可知，女子聽到音樂會的低出席率後感到驚
訝。以 a low turnout 表示低出席率的 (C) 為正確答案。

W : What do you think the reason was?
M1 : Well, the critics are saying that the tickets were way
overpriced. The venue, the Golden Lion Theater, does have
high prices.

男1：你們昨天有聽到電臺提到的藍調爵士音樂會
　　　嗎？
女：嗯，我聽了。我以為門票一定會賣光。真令人驚
　　訝！
男2：我懂。每個人都很期待這場音樂會。誰想得到
　　　才那麼少人參加？
女：你們覺得原因是什麼？
男1：嗯，評論家都在說票價太高了。那個地點，金
　　　獅戲院的價位是滿高的。

單字　sell out 售罄　critic 評論家　overpriced 定價過高的
venue（演唱會、運動賽事等）地點　personally 個人地
breakup 解散　overbooked 超額預訂　turnout 出席人數

1. 這段對話主要是關於什麼？
(A) 近期的表演
(B) 即將到來的表演
(C) 售罄的音樂會
(D) 樂團解散

解答　(A)

2. 女子為什麼說「真令人驚訝」？
(A) 她覺得某個表演的品質很糟。
(B) 她聽說某個表演的席位超賣。
(C) 她發現出席人數很少。
(D) 她發現音樂會取消了。

解答　(C)

Questions 3-4 refer to the following conversation with three speakers. 第3-4題請參照以下三人的對話。

W : Hello. I'd like to discuss a mortgage application. Could I speak to Marianne Lemoute, please?

M1 : I'm sorry, but Ms. Lemoute no longer works here.

W : Really? ³I can't believe it! I have always gotten excellent advice and service from her as my financial advisor.

▶ 上一句男子一說莫勒提不在這裡工作，女子便說「真不敢相信」，提到自己接受過她的建議和服務。由此可知，女子對於莫勒提離職的事實感到可惜和驚訝。正確答案為 (A)。

M2 : She doesn't work in the banking industry anymore from what I understand.

W : Oh, that's too bad. Well, then who can I talk to about my mortgage?

M2 : ⁴It's best if you consult with Flooder. He is the new regional manager.

▶ 請求、提議句的答題線索，通常可以在後半段找到。這是詢問男子建議什麼的題目，所以要從男子的發言中找線索。女子表示沒辦法跟她諮詢很可惜後，男子說跟新的區域經理佛羅德討論應該不錯。正確答案為將新員工改述成接替者（replacement）的 (B)。

女：你好，我想討論房貸申請的事。請問我可以跟瑪麗安‧勒莫提談談嗎？

男1：抱歉，瑪麗安‧莫勒提女士已經不在這邊工作了。

女：真的嗎？真不敢相信！我總是把她當作我的財務顧問，從她那裡得到很好的建議和服務。

男2：據我所知，她不在銀行界工作了。

女：噢，太可惜了。嗯，那我可以跟誰討論我的房貸？

男2：向佛羅德諮詢是最好的。他是新來的區經理。

單字 mortgage 抵押，融資 take over 接收 ownership 所有權 loan 貸款 equally 公平地，相同地 helpful 有幫助的 extension 延長 merger 合併 maternity leave 產假 out of the office 不在辦公室 account number 帳戶號碼 replacement 代替者，接替者

3. 為什麼女子說「真不敢相信」？

(A) 她很驚訝有個員工離開公司了。
(B) 她不信任那個男子。
(C) 她收到一些錯誤的資訊。
(D) 她很開心聽到某些消息。

解答　(A)

4. 男子建議女子做什麼？

(A) 準備好帳戶號碼
(B) 跟勒莫提女士的接替者談話
(C) 寄出申請表格
(D) 親自拜訪銀行

解答　(B)

Step 3 實戰演練

Questions 1-2 refer to the following conversation and list. 第1-2題請參照以下的對話和清單。

W : Charles, ¹I'm really looking forward to the marathon we're sponsoring next month. I bet it'll be great publicity.

▶ 對話主題會在前半段出現。以上面這句為依據，我們可以知道說話者贊助的活動是馬拉松，所以正確答案為 (B)。

M : Yeah, I'm excited, too. We need to hire a company to design the tumblers that we'll give out to the participants. Have you looked over the list of design firms? We have to decide one by the end of this week.

W : I know. I think Fine Art does a very good job, but I heard it is quite pricy. And management has reduced our budget to spend on souvenirs this year.

M : That's true. ²Let's just give the job to the firm here in San Diego. We can reduce the shipping costs, and its prices are pretty reasonable, too.

▶ 兩人聊到精細藝術公司收費昂貴，男子說「Let's just give the job to the firm here in San Diego.」，表示要將工作交給聖地牙哥的當地業者做。確認表格中位於聖地牙哥的公司之後，即可知道正確答案為(C)。

女：查理斯，我真的很期待我們下個月贊助的馬拉松。我敢肯定這會是很棒的宣傳。

男：對啊，我也很激動。我們需要請一間公司來設計我們要發給參加者的隨行杯。妳看過設計公司名單了嗎？我們要在這週內做決定。

女：我知道。我覺得精細藝術公司做得很好，但我聽說滿貴的。而且管理階層削減了我們今年可以花在紀念品上的預算。

男：沒錯。我們就把工作交給聖地牙哥這裡的公司做吧。我們可以降低運費，而且價格也很合理。

單字 sponsor 贊助 judge by 由～判斷 register 報名 bet 確信 publicity 宣傳 participant 參加者 souvenir 紀念品 pricy 昂貴的 reduce 減少 reasonable 合理的

1. 說話者贊助的是什麼種類的活動？

(A) 拍賣會
(B) 跑步比賽
(C) 設計比賽
(D) 藝術展

解答　(B)

公司	位置
精細藝術	新澤西
W設計	舊金山
瓦瑞森	聖地牙哥
葛瑞芬諾	洛杉磯

2. 請看圖表。說話者會跟哪間公司做生意？

(A) 精細藝術
(B) W設計
(C) 瓦瑞森
(D) 葛瑞芬諾

解答　(C)

Questions 3-4 refer to the following conversation and map. 第3-4題請參照以下的對話和地圖。

M : Excuse me, Amanda. ³I have a problem with my ID. It doesn't open the doors to the building, so I have to get someone on the front desk staff to let me in. Could you add my information to the security system?

▶ 男子正在說自己的問題，他無法用自己的證件進出大樓。正確答案為 (C)。

W : Well, the staff in Human Resources is only in charge of IDs for our building, ⁴Why don't you go to the personnel office? Someone there should be able to save you on the database.

▶ 男子被建議去人事部門，人事部的辦公室在三號室。

M : Okay. I'll try. Thanks.

男：不好意思，亞曼達。我的證件有個問題，它打不開通往大樓的門，所以我必須請櫃檯員工放我進來。妳可以把我的資訊加到保全系統裡嗎？
女：嗯，只有人事部的員工負責進出大樓的證件。你何不去人事部辦公室看看？那邊的人應該可以把你存到資料庫中。
男：好，我試試。謝謝。

單字　distribution 分銷　security 保全　in charge of 負責　give it a try 嘗試，試試看　human resource 人力資源　personel office 人事部辦公室

3. 男子的問題是什麼？

(A) 他沒有收到額外的薪水。
(B) 他需要人事部的電話號碼。
(C) 他沒辦法使用他的證件。
(D) 他不記得電腦系統的密碼。

解答　(C)

4. 請看圖表。男子被告知去哪個地方？

(A) 1號室
(B) 2號室
(C) 3號室
(D) 4號室

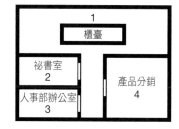

解答　(C)

Questions 1-3 refer to the following conversation. 第1-3題請參照以下的對話。

W : Hi, Michael. ¹/²Did you hear that our office will be painted this evening? The workers will move all the office furniture, so we have to clean everything up on our desks before we leave today.

▶ 請記住對話主題和地點會在前半段出現，所以第一題和第二題的正確答案，很有可能在第一個說話者的發言中出現。要一邊聆聽第一句，一邊在同個地方尋找這兩題的答題線索。第一題的答案是 (C)，第二題則是 (B)。

M : Really? I heard from Ms. Bunny that the painting work will start next weekend.

W : Hmm. ³I had better call the Maintenance Department to make sure.

▶ 遇到 next 題型時，須專心聆聽後半段，尤其是最後一句話。女子說打電話給維修部比較好，所以 (D) 為正確答案。

女：嗨，邁可。你聽說我們辦公室今晚要油漆的事了嗎？工人會搬走所有辦公家具，所以我們今天離開前要清空桌上的所有東西。
男：真的嗎？我從邦妮女士那裡聽說油漆作業會在下週末開始。
女：嗯，我最好打電話給維修部做個確認。

單字　office furniture 辦公家具　painting work 油漆作業　make sure 確保

1. 說話者主要在討論什麼？

(A) 搬遷辦公室
(B) 移除舊家具
(C) 油漆辦公室
(D) 僱用新員工

解答　(C)

2. 對話發生地點可能在哪裡？

(A) 博物館
(B) 辦公室
(C) 餐廳
(D) 機場

解答　(B)

3. 根據對話，女子接下來可能會做什麼？

(A) 移除所有文件
(B) 離開辦公室
(C) 寄電子郵件給邦妮女士
(D) 聯絡特定部門

解答 (D)

Questions 4-6 refer to the following conversation.
第4-6題請參照以下的對話。

> W：Hi, Mr. Anderson. I'm sorry. [4]I was late for the meeting this morning because of the traffic jam. What did I miss?
> ▶ 詢問理由的題目，答題線索會在前半段出現。將 traffic jam 改述成 stuck in traffic 的 (C) 為正確答案。
>
> M：Oh, [5]on Thursday, we are going to install a new program for all of the computers in the Sales Department.
> ▶ 遇到詢問星期、時間等特定時間點的細節題時，出題順序很重要。這題是第二題，所以線索會在中間出現。男子說會在星期四安裝電腦程式，所以 (D) 為正確答案。
>
> W：So is there anything we have to do to prepare for it?
> M：No, but [6]I suggest that you come early on that day. We will have a lot of work to do.
> ▶ 請求、建議題的答題線索，會在後半段提到 suggest、ask、please、could you 等地方出現。that day 指的是 Thursday，(A) 為正確答案。
>
> ----
>
> 女：嗨，安德森先生。抱歉，我因為塞車的緣故，今天早上開會遲到了。我錯過了什麼？
> 男：喔，我們禮拜四的時候，要替銷售部的所有電腦安裝新程式。
> 女：那我們需要準備什麼嗎？
> 男：不用，但是我建議妳那天早一點來。我們會有很多事情要做。

單字　traffic jam 塞車　install 安裝　Sales Department 銷售部

4. 女子為什麼開會遲到了？
　(A) 她搭乘大眾交通工具。
　(B) 她剛度假回來。
　(C) 她被困在車陣中。
　(D) 她住得離公司很遠。

解答 (C)

5. 說話者會在什麼時候安裝新程式？
　(A) 星期一
　(B) 星期二
　(C) 星期三
　(D) 星期四

解答 (D)

6. 根據對話，男子建議做什麼？

　(A) 星期四早點到
　(B) 拜訪銷售部門
　(C) 買機票
　(D) 去出差

解答 (A)

Questions 7-9 refer to the following conversation with three speakers. 第7-9題請參照以下三人的對話。

> M1：[7]Have you guys visited the new company fitness room on the 15th floor?
> ▶ 這是詢問對話地點的題目，男子問其他人有沒有去過新的健身房。從對話的前半段可以知道這三人是職場同事，所以正確答案是 (A) 辦公室。這不是正在健身房進行的對話，所以 (C) 不是答案。
>
> W：I haven't been there yet, but I heard that it's gotten much better than before.
> M2：Yeah, it has. I started working out there this Monday, and [8]I was really impressed by all the cutting-edge equipment.
> M1：[8]And don't forget the view. It's fantastic! You can see the entire city while you're on a bicycle.
> ▶ 這是詢問男子對新器材的意見的題目，出題順序為第二題，所以對話的中間會出現線索。題目中提到的不是 What does the man，而是 What do the men（男子們），所以要專心聆聽這兩名男子的對話內容。其中一個男子說對最新型的運動器材感到印象深刻，另一個人則說搬到樓上後視野很好，所以綜合這兩點，可以知道健身房在許多方面都變好了。正確答案為 (C)。
>
> M2：I know. It was a great idea to move the facility up from the first floor.
> W：Wow, it sounds amazing. [9]I'm definitely stopping by there after work today.
> ▶ 第三題的答題線索經常在後半段出現，須留意女子在後半段說的話。女子聽完男子說的話，最後表示下班後要去健身房看看，所以正確答案為 (B)。
>
> ----
>
> 男1：你們去過在十五樓的新公司健身房了嗎？
> 女：我還沒去過，但是我聽說比以前好很多。
> 男2：對，好很多。我從這個禮拜一開始在那裡健身，所有的最新型器材都讓我印象深刻。
> 男1：別忘了視野，超美的！踩腳踏車的時候，整個城市盡收眼底。
> 男2：我知道。把設施從一樓搬到樓上是個很棒的主意。
> 女：哇，聽起來很棒。我今天下班一定要順路去看看。

單字　be impressed by 對～印象深刻　cutting-edge 最新型的　definitely 一定　stop by 順路造訪　facility 設施

7. 此對話最有可能在哪裡發生？

    (A) 辦公室
    (B) 保健護理研討會
    (C) 健身中心
    (D) 運動器材店

解答　(A)

8. 男子說了關於新設施的什麼？

    (A) 有些二手運動器材。
    (B) 在一樓的時候比較擠。
    (C) 很多方面都升級了。
    (D) 昂貴的器材比以前多。

解答　(C)

9. 女子說她會做什麼？

    (A) 去一樓
    (B) 去某個設施
    (C) 在公園健身
    (D) 打電話給健身中心

解答　(B)

Questions 10-12 refer to the following conversation.
第10-12題請參照以下的對話。

M : Welcome back to Music Hour. Let's continue the interview with our special guest, Michelle O'Conner. Michelle, can you tell us more about your newly released album?
W : Sure! It's a contemporary crossover album of pop and jazz, and [10] I think the best part is that you can all enjoy the songs no matter how old you are.

▶ 這是詢問細節的題目，在第一題出現，所以要從前半段的女子發言中找線索。女子一邊介紹專輯，一邊說這些歌曲無論幾歲都能享受，所以正確答案為 (A)。這不是傳統的爵士樂，而是爵士樂和流行樂的當代混合音樂類型，所以 (C) 不是答案。

M : That sounds great. Now, [11] I heard that you're planning to hold a nationwide tour concert. Which states will you be visiting?

▶ 詢問女子會做什麼事的題目，出題順序為第二題，中間的時候男子向女子表示知道她計劃開演唱會，接著問會去哪裡。將演唱會改述成 performance 的 (B) 為正確答案。

W : [12] Thanks for asking. Right now, we're still deciding which cities to visit. The details will be announced next week.

▶ 這是掌握意圖的題目，所以要知道對話的鋪陳才能解題。男子在前面的對話中詢問會在哪裡開全國巡迴演唱會，女子先謝謝對方的提問，再說自己正在煩惱要去哪些城市。因此，女子的真正意思是還不知道會

去哪，所以無法回答。正確答案為 (D)。

男：歡迎回到音樂時間。讓我們繼續採訪我們的特別來賓米雪兒・歐康納。米雪兒，妳可以跟我們多說一些妳的最新專輯的事嗎？
女：沒問題！這是一張流行樂和爵士樂的當代混合音樂專輯，我覺得最棒的是無論你幾歲，都能享受這些歌曲。
男：聽起來很棒。我聽說妳計劃舉辦全國巡迴演唱會。妳會去哪些州？
女：謝謝你的提問。我們目前還在決定要去哪些城市。細節會在下個禮拜公布。

單字　release 發行，上映　contemporary 當代的　no matter how 無論如何　be planning to 計劃～　nationwide 全國的

10. 女子喜歡她的專輯的什麼地方？

    (A) 可以引起所有年齡層的興趣。
    (B) 這是她目前為止最暢銷的專輯。
    (C) 只聚焦於傳統爵士樂。
    (D) 這是她的第一張專輯。

解答　(A)

11. 女子計劃做什麼？

    (A) 發行下一張專輯
    (B) 表演
    (C) 拜訪故鄉
    (D) 暫停音樂生涯休息一下

解答　(B)

12. 女子說「謝謝你的提問」是什麼意思？

    (A) 她想問同樣的問題。
    (B) 她想談論新的話題。
    (C) 那個問題她聽過很多遍了。
    (D) 她現在沒辦法給答覆。

解答　(D)

Questions 13-15 refer to the following conversation and directory. 第13-15題請參照以下的對話和樓層介紹。

W : Hello. I'm here for a job interview at noon. The person I spoke to told me I need to sign in at the reception desk to gain access to the building.
M : [13] Well, you're in the right place. Please sign your name here and show me your ID. Which suite are you going to?

▶ 可以預測職業的線索通常會在前半段出現，男子跟來面試的女子說來對地方了，而且請她簽名和出示身分證，所以男子是接待人員。正確答案為 (C)。

W : ¹⁴Office 406. I'm meeting with Mr. Landon.

▶ 女子說要去四〇六號辦公室，樓層介紹的四〇六號辦公室是卡森法律事務所，由此可知女子要在律師的辦公室面試。正確答案為 (D)。

M : Okay, you can use the elevator. Our building is repainting the walls in the hallway right now, and there's a lot of equipment on the floor. Hold on... ¹⁵Let me move this ladder out of your way. Otherwise, you might bump into it.

▶ 男子說地板上有很多東西，要幫她移走梯子。正確答案為 (A)。

女：哈囉，我是來參加中午的工作面試的。跟我交談的人告訴我，需要在接待處簽到，才能取得進入大樓的權限。

男：嗯，您來對地方了。請在這裡簽名並出示您的身分證。您要去幾號辦公室？

女：四〇六號辦公室。我要跟蘭登先生見面。

男：好的，您可以使用電梯。我們大樓目前正在重新油漆走廊的牆壁，地上有很多設備。等一下……我替您移走路上的梯子，不然您有可能會撞到。

單字　reception desk = front desk（飯店、辦公大樓等的）接待處，櫃臺　sign in 簽到，登記名字　gain access 取得權限　suite 號，室　bump into 撞到

13. 男子最有可能是誰？
(A) 面試官
(B) 維修技師
(C) 接待人員
(D) 畫家

解答　(C)

14. 請看圖表。女子最有可能在哪裡面試？
(A) 醫生的診所
(B) 行銷公司
(C) 建築公司
(D) 律師的辦公室

樓層介紹
室號
401　楊醫師診所
402　里德＆肯行銷公司
403　R&J 建築公司
405　出租中
406　卡森法律事務所

解答　(D)

15. 男子接下來可能會做什麼？
(A) 搬梯子
(B) 簽名
(C) 重新油漆牆壁
(D) 使用樓梯

解答　(A)

Unit 13　詢問主題、目的的題目

Q1. M: How are you doing with the computer program you use to enter customer data?

W: I'm quite familiar with it. I did the same kind of data entry at my last job.

M: That sounds really great! If you have any problems, don't hesitate to call me.

Q2. W: Hello. I bought a refrigerator at your store this morning, and I heard from the store that you'll be delivering my new refrigerator today.

M: Yes, we will. You are Mrs. Jackson, right?

W: Yes, I am. Can you take away my old refrigerator as well?

M: Sure. There will be an additional cost for that service though.

Unit 14　詢問職業／對話地點的題目

Q1. W: Excuse me. I'd like to go to the Central Shopping Mall. Will your bus take me there?

M: No, it won't. You'll have to take the number 50 bus. It will bring you there.

W: Thank you. Does the bus stop at this station? I totally have no idea about taking the bus.

M: You have to go across the road. You can see the bus station with the yellow roof.

Q2. M: Hi. This is Kim from Daily Plumbing. We got a call from the restaurant manager saying that there is a problem with the toilet.

W: Oh, thanks for coming so quickly. I was cleaning the restroom and noticed that the water in the toilet had overflowed.

M: Okay. I just have to get some equipment from my truck. I'll be back in a minute.

Unit 15　詢問說話者的建議的題目

Q1-2. W: I was almost late again this morning. I got stuck in a terrible traffic jam.

M: Really? It's even worse than taking the subway.

W: I wish I could take the subway, too, but my house is quite far from the subway station.

M: Maybe someone who lives near you would like to carpool to the station. Why don't you talk with our colleagues?

Unit 16　詢問接下來會做的事的題目

Q1-2. M: Doris, did you know that the post office on Park

Avenue has relocated? Now, a restaurant is being built in its place.

W: Yes. The post office just moved to a new location on Main Street two weeks ago.

M: Oh, really? Do you know the address? I have to send this parcel today.

W: No, I don't, but I can make you a rough map.

Unit 17　詢問細節的題目

Q1-3. M: Hello there. I moved in to the apartment complex last month. I'd like to register for the fitness center.

W: No problem. I'll need a copy of your lease or a utility bill anything that proves you are currently living in your apartment.

M: Unfortunately, I didn't bring anything with me. Can I come back after work?

W: Of course. We close early on Wednesdays though, so try to make it by 7 o'clock. This information brochure lists our gym hours and the office hours.

Unit 18　掌握句子意圖的題目

Q1-2. M1: Did you hear the radio yesterday about the blue jazz concert?

W: Yes, I did. I thought the show would definitely sell out. How shocking!

M2: I know. Everyone was so excited about the concert. Who would've imagined that so few people would attend?

W: What do you think the reason was?

M1: Well, the critics are saying that the tickets were way overpriced. The venue, the Golden Lion Theater, does have high prices.

Q3-4. W: Hello. I'd like to discuss a mortgage application. Could I speak to Marianne Lemoute, please?

M: I'm sorry, but Ms. Lemoute no longer works here.

W: Really? I can't believe it! I have always gotten excellent advice and service from her as my financial advisor.

M: She doesn't work in the banking industry anymore from what I understand.

W: Oh, that's too bad. Well, then who can I talk to about my mortgage?

M: It's best if you consult with Flooder. He is the new regional manager.

Unit 19　結合視覺資料的題目

Q1-2. W: Charles, I'm really looking forward to the marathon we're sponsoring next month. I bet it'll be great publicity.

M: Yeah, I'm excited, too. We need to hire a company to design the tumblers that we'll give out to the participants. Have you looked over the list of design firms? We have to decide one by the end of this week.

W: I know. I think Fine Art does a very good job, but I heard it is quite pricy. And management has reduced our budget to spend on souvenirs this year.

M: That's true. Let's just give the job to the firm here in San Diego. We can reduce the shipping costs, and its prices are pretty reasonable, too.

Q3-4. M: Excuse me, Amanda. I have a problem with my ID. It doesn't open the doors to the building, so I have to get someone on the front desk staff to let me in. Could you add my information to the security system?

W: Well, the staff in Human Resources is only in charge of IDs for our building, Why don't you go to the personnel office? Someone there should be able to save you on the database.

M: Okay. I'll try. Thanks.

Review Test

Q1-3. W: Hi, Michael. Did you hear that our office will be painted this evening? The workers will move all the office furniture, so we have to clean everything up on our desks before we leave today.

M: Really? I heard from Ms. Bunny that the painting work will start next weekend.

W: Hmm. I had better call the Maintenance Department to make sure.

Q4-6. W: Hi, Mr. Anderson. I'm sorry. I was late for the meeting this morning because of the traffic jam. What did I miss?

M: Oh, on Thursday, we are going to install a new program for all of the computers in the Sales Department.

W: So is there anything we have to do to prepare for it?

M: No, but I suggest that you come early on that day. We will have a lot of work to do.

Q7-9. M1: Have you guys visited the new company fitness room on the 15th floor?

W: I haven't been there yet, but I heard that it's gotten much better than before.

M2: Yeah, it has. I started working out there this Monday, and I was really impressed by all the cutting-edge equipment.

M1: And don't forget the view. It's fantastic! You can see the entire city while you're on a bicycle.

M2: I know. It was a great idea to move the facility up from the first floor.

W: Wow, it sounds amazing. I'm definitely stopping by there after work today.

Q10-12. M: Welcome back to Music Hour. Let's continue the interview with our special guest, Michelle O'Conner. Michelle, can you tell us more about your newly released album?

W: Sure! It's a contemporary crossover album of pop and jazz, and I think the best part is that you can all enjoy the songs no matter how old you are.

M: That sounds great. Now, I heard that you're planning to hold a nationwide tour concert. Which states will you be visiting?

W: Thanks for asking. Right now, we're still deciding which cities to visit. The details will be announced next week.

Q13-15. W: Hello. I'm here for a job interview at noon. The person I spoke to told me I need to sign in at the reception desk to gain access to the building.

M: Well, you're in the right place. Please sign your name here and show me your ID. Which suite are you going to?

W: Office 406. I'm meeting with Mr. Landon.

M: Okay, you can use the elevator. Our building is repainting the walls in the hallway right now, and there's a lot of equipment on the floor. Hold on… Let me move this ladder out of your way. Otherwise, you might bump into it.

類型分析 8　各大主題攻略一服務
Unit 20　餐廳

Step 3 實戰演練

Questions 1-3 refer to the following conversation.
第1-3題請參照以下的對話。

M: Excuse me. ²Do you have any special spaces for large groups? I want to bring about 10 clients who are visiting my company this weekend here for dinner.
▶ 這題問的是男子的要求／提議，需仔細聆聽男子的發言。作答請求／建議題的時候，須專心聆聽提議（I want）的句子。男子的第一句話是在問有沒有可以容納十人的座位，所以第二題的正確答案為 (A)。

W: Yes, we have a private ¹dining area that seats up to 20 people.
▶ 聽到 dining area 後可以確定對話地點是餐廳。第一題的正確答案為 (A)。

M: That's great. But before I make a reservation, I need to check the prices first.

W: Then ³ you should consider getting our course menu for groups. It's limited in its selection, but the price is affordable.
▶ 這題問的是女子的推薦事項，所以要仔細聆聽女子的發言中表示提議（you should、you could、why

don't you）的部分。女子建議「看看團體客套餐菜單」，所以 (C) 為正確答案。

男：不好意思，請問你們有提供給團體客的特別空間嗎？我這個週末想帶十位拜訪我們公司的客戶來這裡用晚餐。

女：有的，我們有私人用餐區，最多可供二十人入座。

男：太好了。但是在我預約之前，我需要先確認一下價格。

女：那您可以考慮看我們的團體客套餐菜單。選擇有限，但是價格實惠。

單字　space 空間　client 客人，客戶　private 私人的，私下的　dining 用餐　up to 到～為止　consider 考慮　affordable 可負擔的

1. 說話者有可能在哪裡？
(A) 餐廳
(B) 辦公室
(C) 電影院
(D) 書店

解答　(A)

2. 根據對話，男子要求什麼？
(A) 合適的空間
(B) 特別菜單
(C) 折扣
(D) 合理的價格

解答　(A)

3. 女子推薦了什麼？
(A) 兒童菜單
(B) 新菜單
(C) 特別組合菜單
(D) 折扣時段菜單

解答　(C)

Unit 21　飯店

Step 3 實戰演練

Questions 1-3 refer to the following conversation.
第1-3題請參照以下的對話。

W: ¹Our overseas clients are here next week. I'd like to book some rooms in the Manchester Hotel for them. What do you think about that hotel?
▶ 請記住題目中有專有名詞的話，線索會在聽到專有

名詞的地方出現。女子說想帶客戶去曼徹斯特飯店，所以 (D) 為正確答案。

M：I like it, but [2]I want to know about the facilities at the hotel.
▶ 隨時都要注意帶有轉折語氣的對比連接詞（but）後面的內容。男子想了解飯店的設施，所以 (C) 為正確答案。

W：[3]We can check them online to find out about them. We can use the computer in my office if you don't mind.
▶ 建議題的答題線索，會在提出建議的對話中（I / we can~）出現。女子提議到辦公室用電腦，所以 (A) 為正確答案。

女：我們的海外客戶下個禮拜要來。我想替他們預約曼徹斯特飯店的房間。你覺得那間飯店怎麼樣？
男：我很喜歡，但我想知道飯店裡有哪些設施。
女：我們可以上網查。你不介意的話，我們可以用我辦公室的電腦。

單字　overseas 海外，海外的　client 客戶　facility 設施

1. 女子想讓誰住在曼徹斯特飯店？

(A) 她的同事
(B) 她的家人
(C) 她的朋友
(D) 她的客戶

解答　(D)

2. 男子想知道飯店的什麼？

(A) 位置
(B) 收益
(C) 設施
(D) 價格

解答　(C)

3. 女子為什麼提議去她的辦公室？

(A) 為了確認網站
(B) 為了見客戶
(C) 為了預約
(D) 為了準備會議

解答　(A)

Review Test

Questions 1-3 refer to the following conversation.
第1-3題請參照以下的對話。

W：Hi. Before we order our meal, [1]could you please check

---

this coupon that I printed out from the website? It indicates that if we order at least two meals, we can get some free drinks.
▶ 跟來源有關、詢問細節的題目是第一題，所以線索會在前半段出現。女子說從網站拿到優惠券，所以 (D) 為正確答案。

M：[2]I'm so sorry, but that coupon is only good during lunch.
▶ but 後面常常出現重要的線索，這裡提到優惠券只在午餐時間有效，所以 (A) 為正確答案。

W：Really? I thought I can use this coupon. That's a shame.
M：But don't be disappointed. [3] We are having a special offer today, so you can get 20% off any meal.
▶ 題目跟男子的發言有關，而且是三題中的最後一題，所以要專心聆聽後半段。男子說會提供 special offer，所以 (D) 為正確答案。

女：嗨，在我們點餐之前，可以請你確認一下這張我從網站上列印出來的優惠券嗎？上面顯示我們點兩份餐點的話，可以享有免費的飲料。
男：抱歉，這個優惠券只能在午餐時間使用。
女：真的嗎？我還以為我可以用這張優惠券。好可惜。
男：但是不用失望，我們今天有特別折扣，所以任何餐點都可以打八折。

單字　meal 用餐　print out 列印　indicate 表明
disappoint 失望　special offer 特別折扣

1. 女子從哪裡獲得優惠券的？

(A) 書
(B) 雜誌
(C) 報紙
(D) 網站

解答　(D)

2. 男子提到優惠券有什麼問題？

(A) 只能在午餐時間使用。
(B) 只能在週末使用。
(C) 過期了。
(D) 適用於別家餐廳。

解答　(A)

3. 男子說目前正在進行什麼？

(A) 開幕折扣
(B) 清倉特賣
(C) 減價時段
(D) 特別折扣

解答　(D)

Questions 4-6 refer to the following conversation.
第4-6題請參照以下的對話。

M : Hi. My name is Dean, and ⁴I'm calling to book a suite for my family vacation.
▶ 打電話的原因或目的會在前半段出現，須特別注意聽「I'm calling~」的句子。(A) 為正確答案。

W : Thank you for calling the WD Hotel. ⁵For how long would you like to stay, sir?

M : ⁵For seven days. How much is the charge, including breakfast?
▶ 作答跟細節有關的第二題時，要專心聆聽中間的對話。將 7 days 改述成 1 week 的 (A) 為正確答案。

W : It's $500, and breakfast is complimentary. ⁶Could you please give me your name and phone number?
▶ 這是需要類推的 next 題型，須專心聆聽最後一句話。女子要求提供聯絡方式，可以預測到男子會對此做出回覆，所以 (D) 為正確答案。

男：嗨，我叫做汀。我來電來是想替家族旅遊預約一間套房。
女：感謝您來電WD飯店。先生，請問您預計停留多久？
男：七天。含早餐多少錢？
女：五百美元，早餐是免費的。可以給我您的姓名和電話號碼嗎？

單字　book 預約　family vacation 家族旅遊　stay 暫住，停留　charge 費用，價錢　complimentary 免費的

4. 男子為什麼打電話？
(A) 為了預約
(B) 為了找遺失的個人物品
(C) 為了取消預約
(D) 為了付款

解答　(A)

5. 男子會在飯店停留多久？
(A) 一週
(B) 兩週
(C) 三天
(D) 五天

解答　(A)

6. 男子接下來最有可能做什麼？
(A) 寄出關於預約的電子郵件
(B) 去飯店的櫃臺
(C) 給他的信用卡資訊
(D) 提到他的聯絡資訊

解答　(D)

Questions 7-9 refer to the following conversation.
第7-9題請參照以下的對話。

W : Excuse me. ⁷Where can I get information about the tourist attractions around your hotel?

M : ⁷/⁸You could go to the concierge near the main entrance. He can give you a travel map.
▶ 職業、公司等資訊會在前半段出現。女子正在問觀光景點的資訊，可以推測能夠回答這種問題的人是飯店員工。因此，第七題的正確答案為 (C)。地點和位置的相關線索會在前半段出現，但是三道題目中的第二題是詢問地點的題目，所以要能預測到對話的中間會出現線索。concierge 意即禮賓接待員，在這裡能得知他在正門附近。(D) 為正確答案。

W : How about transportation? Do you provide any transportation services?

M : Yes. ⁹You can get a timetable for the shuttle bus from the concierge as well. It runs from our hotel to the downtown area.
▶ 作答關於未來計畫（next、after）的題目時，要仔細聆聽後半段，特別是最後一句話。男子說可以從禮賓接待員那裡拿到時間表，所以可以推測女子會去找禮賓接待員。(A) 為正確答案。

女：不好意思，請問我可以在哪裡獲得關於你們飯店附近的觀光景點資訊？
男：您可以去找正門附近的禮賓接待員。他會給您旅遊地圖。
女：那交通呢？你們有提供任何交通工具服務嗎？
男：有的，您同樣可以從禮賓接待員那裡拿到接駁巴士的時間表。運行路線是從我們飯店到市區。

單字　tourist attraction 觀光景點　main entrance 正門　timetable 時間表，行程表　run 運行

7. 男子最有可能是誰？
(A) 銷售員
(B) 辦公室員工
(C) 飯店員工
(D) 房客

解答　(C)

8. 根據對話，禮賓接待員在哪裡？
(A) 游泳池附近
(B) 櫃臺旁邊
(C) 男子房間附近
(D) 入口附近

解答　(D)

9. 女子在對話結束後會做什麼？

(A) 去找禮賓接待員
(B) 找司機
(C) 打電話給旅行社
(D) 跟其他客人說話

解答　(A)

Questions 10-12 refer to the following conversation.
第10-12題請參照以下的對話。

M: Hello. ¹⁰/¹¹The fridge in my room is making a strange noise. I can't put up with the noise. I think it's broken.

▶ 對話地點的答題依據會在第一句話出現。透過男子說的 in my room（我的房間）可以知道對話地點在飯店裡，所以 (B) 為正確答案。

▶ 透過前半段的對話，可以知道男子受不了冰箱發出的噪音，由此可知男子說這句話是希望冰箱可以快點修好。(A) 為正確答案。

W: I'm very sorry about the inconvenience. I'll send one of our maintenance workers to check it out. Is there anything else I can do for you?

M: ¹²Can you bring me a bottle of iced water? All the water in the fridge is getting warm.

W: ¹²Of course. I'll get that for you right away.

▶ 最後一題詢問接下來要做什麼事的題目，答題線索會在後半段出現。男子請對方拿一瓶冰水來，女子回覆會馬上拿過去，所以 (C) 為正確答案。

男：哈囉，我房間的冰箱一直發出奇怪的噪音。我無法忍受這個噪音。我覺得它故障了。
女：非常抱歉造成您的不便，我會派一個維修員前去檢查。還有任何我能為您效勞的地方嗎？
男：可以給我一瓶冰水嗎？所有冰箱裡的水都慢慢變溫的了。
女：沒問題，我馬上拿給您。

單字　fridge 冰箱　make a noise 發出噪音　put up with 忍受，忍耐　broken 故障的　inconvenience 不便　maintenance 維修，保持，維護　check out 確認　bring 攜帶，拿去　right away 立刻，馬上　electronic 電子的　fix 修理　immediately 立刻，馬上　for long 長久　be satisfied with 對～感到滿意　reservation 預約

10. 說話者在哪裡？

(A) 餐廳
(B) 飯店
(C) 辦公室
(D) 電子產品店

解答　(B)

11. 男子說「我無法忍受這個噪音」的意思是什麼？

(A) 他希望冰箱可以立刻被修好。
(B) 他沒辦法跟女子講太久。
(C) 他很滿意客房服務。
(D) 他會取消預約。

解答　(A)

12. 女子接下來最有可能會做什麼？

(A) 上甜點
(B) 取消訂單
(C) 拿一些水
(D) 確認行程表

解答　(C)

聽寫訓練

Unit 20 餐廳

M: Excuse me. Do you have any special spaces for large groups? I want to bring about 10 clients who are visiting my company this weekend here for dinner.

W: Yes, we have a private dining area that seats up to 20 people.

M: That's great. But before I make a reservation, I need to check the prices first.

W: Then you should consider getting our course menu for groups. It's limited in its selection, but the price is affordable.

Unit 21 飯店

W: Our overseas clients are here next week. I'd like to book some rooms in the Manchester Hotel for them. What do you think about that hotel?

M: I like it, but I want to know about the facilities at the hotel.

W: We can check them online to find out about them. We can use the computer in my office if you don't mind.

Review Test

Q1-3. W : Hi. Before we order our meal, could you please check this coupon that I printed out from the website? It indicates that if we order at least two meals, we can get some free drinks.

M : I'm so sorry, but that coupon is only good during lunch.

W : Really? I thought I can use this coupon. That's a shame.

M : But don't be disappointed. We are having a special offer today, so you can get 20% off any meal.

Q4-6. M : Hi. My name is Dean, and I'm calling to book a suite for my family vacation.

W : Thank you for calling the WD Hotel. For how long

would you like to stay, sir?

M : For seven days. How much is the charge, including breakfast?

W : It's $500, and breakfast is complimentary. Could you please give me your name and phone number?

Q7-9. W : Excuse me. Where can I get information about the tourist attractions around your hotel?

M : You could go to the concierge near the main entrance. He can give you a travel map.

W : How about transportation? Do you provide any transportation services?

M : Yes. You can get a timetable for the shuttle bus from the concierge as well. It runs from our hotel to the downtown area.

Q10-12. M: Hello. The fridge in my room is making a strange noise. I can't put up with the noise. I think it's broken.

W: I am very sorry about the inconvenience. I'll send one of our maintenance workers to check it out. Is there anything else I can do for you?

M: Can you bring me a bottle of iced water? All the water in the fridge is getting warm.

W: Of course. I'll get that for you right away.

類型分析 9　各大主題攻略─購物
Unit 22　購物

Step 3 實戰演練

Questions 1-3 refer to the following conversation.
第1-3題請參照以下的對話。

W : I am looking for a new digital camera. ¹Can you tell me what kind of battery this one uses?
▶ 題目問了女子想知道關於相機的什麼，這是詢問細節的題目，所以要聽女子前半段的發言。「可以告訴我這是用哪種電池嗎」，所以 (B) 為正確答案。

M : It uses a rechargeable battery. And the battery is free with the purchase of any digital camera.
W : Wow, that's what I want. Do you have any special events that are going on now?
M : Yes, ²we are giving away camera cases in various colors for free.
▶ 女子詢問購買相機可以獲得什麼，男子說「會免費贈送相機包」，所以 (D) 為正確答案。

³They are displayed at the front of the store. Let me show you where they are.
▶ 這是 next 題型的題目，所以要專心聆聽最後面的對話。男子跟女子說「不同顏色的相機包擺在商店前

面」，要帶她去看，所以 (B) 為正確答案。

女：我正在找新的數位相機。你可以告訴我這是用哪種電池嗎？
男：這是使用可充電電池，而且購買任何數位相機都會免費贈送電池。
女：哇，這就是我想要的。你們現在有舉辦任何的特別活動嗎？
男：有，我們正在免費贈送多種顏色的相機包。它們被擺在商店前面。我帶您去看在哪。

單字　rechargeable 可重新充電的 purchase 購買 various 多種的，不同的 display 陳列

1. 女子想知道關於相機的什麼？
(A) 多少錢
(B) 使用什麼電池
(C) 是什麼顏色
(D) 在哪製作的

解答　(B)

2. 女子購買相機的話，可以獲得什麼？
(A) 會員卡
(B) 電影票
(C) 折扣券
(D) 免費商品

解答　(D)

3. 女子接下來可能會做什麼？
(A) 支付相機的錢
(B) 看相機包
(C) 聯絡她的朋友
(D) 購買其他物品

解答　(B)

Unit 23　購票

Step 3 實戰演練

Questions 1-3 refer to the following conversation.
第1-3題請參照以下的對話。

W : Hello. ¹I'm calling to buy tickets for the concert tomorrow. Can I buy them over the phone?
▶ 以「I'm calling~」開頭的對話，都是會出現打電話目的的句子，所以要注意聆聽。女子想要買票，所以 (D) 為正確答案。

M : I'm sorry, but ²we don't sell tickets over the phone. Why don't you come and buy them tomorrow?

▶ 詢問理由的題目，前兩句會出現相關的答題線索。男子說「不能透過電話售票，要親自購票」，所以 (B) 為正確答案。

W：Then can I get a discount on them?

M：Sure, but you had better come early tomorrow. ³The discounted tickets are limited in number.

▶ 這題跟男子的發言有關，所以要專心聆聽這個部分。男子說折扣票的數量有限，所以 (B) 為正確答案。

女：你好，我來電是想買明天的演奏會門票。我可以透過電話購買嗎？
男：抱歉，我們不透過電話售票。您要不要明天來了再買呢？
女：那我可以享有折扣嗎？
男：當然，但您明天早一點來比較好。折扣票數量有限。

單字　concert 演奏會　discount 折扣　be limited in number 數量有限

1. 女子想做什麼？
(A) 預約
(B) 線上購物
(C) 取消訂票
(D) 購票

解答　(D)

2. 男子為什麼說沒辦法協助女子？
(A) 他從上週就開始休假。
(B) 他只能在售票處賣票。
(C) 他不負責售票。
(D) 他必須獲得經理的批准。

解答　(B)

3. 男子告訴女子什麼？
(A) 座位有限
(B) 票券有限
(C) 預訂系統
(D) 付款方式

解答　(B)

Review Test

Questions 1-3 refer to the following conversation.
第1-3題請參照以下的對話。

W：Excuse me. ¹I'm looking for men's pants. Could you please help me to find a pair just like these?

▶ 詢問對話地點的題目，答題線索會在前半段出現。聽到 pants 的話，可以知道 (C) 為正確答案。

M：²Oh, all of the ones with that design are sold out. Do you want to see another design?

▶ 職業、公司、部門等會在前半段出現。這題問的是男子的職業，所以要專心聆聽男子的第一句話。(D) 為正確答案。

W：No, thanks. Is there any place where I can find these?

M：Um... ³Why don't you visit our other store on Brit Street? Or if you can wait until next week, I can order them and have them delivered to your house.

▶ 要求、建議會在後半段出現，必須特別仔細聽包含疑問句「Why don't~?」、Could / Would you~?」的對話。(B) 為正確答案。

女：不好意思，我正在找男褲。你可以幫我找跟這個一樣的嗎？
男：噢，那個款式的全部都賣完了。您要看看另一個款式嗎？
女：不用，謝謝。有其他我可以找到這件褲子的地方嗎？
男：嗯……您要不要去我們布里街上的另一間店？或是您可以等到下個禮拜的話，我可以下訂然後寄到您府上。

單字　pants 褲子　like 像～的　sold out 賣完的，缺貨的　deliver 運送，寄送

1. 對話者最有可能在哪裡？
(A) 餐廳
(B) 辦公室
(C) 服飾店
(D) 飯店

解答　(C)

2. 男子的職業是什麼？
(A) 祕書
(B) 圖書館員
(C) 辦公室員工
(D) 店員

解答　(D)

3. 男子建議女子做什麼？
(A) 跟其他店員說
(B) 拜訪另一間店
(C) 在線上商店購買物品
(D) 填寫表格

解答　(B)

Questions 4-6 refer to the following conversation.
第4-6題請參照以下的對話。

M : Hello. ⁴I'm calling to book a ticket to go to Chicago on October 1.
▶ 打電話的理由會在來電者的第一句話中出現，所以要特別仔細聽「I'm calling~、I hope / wish~」這類的句子。(A) 為正確答案。

W : Okay, let me check to see if any seats are available. Sometimes it's full because of groups of tourists.

M : Oh, and ⁵could you please check whether a window seat is available or not?
▶ 要求、建議會在後半段出現，要特別仔細聽「Could you~?、Why don't you~?」這類的句子。男子詢問是否有靠窗的座位，所以 (B) 為正確答案。

W : Sure. But before I do that, ⁶ could you please give me your full name, passport number, and phone number?
▶ 遇到 next 題型時，要仔細聆聽最後面的對話。女子要求對方提供個人資訊，所以男子會對此做出答覆。(A) 為正確答案。

男：嗨，我來電來是想訂一張十月一日飛往芝加哥的票。
女：好的，讓我確認一下是否有座位。有時候會因為團體遊客而客滿。
男：噢，還有可以麻煩妳確認是否還有靠窗的位置嗎？
女：沒問題，但是在這之前，可以給我您的全名、護照號碼和電話號碼嗎？

單字 book a ticket 訂票 seat 座位 available 可購買的，可使用的 passport number 護照號碼

4. 男子為什麼會打電話？
(A) 為了預訂
(B) 為了改位置
(C) 為了確認預約
(D) 為了付款

解答 (A)

5. 男子要求什麼？
(A) 折扣
(B) 靠窗座位
(C) 走道座位
(D) 素食餐

解答 (B)

6. 根據對話，男子接下來可能會做什麼？
(A) 提供個人資訊
(B) 付機票錢
(C) 去機場

(D) 打電話給另一間航空公司

解答 (A)

Questions 7-9 refer to the following conversation.
第7-9題請參照以下的對話。

W : Hi. ⁷I need to get a new laptop for my daughter, and my friend recommended your store.
▶ 前半段會出現特定地點的提示詞。聽到 laptop 的話，就能知道 (C) 為正確答案。

M : You are lucky ⁸because a special promotion just started yesterday. You can get 30% off everything.
▶ 具體資訊會在中間的部分出現，而這題是跟男子發言有關的題目，所以要專心聆聽男子的對話。男子說從昨天開始進行活動，可以享有折扣，所以 (D) 為正確答案。

W : Wow, that sounds great! So ⁹could you recommend the newest product?
▶ 回答請求、建議題時，要聆聽在後半段出現的提議問句。女子請對方展示最新商品，所以 (A) 為正確答案。

M : Sure. Let me show you the laptop that just arrived. I'm sure you'll love it.

女：嗨，我需要一台給我女兒用的新筆電，我朋友推薦了你們的店。
男：您很幸運，因為特別促銷昨天才剛開始。任何東西都可以打七折。
女：哇，聽起來很棒！那你可以推薦最新產品給我嗎？
男：沒問題。我給您看看剛到的筆電。我確定您會喜歡的。

單字 laptop 筆記型電腦 recommend 推薦 special promotion 特別促銷 newest 最新的

7. 此對話最有可能在哪裡發生？
(A) 超市
(B) 家具店
(C) 電子商品店
(D) 服飾店

解答 (C)

8. 男子說店裡正在舉辦什麼？
(A) 維修作業
(B) 開幕特賣
(C) 清倉特賣
(D) 特別促銷

解答 (D)

9. 女子要求什麼？

(A) 最新的筆記型電腦
(B) 最便宜的筆記型電腦
(C) 最輕的筆記型電腦
(D) 最小的筆記型電腦

解答　(A)

Questions 10-12 refer to the following conversation and coupon. 第10-12題請參照以下的對話和折扣券。

W: [10]Hi. I'm going to redecorate my apartment. And I'd like to buy a sofa by using this coupon that I saw in your catalog.

▶ 這題問的是女子的計畫，所以線索會在女子的發言中出現。女子說要重新裝飾公寓。改述 redecorate my apartment 的 (A) 為正確答案。

M: What price range do you have in mind?

W: I am planning to spend no more than $600. And I need to make sure the furniture goes well with my green wallpaper.

M: I think white or beige will suit the color of the wall. [11]The model in the window display costs $570. It comes in three colors, white, beige, and brown. It has been very popular since last year.

W: [11]I like the design and the size. And I'll choose beige color. When should I expect delivery?

▶ 優惠券寫明了消費金額的對應折扣率。男子推薦五百七十美元的沙發，女子說很喜歡，並說要選米黃色的。由此可知女子會支付五百七十美元。表格中介於五百零一至六百美元的商品折扣率是二十％，所以 (D) 為正確答案。

M: One moment, please. [12]Let me check the computer to see the exact delivery date.

▶ 詢問接下來會做什麼事的最後一題，答題線索會在後半段出現。男子說要用電腦查確切的寄送日期，所以 (B) 為正確答案。

女：嗨，我要重新裝飾我的公寓。我想用這張在你們的目錄上看到的優惠券購買沙發。
男：您預想的價格範圍落在哪裡？
女：我打算不花費超過六百美元。而且我需要確保家具適合我的綠色壁紙。
男：我覺得白色或米黃色會適合那面牆的顏色。櫥窗中的那個樣式是五百七十美元。有三種顏色，白色、米黃色和棕色。從去年開始就非常受歡迎。
女：我喜歡它的設計和大小。我要選米黃色的。沙發什麼時候會寄送？
男：請稍等。讓我確認一下電腦，看看確切的寄送日期。

單字 redecorate 重新裝飾 price range 價格範圍 have

---

in mind 想到～ make sure 確保～ go well with 適合～ wallpaper 壁紙 delivery 寄送 renovate 翻修 own 自己的 request 索取，要求 demonstration 示範操作，説明

10. 女子說她打算做什麼？

(A) 翻修她的房子
(B) 搬到新房子
(C) 開始自己的事業
(D) 設計家具

解答　(A)

11. 請看圖表。女子將享有哪個折扣？

萊斯麗家具 春季折扣券			
5% 折扣 ~$300	10% 折扣 $301~$400	15% 折扣 $401~$500	20% 折扣 $501~$600

* 有效期限至 4 月 30 日

(A) 5%折扣
(B) 10%折扣
(C) 15%折扣
(D) 20%折扣

解答　(D)

12. 男子接下來最有可能會做什麼？

(A) 跟經理說話
(B) 確認寄送日期
(C) 索取文件
(D) 示範操作產品

解答　(B)

聽寫訓練

Unit 22 購物

W: I am looking for a new digital camera. Can you tell me what kind of battery this one uses?

M: It uses a rechargeable battery. And the battery is free with the purchase of any digital camera.

W: Wow, that's what I want. Do you have any special events that are going on now?

M: Yes, we are giving away camera cases in various colors for free. They are displayed at the front of the store. Let me show you where they are.

Unit 23 購票

W: Hello. I'm calling to buy tickets for the concert tomorrow. Can I buy them over the phone?

M: I'm sorry, but we don't sell tickets over the phone. Why don't you come and buy them tomorrow?

W: Then can I get a discount on them?

M: Sure, but you had better come early tomorrow. The discounted tickets are limited in number.

Review Test

Q1-3. W: Excuse me. I'm looking for men's pants. Could you please help me to find a pair just like these?

M: Oh, all of the ones with that design are sold out. Do you want to see another design?

W: No, thanks. Is there any place where I can find these?

M: Um... Why don't you visit our other store on Brit Street? Or if you can wait until next week, I can order them and have them delivered to your house.

Q4-6. M: Hello. I'm calling to book a ticket to go to Chicago on October 1.

W: Okay, let me check to see if any seats are available. Sometimes it's full because of groups of tourists.

M: Oh, and could you please check whether a window seat is available or not?

W: Sure. But before I do that, could you please give me your full name, passport number, and phone number?

Q7-9. W: Hi. I need to get a new laptop for my daughter, and my friend recommended your store.

M: You are lucky because a special promotion just started yesterday. You can get 30% off everything.

W: Wow, that sounds great! So could you recommend the newest product?

M: Sure. Let me show you the laptop that just arrived. I'm sure you'll love it.

Q10-12.

W: Hi. I'm going to redecorate my apartment. And I'd like to buy a sofa by using this coupon that I saw in your catalog.

M: What price range do you have in mind?

W: I am planning to spend no more than $600. And I need to make sure the furniture goes well with my green wallpaper.

M: I think white or beige will suit the color of the wall. The model in the window display costs $570. It comes in three colors, white, beige, and brown. It has been very popular since last year.

W: I like the design and the size. And I'll go with the model in beige. When should I expect delivery?

M: One moment, please. Let me check the computer to see the exact delivery date.

類型分析10　各大主題攻略一職場

Unit 24　徵人、辭職

Step 3 實戰演練

Questions 1-3 refer to the following conversation.

第1-3題請參照以下的對話。

> M：Hello. My name is Jason, and ¹I'm calling about the sales position you advertised on your website.
>
> ▶ 這題問的是對話主題，所以要仔細聆聽第一句話。男子的第一句話「I'm calling about the sales position you advertised on your website.」的意思是，看到「徵才廣告」後打了電話，所以 (D) 為正確答案。
>
> W：Thank you for calling. As you read in the advertisement, ²we're looking for someone with experience selling computers.
>
> ▶ 這題問的是地點，所以要仔細聽地點詞彙。從女子的這句話「we're looking for someone with experience selling computers.」可以得知正在找「有電腦銷售經驗的人」，由此可知女子在「電子產品店」工作。(C) 為正確答案。
>
> M：Don't worry about that. I've worked at a computer shop as a salesman for 3 years.
>
> W：That's really good news! ³Why don't you send us your resume?
>
> ▶ 這是詢問提議／請求內容的題目，所以要專心聆聽出現提議問句的地方。提議問句通常會在後半段出現。最後一句話「Why don't you send us your resume?」的意思是「叫對方寄履歷」，所以 (D) 為正確答案。
>
> ---
>
> 男：嗨，我叫做傑森。我來電是關於我在您的網站上看到銷售職缺的廣告。
>
> 女：謝謝您的來電。正如您在廣告上看到的，我們正在找有電腦銷售經驗的人。
>
> 男：這點您不用擔心。我在電腦賣場當過三年的銷售員。
>
> 女：那真是好消息！您何不寄一份履歷給我們呢！

單字　call about 打電話討論～　look for 尋找　resume 履歷

1. 說話者主要在討論什麼？

(A) 電腦諮詢
(B) 抱怨某個員工
(C) 買電腦
(D) 應徵職位

解答　(D)

2. 女子有可能在哪裡工作？

(A) 超市

(B) 辦公室
(C) 電子產品店
(D) 電腦工廠

解答　(C)

3. 女子建議男子做什麼？

　　(A) 拜訪商店
　　(B) 改天再打
　　(C) 前往面試
　　(D) 繳交文件

解答　(D)

Unit 25　教育、宣傳

Step 3　實戰演練

Questions 1-3 refer to the following conversation.
第1-3題請參照以下的對話。

W : This is Susanna from the AA Advertising Company. [1]I'm calling about an idea I have to promote your restaurant.
▶ 女子說打電話是為了討論關於男子的餐廳的宣傳策略，所以正確答案為 (D)。

M : Oh, that's interesting! Because we recently remodeled the restaurant, I want you to see it. [2]Can you come by to see it?
▶ 男子說最近翻修了餐廳，並提議女子來參觀。正確答案為 (A)。

W : Sure, I'll go there tomorrow, and, while I'm there, [3]we can discuss the script for the advertisement.
▶ 詢問接下來要做什麼事的題目，答題線索會在最後面出現。女子說可以討論廣告內容，所以正確答案為 (D)。

女：我是AA廣告公司的蘇珊娜。我來電是關於一個宣傳貴餐廳的點子。
男：噢，真有趣！因為我們最近翻修了餐廳，所以我想讓妳看看。妳可以過來看嗎？
女：沒問題，我明天過去。到時候我們可以討論廣告的腳本。

單字　promote 宣傳　remodel 翻修，改造　script 腳本　advertisement 廣告

1. 說話者主要在討論什麼？

　　(A) 翻修過的餐廳
　　(B) 廣告公司
　　(C) 新餐廳
　　(D) 廣告活動

解答　(D)

2. 男子建議做什麼？

　　(A) 看看餐廳
　　(B) 拜訪她的廣告公司
　　(C) 下個禮拜討論腳本
　　(D) 在她的餐廳吃晚餐

解答　(A)

3. 說話者接下來會做什麼？

　　(A) 討論付款
　　(B) 拜訪競爭者的餐廳
　　(C) 翻修餐廳
　　(D) 討論廣告

解答　(D)

Unit 26　設施、網絡管理

Step 3　實戰演練

Questions 1-3 refer to the following conversation.
第1-3題請參照以下的對話。

M : Do you know [1]when the mechanic will come to fix the air conditioner?
▶ 這題問的是男子在詢問什麼，所以要仔細聆聽男子的發言。男子正在說關於「冷氣維修問題」的事，所以 (C) 為正確答案。

W : Tomorrow afternoon, I guess. Is there a problem?
M : I'm concerned about my meeting. [2]If it isn't working by today, I'll have to reschedule my meeting. I'd rather postpone it.
▶ 這題問的是男子會延後什麼。男子說要延後開會時間，所以 (D) 為正確答案。

W : Don't worry about it. [3]I can call someone else and check whether he can fix it by this afternoon or not.
▶ 這題問的是接下來會做的事，所以要仔細聆聽最後一句話。女子說「會打電話問其他人」，所以 (B) 為正確答案。

男：妳知道技師什麼時候會來修冷氣機嗎？
女：我猜明天下午吧。有什麼問題嗎？
男：我很擔心我的會議。如果今天還沒辦法運作的話，我需要重新安排我的會議時間。我寧願延期。
女：別擔心。我可以打電話給其他人，看對方能不能在今天下午之前修好。

單字　fix 修理　guess 猜測，猜中　postpone 延期，延後　reschedule 重新安排日程　be concerned about 擔心～

1. 男子在詢問什麼？
   (A) 員工會議
   (B) 新祕書
   (C) 維修問題
   (D) 國際會議

解答　(C)

2. 男子說他想延後什麼？
   (A) 預約
   (B) 培訓
   (C) 出差
   (D) 會議

解答　(D)

3. 女子接下來有可能會做什麼？
   (A) 繳交報告
   (B) 打電話給維修人員
   (C) 準備會議
   (D) 開窗戶

解答　(B)

Unit 27　會計、預算

Step 3 實戰演練

Questions 1-3 refer to the following conversation.
第1-3題請參照以下的對話。

> M : Tracy, I just heard that we have to [1]reduce our expenses by 20 percent. How do you think we can do that?

▶ 這題問的是對話主題，所以要專心聆聽第一句話。這種對話內容通常都跟「經費刪減」有關，所以 (B) 為正確答案。

> W : Really? I haven't heard that yet. How are we going to pay for the dinner for our department?
> M : Hmm, [2]I think we need to reconsider the budget for it again. We have to look for another supplier.

▶ 這是詢問建議的題目，所以要專心聆聽提及建議句（We need to）的部分。男子說「需要重新考慮預算」，所以 (B) 為正確答案。

> W : [3]I should call the supplier as soon as possible to notify them that we have to break the contract.

▶ 這是 next 題型，所以要專注於最後一句話。女子說「要打電話給供應商」，所以 (A) 為正確答案。

男：特蕾西，我剛才聽說我們要減少二十％的開支。妳覺得我們能做什麼呢？
女：真的嗎？我還沒聽說那件事。我們要怎麼付我們部門的晚餐錢？

男：嗯，我覺得我們需要重新考慮這個預算。我們必須尋找另一個供應商。
女：我應該要盡快打電話給供應商，告知他們我們會違約。

單字　**reduce** 減少，縮小　**expense** 費用，經費　**reconsider** 重新考慮　**budget** 預算　**notify** 通知，告知　**break** 破壞，打破　**contract** 合約

1. 說話者在討論什麼？
   (A) 預約
   (B) 減少晚餐費用
   (C) 重新安排晚餐的時間
   (D) 翻修餐廳

解答　(B)

2. 男子建議做什麼？
   (A) 預定另一間餐廳
   (B) 重新做估價
   (C) 要求捐款
   (D) 取消晚餐

解答　(B)

3. 女子接下來可能會做什麼？
   (A) 聯絡餐廳
   (B) 告知所有員工
   (C) 拜訪另一個部門
   (D) 取消預約

解答　(A)

Unit 28 事業規劃

Step 3 實戰演練

Questions 1-3 refer to the following conversation.
第1-3題請參照以下的對話。

> W : Did you already sign the contract with the agent for your new restaurant?
> M : Well, I sent an email to the agent yesterday [1]to get some information about the renovations. But I still haven't got a response.

▶ 這題問的是男子索取的東西是什麼，所以要專注於男子的發言。男子說寄信想取得翻修的資訊，所以 (A) 為正確答案。

> W : [2]I think you should give her a call.

▶ 這是詢問建議事項的題目，所以要從建議句（you should）之中尋找線索。女子建議打電話，所以 (C) 為正確答案。

Anyway, [3] I'm worried that buying it is going to be complicated.

▶ 這題問的是女子擔心的事，所以答題線索會在情緒詞彙、否定語氣的句子附近出現。女子說「擔心買下這間餐廳會變得複雜」，所以 (B) 為正確答案。

女：你已經跟仲介簽新餐廳的合約了嗎？
男：呃，我昨天寄電子郵件給仲介，想取得翻修的資訊，但我還沒收到回覆。
女：我覺得你應該要打給她。總之，我擔心買下這間餐廳會變得複雜。

單字 renovation 翻修，改造 still 還，尚且 anyway 無論如何，總之 complicated 複雜的

1. 男子索取了什麼？

(A) 關於翻修的資訊
(B) 屋主的聯絡方式
(C) 餐廳的位置
(D) 房地產的價格

解答 (A)

2. 女子建議男子做什麼？

(A) 改變營業時間
(B) 製作邀請函
(C) 聯絡不動產仲介
(D) 明天去拜訪仲介

解答 (C)

3. 女子擔心做什麼事？

(A) 找室內設計師
(B) 購買餐廳
(C) 搬走舊家具
(D) 僱用新員工

解答 (B)

Review Test

Questions 1-3 refer to the following conversation.
第1-3題請參照以下的對話。

M : [1] Hi. This is Martin from the technical support team. [2] I got a call from someone in your staff that a computer isn't working.
▶ 職業、公司、部門等會在前半段出現。男子說自己是技術支援組的人，所以 (D) 為正確答案。

W : Thanks for coming. [2] Suddenly, the computer shut down when I was about to complete my project. After that, I couldn't turn it back on.

▶ 問題、抱怨事項等會在前半段出現。綜合兩人的對話來看是電腦故障，所以 (B) 為正確答案。

M : I think I should take your computer to my office to check it out.
W : Okay. [3] But can you fix it by tomorrow? I have to finish my work before this weekend.
▶ 作答請求或建議題時，要專注於建議句（can you、could you、why don't you~）。(D) 為正確答案。

男：嗨，我是技術支援組的馬汀。我接到你們員工打來的電話，說有台電腦無法運作。
女：謝謝你過來。在我快完成專案的時候，電腦就突然關機了。在那之後我沒辦法打開電腦。
男：我覺得我應該要把妳的電腦拿到我的辦公室檢查。
女：好。不過，你可以在明天之前修好嗎？我必須在這個週末之前完成我的工作。

單字 technical support team 技術支援組 suddenly 突然 shut down （電腦）關機，關閉 complete 完成，結束 fix 修理，收拾

1. 男子最有可能是誰？

(A) 會計師
(B) 建築師
(C) 銀行員
(D) 技師

解答 (D)

2. 女子的問題是什麼？

(A) 她最近跟同事吵架了。
(B) 她的電腦故障了。
(C) 她需要一些參考資料來完成專案。
(D) 她因為技術支援組而遺失了文件。

解答 (B)

3. 女子要求男子做什麼？

(A) 安裝新程式
(B) 邀請她參加國際研討會
(C) 代替她出席會議
(D) 在明天之前修好電腦

解答 (D)

Questions 4-6 refer to the following conversation.
第4-6題請參照以下的對話。

M : Hello, Ms. Vera. [5] I'm John from the Human Resources Department at TACC.
▶ 職業、公司、部門等會在前半段出現。男子說自

是人事部的人，由此可知他是辦公室員工。第五題的正確答案是 (B)。

I was very impressed with your resume, [4]and I want you to come in for an interview on Friday.

▶ 兩人正在討論面試的事。第四題的正確答案是 (C)。

W : Thank you. I was waiting for your call. Do I need to bring anything for the interview?

M : [6]You need to come with a printed copy of your resume.

▶ 這是詢問細節的題目，男子說需要履歷，所以女子會帶履歷過去。(A) 為正確答案。

男：哈囉，薇拉女士。我是 TACC 人事部的約翰。我對您的履歷感到印象深刻，想請您星期五來面試。

女：謝謝。我一直在等您的來電。我需要帶什麼東西去面試嗎？

男：您需要帶一份履歷影本過來。

單字　Human Resources Department 人事部　impressed 對～感到印象深刻的　interview 面試　printed 列印的

4. 對話者主要在討論什麼？

　(A) 週年派對
　(B) 特別促銷
　(C) 面試
　(D) 演講

解答　(C)

5. 男子的工作是什麼？

　(A) 律師
　(B) 辦公室員工
　(C) 店員
　(D) 講師

解答　(B)

6. 女子需要帶什麼？

　(A) 個人簡歷
　(B) 辦公用品
　(C) 推薦函
　(D) 照片

解答　(A)

Questions 7-9 refer to the following conversation with three speakers. 第7-9題請參照以下三人的對話。

W : [7]Our magazine is planning a special feature on newly listed companies in the state next month. Are you interested in this assignment?

▶ 這題問的是對話主題，所以要在前半段找線索，可

以知道這段是關於特輯報導的取材。也就是說，他們正在討論接下來的專案，所以正確答案為 (C)。

M1 : Yes, I am. [8]I want to write about the IT firm Stargate. It won the new company of the year award at last year's industry conference.

▶ 這是詢問星門公司的細節題，必須仔細聆聽出現關鍵字 Stargate 這個公司名稱的部分。男子說想採訪在去年的產業會議上得獎的 Stargate。正確答案為 (B)。

W : Okay, Ken. That sounds great. [9]And, Andrew, why don't you go along and take some photos for the article?

▶ 詢問安德魯被要求做什麼事的題目是第三題，所以要專注於安德魯的對話對象所說的話。女子要他跟寫報導的員工一起去拍照，所以正確答案為 (D)。

M2 : Sure, I'd be glad to. When are you planning to visit the company, Ken?

M1 : I'll check my schedule and get back to you right away.

女：我們雜誌計劃下個月做這個州的新上市公司的特別報導。你對這個工作有興趣嗎？

男1：是，我有興趣。我想寫關於星門科技公司的報導。它在去年的產業會議上贏得年度新公司獎。

女：好，肯。太好了。那麼，安德魯，你一起去拍報導用的照片吧？

男2：沒問題，我很樂意。肯，你打算什麼時候去拜訪那間公司？

男1：我確認一下我的行程，再馬上跟你說。

單字　feature 特輯　listed company 上市公司 assignment 工作

7. 說話者主要在討論什麼？

　(A) 新的出版社
　(B) 攝影獎
　(C) 即將到來的專案
　(D) 近期的產業會議

解答　(C)

8. 提到了關於星門公司的什麼？

　(A) 經歷了重整。
　(B) 最近獲獎了。
　(C) 僱用了一些新員工。
　(D) 會參加即將到來的會議

解答　(B)

9. 安德魯被要求做什麼？

　(A) 寫報導
　(B) 聯絡科技公司
　(C) 買午餐
　(D) 拍照

解答　(D)

Questions 10-12 refer to the following conversation and chart. 第10-12題請參照以下的對話和圖表。

W: Hi, Steve. Sorry to interrupt. ¹⁰I just got out of a budget meeting. I heard that we would scale down our corporate fitness programs due to the recent budget cuts.

▶ 活動種類和對話主題的相關線索，會在對話的前半段出現。女子說剛開完預算會議，所以 (C) 為正確答案。

M: I also heard that. ¹¹Mr. Olson said we are going to cut the most expensive class to operate.

W: That doesn't make sense. ¹¹According to the survey we took last month, that is the most popular class with employees.

▶ 男子說，從奧爾森先生那裡聽說要中斷經費最貴的課，女子則回覆根據調查結果，那是最受員工歡迎的課程。透過圖表可以知道最受員工歡迎的課是拉丁舞，所以 (B) 為正確答案。

M: I know what you're saying. ¹²Many employees will be disappointed to learn that we are not going to offer the program anymore.

▶ 男子擔心公司不再提供拉丁舞課，會讓很多員工失望，所以 (D) 為正確答案。

女：嗨，史蒂夫。抱歉打斷你，我剛開完預算會議。我聽到因為最近預算刪減，我們要縮小公司健身課程的規模。
男：我也聽說了。奧爾森先生說我們要中斷經費最貴的課。
女：這不合理啊。根據我們上個月做的調查，這是最受員工歡迎的課程。
男：我明白妳的意思。如果知道我們不再提供那個課程的話，很多員工都會感到失望的。

單字 **interrupt** 妨礙 **budget** 預算 **scale down** 縮小規模 **corporate** 公司的 **fitness** 健身，健康 **due to** 由於～ **recent** 最近的 **budget cut** 預算刪減 **operate** 經營，運作 **make sense** 有道理，合理 **according to** 根據～ **survey** 調查 **be disappointed** 感到失望的 **trade fair** 貿易博覽會 **award** 獎項 **ceremony** 儀式，典禮 **be concerned** 感到擔心的 **behind schedule** 進度落後的 **upcoming** 即將到來的 **be ready for** 準備好～ **let down** 使失望

10. 女子剛參加完什麼活動？

　(A) 研討會
　(B) 貿易博覽會
　(C) 會議
　(D) 頒獎典禮

解答　(C)

11. 請看圖表。哪個課程會被中斷？

　(A) 瑜珈

(B) 拉丁舞
(C) 有氧舞蹈
(D) 芭蕾

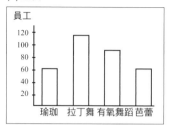

解答　(B)

12. 為什麼男子感到擔心？

　(A) 調查的進度落後太多。
　(B) 等一下要開的會議他會遲到。
　(C) 他還沒準備好做簡報。
　(D) 最近的一項決定會讓員工感到失望。

解答　(D)

聽寫訓練

Unit 24　徵人、辭職

M: Hello. My name is Jason, and I'm calling about the sales position you advertised on your website.

W: Thank you for calling. As you read in the advertisement, we're looking for someone with experience selling computers.

M: Don't worry about that. I've worked at a computer shop as a salesman for 3 years.

W: That's really good news! Why don't you send us your resume?

Unit 25　教育、宣傳

W: This is Susanna from the AA Advertising Company. I'm calling about an idea I have to promote your restaurant.

M: Oh, that's interesting! Because we recently remodeled the restaurant, I want you to see it. Can you come by to see it?

W: Sure, I'll go there tomorrow, and, while I'm there, we can discuss the script for the advertisement.

Unit 26　設施、網絡管理

M: Do you know when the mechanic will come to fix the air conditioner?

W: Tomorrow afternoon, I guess. Is there a problem?

M: I'm concerned about my meeting. If it isn't working by today, I'll have to reschedule my meeting. I'd rather postpone it.

W: Don't worry about it. I can call someone else and check whether he can fix it by this afternoon or not.

Unit 27　會計、預算

M: Tracy, I just heard that we have to reduce our expenses by 20 percent. How do you think we can do that?

W: Really? I haven't heard that yet. How are we going to pay for the dinner for our department?

M: Hmm, I think we need to reconsider the budget for it again. We have to look for another supplier.

W: I should call the supplier as soon as possible to notify them that we have to break the contract.

Unit 28　事業規劃

W: Did you already sign the contract with the agent for your new restaurant?

M: Well, I sent an email to the agent yesterday to get some information about the renovations. But I still haven't got a response.

W: I think you should give her a call. Anyway, I'm worried that buying it is going to be complicated.

Review Test

Q1-3. M: Hi. This is Martin from the technical support team. I got a call from someone in your staff that a computer isn't working.

W: Thanks for coming. Suddenly, the computer shut down when I was about to complete my project. After that, I couldn't turn it back on.

M: I think I should take your computer to my office to check it out.

W: Okay. But can you fix it by tomorrow? I have to finish my work before this weekend.

Q4-6. M : Hello, Ms. Vera. I'm John from the Human Resources Department at TACC. I was very impressed with your resume, and I want you to come in for an interview on Friday.

W: Thank you. I was waiting for your call. Do I need to bring anything for the interview?

M: You need to come with a printed copy of your resume.

Q7-9. W: Our magazine is planning a special feature on newly listed companies in the state next month. Are you interested in this assignment?

M1: Yes, I am. I want to write about the IT firm Stargate. It won the new company of the year award at last year's industry conference.

W: Okay, Ken. That sounds great. And, Andrew, why don't

you go along and take some photos for the article?

M2: Sure, I'd be glad to. When are you planning to visit the company, Ken?

M1: I'll check my schedule and get back to you right away.

Q10-12. W: Hi, Steve. Sorry to interrupt. I just got out of a budget meeting. I heard that we would scale down our corporate fitness programs due to the recent budget cuts.

M: I also heard that. Mr. Olson said we are going to cut the most expensive class to operate.

W: That doesn't make sense. According to the survey we took last month, that is the most popular class with employees.

M: I know what you're saying. Many employees will be disappointed to learn that we are not going to offer the program anymore.

PART 3 FINAL TEST - 1

Questions 32-34 refer to the following conversation.
第32-34題請參照以下的對話。

M : Excuse me. [32] How much will it cost to send this package to Washington? I want it to arrive there by tomorrow.
▶ 這是詢問對話主題的題目，所以要專心聆聽前半段。(C) 為正確答案。

W : $20, but to get it there by tomorrow, [33] I suggest using express delivery service. But that will be an additional $10.
▶ 雖然建議事項通常會在後半段出現，但是請記住，建議題的出題順序是第二題時，相關內容可能會在中間出現。女子建議使用快遞，所以 (A) 為正確答案。

M : Oh, that's quite expensive. [34] I'd rather not use express delivery.
▶ 關於未來的行動要仔細聆聽後半段。因為快遞服務太貴，男子打算使用比較便宜的服務，所以 (B) 為正確答案。

W : Then please write your name, address, and phone number on the package.

男：不好意思，請問寄這個包裹到華盛頓要多少錢？我希望明天可以到。
女：二十美元，不過明天到的話，我建議使用快遞服務。但是那個要再加十美元。
男：喔，那滿貴的。我還是不要用快遞好了。
女：那請您在包裹上寫下您的姓名、地址和電話號碼。

單字　package 包裹　suggest 建議　express delivery 快遞　additional 追加的，額外的　rather 寧願，倒不如

32. 說話者主要在討論什麼？

(A) 寄信
(B) 去華盛頓
(C) 寄包裹
(D) 買禮物

解答　(C)

33. 女子建議做什麼？

(A) 使用快遞
(B) 下個禮拜前寄包裹
(C) 用另一個箱子裝物品
(D) 請另一個人幫忙

解答　(A)

34. 男子最有可能決定做什麼？

(A) 用快遞寄包裹
(B) 選擇比較不貴的服務
(C) 把包裹拿回家
(D) 預約其他服務

解答　(B)

Questions 35-37 refer to the following conversation with three speakers. 第35-37題請參照以下的三人對話。

W : Hi, Tom. [35] How's the design work for our new brochure going?
▶ 對話主題或相關線索會在對話的前半段出現。透過女子的第一句話，可以知道三人正在進行新冊子的設計作業，所以 (B) 為正確答案。

M1 : I've completed most of it. I can e-mail you the final design within a couple of hours.
W : Sounds good. Then we can send it to the printing office tomorrow at the latest. [36] Come to think of it, we should put some customer reviews on the last page.
▶ 女子提議把客人的心得加到冊子中，所以改述了 put some customer reviews 的 (B) 為正確答案。

M1 : That makes sense. I'll add some testimonials from our satisfied customers on the back page.
W : [37] Daniell, please contact B&M Printers and find out how long the printing will take and how much it will cost. I have always been happy with its high-quality work.
▶ 女子請對方聯絡 B&M 影印店，並補充自己對他們的高品質服務很滿意。(A) 為正確答案。

M2 : Okay, I'll call the store right away.

女：嗨，湯姆。我們的新冊子設計得如何了？
男1：我已經完成大部分了。我幾個小時內就可以寄最終版的設計給妳。
女：聽起來很棒。那我們最慢可以明天寄給影印店。

仔細一想，我們應該要把一些客人的心得放在最後一頁。
男1：很有道理。我會把感到滿意的客人的推薦文加到最後一頁。
女：丹尼爾，請聯絡B&M影印店，看印刷要花多久時間和多少錢。我對他們的高品質服務一直都很滿意。
男2：好，我會馬上打給那間店。

單字　brochure 小冊子，指南　complete 完成　most 大部分　final 最終的　within 在～以內　printing office 影印店　at the latest 最晚　come to think of it 仔細一想　review 心得　make sense 有道理　add 新增　testimonial 推薦文　satisfied 滿意的　contact 聯絡　find out 查明　cost 花費　high-quality 高品質的，高級的　right away 馬上，立刻　clothing 衣服　create 創造　advertising 廣告　budget 預算　safety 安全　manual 說明書　reservation 預約　content 內容　conduct 實施，做　customer survey 顧客調查　edit 編輯　entire 整個的　report 報告（書）　positive 正面的　result 結果　upward 向上的　sales 銷售

35. 說話者正在進行什麼作業？

(A) 衣服設計
(B) 製作小冊子
(C) 廣告預算
(D) 安全說明書

解答　(B)

36. 女子建議做什麼？

(A) 取消預約
(B) 新增新的內容
(C) 做顧客調查
(D) 編輯整個報告

解答　(B)

37. 女子說她對什麼感到滿意？

(A) 某間店的高品質服務
(B) 客人的正面評價
(C) 顧客調查結果
(D) 銷售的上升趨勢

解答　(A)

Questions 38-40 refer to the following conversation. 第38-40題請參照以下的對話。

W : David, [38] I've been trying to access my email, but when I enter my password, I get a message that it's invalid.
▶ 遇到詢問問題（problem）的題目時，帶有否定含義的單字（damage、wrong、problem、invalid）出現的地方很有可能是正確答案，所以要專心聽這些單

字。請記住問題經常在對話的前半段出現。女子說「輸入密碼後會收到密碼無效的訊息」，所以她遇到的是「輸入密碼」的問題。(B) 為正確答案。

M : Did you ask the technician about that?

W : [39] I already tried calling technical support, but it appears that no one is working there now.

▶ 具體的資訊通常會在中間出現，所以要仔細聆聽這個部分。女子說已經打電話給技術支援組了，所以 (A) 為正確答案。

M : [40] There is a 24-hour technical service you can call. I can look up the phone number for you.

▶ 提議句會在後半段出現，其答題線索是以「I can~」開頭的句子。男子的第二句話是說「有個二十四小時提供技術服務的地方，可以幫忙查電話號碼」，所以 (D) 為正確答案。

女：大衛，我一直試著要存取我的電子郵件，但是當我輸入密碼後，會收到密碼無效的訊息。
男：妳問過技術人員了嗎？
女：我已經試過打給技術支援組了，但是他們現在似乎都下班了。
男：有個二十四小時提供技術服務的地方。我可以幫妳查電話號碼。

單字　**access** 存取，接近　**password** 密碼　**invalid** 無效的　**technical support** 技術支援　**appear** 似乎

38. 女子遇到什麼問題？

(A) 執行新系統
(B) 輸入密碼
(C) 寄電子郵件
(D) 使用電子裝置

解答　(B)

39. 女子一直嘗試聯絡誰？

(A) 技術支援組
(B) 水管工
(C) 接待人員
(D) 維修組

解答　(A)

40. 男子主動提出要做什麼？

(A) 隔天再幫忙女子
(B) 打給另一個支援組
(C) 幫女子找密碼
(D) 找電話號碼

解答　(D)

Questions 41-43 refer to the following conversation.
第41-43題請參照以下的對話。

M : Nancy, [41] I lost my mobile phone at the restaurant last night, and I need to get a new one. Could you recommend a good store?

▶ 這題問的是對話主題，答題線索會在前半段出現。男子正在說手機的事，所以 (B) 為正確答案。

W : [42] Why don't you try the New Electronics Store? It has very affordable prices.

▶ 作答請求、建議時，要仔細聆聽出現建議句（why don't you?、you could~）的部分。女子說那間的價格很便宜，所以 (A) 為正確答案。

M : [43] I don't remember where the store is though. Could you tell me where it is located?

▶ 這題問的是男子忘了什麼，所以要專注於男子的發言。男子說「不記得那間店在哪裡了」，所以 (A) 為正確答案。

W : Sure, I can take you there if you want.

男：南西，我昨晚在餐廳弄丟手機了，我需要一支新的。妳可以推薦好店給我嗎？
女：你何不試試紐伊電子產品店？它的價格很便宜。
男：但我不記得那間店在哪裡了。妳可以跟我說在哪裡嗎？
女：沒問題，你想要的話，我可以帶你去。

單字　**recommend** 推薦　**affordable price** 可負擔的價格　**though** 然而

41. 說話者主要在討論什麼？

(A) 電子辭典
(B) 手機
(C) 筆記型電腦
(D) MP3播放器

解答　(B)

42. 女子為什麼推薦紐伊電子產品店？

(A) 價格合理。
(B) 那間店離他們很近。
(C) 那間店正在打折。
(D) 老闆是她朋友。

解答　(A)

43. 男子忘記什麼了？

(A) 商店的位置
(B) 手機價格
(C) 他弄丟手機的地方
(D) 店名

解答　(A)

Questions 44-46 refer to the following conversation.
第44-46題請參照以下的對話。

W: ⁴⁴ It looks like we are almost at the art gallery. We should start to look for a place to park.
▶ 作答「What＋名詞」的題目時，要仔細聆聽跟該名詞（event）有關的部分。女子的第一句話說好像快抵達美術館了，由此可知說話者計劃參觀美術展，所以 (D) 為正確答案。

M: Okay. I'm really looking forward to seeing the art exhibit. ⁴⁵ I've wanted to see it since I saw the advertisement on TV.
▶ 男子的第一句話說「自從看到電視廣告後就很想看展覽」，所以 (C) 為正確答案。

W: I guess the advertisement succeeded. I don't see any available parking spaces on the street.

M: I think ⁴⁶ there's a parking lot beside that building. Why don't we try parking there?
▶ 作答建議題時，要專心聆聽提到「Why don't~?」的部分。男子的第二句話說「我覺得那棟建築旁邊有停車場。我們去那邊停車看看吧？」所以 (C) 為正確答案。

女：看來我們快到美術館了。我們應該開始找地方停車。
男：好。我真的很期待看美術展。自從我在電視上看到廣告之後，我就一直很想來看。
女：我想廣告做得很成功。我看路上都沒停車位。
男：我覺得那棟建築旁邊有停車場。我們去那邊停車看看吧。

單字　**almost** 幾乎　**gallery** 美術館　**park** 停車　**exhibit** 展覽會，展示品　**advertisement** 廣告　**succeed** 成功

44. 說話者計劃出席什麼活動？
　　(A) 會議
　　(B) 美術課
　　(C) 汽車展
　　(D) 美術展

解答　(D)

45. 男子是怎麼知道這個活動的？
　　(A) 透過藝術雜誌
　　(B) 透過報導
　　(C) 透過電視廣告
　　(D) 透過他的朋友

解答　(C)

46. 男子建議做什麼？
　　(A) 進入展覽會場
　　(B) 放棄看展覽
　　(C) 在停車場停車

　　(D) 找其他展覽會

解答　(C)

Questions 47-49 refer to the following conversation with three speakers. 第47-49題請參照以下三人的對話。

M1: Hey, Donna! ⁴⁷ David and I are on our way to Salero to have lunch together. Would you like to join us?
▶ 對話主題的相關線索會在前半段出現。男子向女子提議一起去叫做 Salero 的餐廳用餐，而且一半以上的對話都跟餐廳有關，所以 (C) 為正確答案。

W: Do you mean the seafood restaurant near city hall? ⁴⁸ It's too far from our office.

M1: Jane told me that a second restaurant opened in Grand Plaza yesterday.

W: That sounds great. ⁴⁸ But I'm afraid the food is way too expensive there.
▶ 女子擔心餐廳離公司太遠和那間餐廳的食物會太貴，所以 (D) 為正確答案。

M1: No worries. ⁴⁹ It is offering a generous discount during its opening week. David, did you bring the discount coupon?
▶ 男子說餐廳開幕週會提供很優惠的折扣，由此可知 (B) 為正確答案。

M2: Of course. I downloaded a 30-percent-off coupon from its website.

男1：嘿，唐娜！我跟大衛正要一起去莎雷洛吃午餐。妳要加入我們嗎？
女：你是指靠近市政府的那間海鮮餐廳嗎？離我們辦公室太遠了。
男1：簡恩告訴我，莎雷洛昨天在葛蘭德廣場開第二間餐廳了。
女：聽起來很棒。但是我怕那邊的食物會很貴。
男1：不用擔心。開幕週會提供很優惠的折扣。大衛，你有帶折價券嗎？
男2：當然。我從他們官網下載了七折優惠券。

單字　**on one's way to** 在去～的路上　**join** 加入，一起　**seafood** 海鮮　**generous** 豐厚的，慷慨的　**discount** 折扣　**during** 在～期間　**bring** 攜帶　**department store** 百貨公司　**local** 當地的　**grocery** 食品雜貨　**nearby** 附近的　**poor** 惡劣的，貧困的　**waiting time** 等候時間　**lack** 不足　**delivery** 寄送　**catering** 提供飲食

47. 他們主要在討論什麼？
　　(A) 百貨公司
　　(B) 當地的雜貨店
　　(C) 附近的餐廳
　　(D) 新網站

解答　(C)

48. 女子擔心什麼？

(A) 服務不佳
(B) 等候時間很久
(C) 停車空間不足
(D) 價格昂貴

解答　(D)

49. 這個禮拜提供什麼？

(A) 免費寄送
(B) 價格折扣
(C) 新菜單
(D) 外燴服務

解答　(B)

Questions 50-52 refer to the following conversation.
第50-52題請參照以下的對話。

W：Hello. ⁵⁰/⁵¹ I'm calling to ask if there are any rental cars available this Friday morning.

▶ 這是詢問主題的題目，所以要專心聆聽第一句話。女子的第一句話是問「有沒有出租車」，所以 (C) 為正確答案。

M：Sure. ⁵¹ We'll have several cars available on Friday. Will you be returning the car on the same day?

▶ 這是詢問職業的題目，所以要專心聆聽前半段。而且問的是男子的職業，所以聆聽男子的發言時，要專心聆聽跟職業有關的單字。女子的第一句話是「關於租車的諮詢」，對話中間穿插提到「rental cars、cars available、return the vehicle」等等，由此可知男子的工作地點是「租車公司」，所以 (A) 為正確答案。

W：No. I'll be using it for 2 weeks as I travel, so can I drop the car off at the airport?
M：That's no problem. However, ⁵² if you return the vehicle to a different location, we charge a $50 fee.

▶ 這題跟男子有關，所以要專心聆聽男子的發言。男子的第二句話說「如果在不同地點還車，會收五十美元」，所以 (D) 為正確答案。

女：哈囉，我來電是想問這個禮拜五早上是否有出租車可以租。
男：當然有。禮拜五有幾台車可以租。您會在同一天還車嗎？
女：不會，我旅遊的這兩週會用到，所以我可以在機場還車嗎？
男：沒問題。不過，如果您在不同地點還車，我們會收五十美元。

單字　rental 租賃，出租　available 可使用的　several 幾個的　drop off at 在～放下　airport 機場　vehicle 車輛，運載工具　charge 收費

50. 說話者在討論什麼？

(A) 機場停車場
(B) 機票
(C) 租車
(D) 旅遊方案

解答　(C)

51. 男子最有可能在哪裡工作？

(A) 租車公司
(B) 機場
(C) 旅行社
(D) 汽車經銷商

解答　(A)

52. 根據男子，收五十美元是為了什麼？

(A) 買回程票
(B) 在長期停車場停車
(C) 提供接送服務
(D) 在不同城市還車

解答　(D)

Questions 53-55 refer to the following conversation.
第53-55題請參照以下的對話。

M：Hi, Rhonda. I just heard from Jordan Mitts, one of the speakers. ⁵³ He said that he cannot make it to the training session for our new employees.

▶ 男子在前半段提到新員工培訓課程的講者之一取消演講的問題，後面的內容則跟問題的解決方法有關。(B) 為正確答案。

W：Oh, that's really short notice. We only have ten days left before the training session. What should we do?
M：Well, why don't we ask Andrew Ling in the Marketing Department? He gave a speech about time management last year. ⁵⁴ The audience response was very positive. I also thought it was a very good speech.

▶ 男子推薦安德魯・凌代替演講，理由是聽眾對他去年的演講反應很好。這表示男子提到的安德魯・凌有資格演講，所以 (D) 為正確答案。

W：That's a great idea. ⁵⁵ I'll give him a call right now.

▶ 詢問接下來要做什麼事的最後一題，答題線索會在對話的後半段出現。透過最後一句話，可以知道女子會打電話給安德魯・凌。(C) 為正確答案。

男：嗨，諾達。我剛才收到講者之一的喬登・米特斯的聯絡。他說他沒辦法出席我們的新員工培訓課程了。
女：噢，這個通知好臨時。在培訓課程之前，我們只剩下十天了。我們該怎麼辦？

男：嗯，我們問問行銷部的安德魯‧凌吧？他去年演講過時間管理的主題。聽眾的反應很好。我也覺得是一場很棒的演講。

女：這是個好主意。我現在就打電話給他。

單字　make it 守約，及時抵達　notice 通知，公告　give a speech 演講　management 管理　audience 聽眾　positive 正面的，積極的　anniversary 紀念日　launch 開始，上市　board 董事會　feedback 回饋　qualified 有資格的　report 報告　make a phone call 打電話　response 反應

53. 說話者正在準備什麼？

(A) 年度活動
(B) 培訓課程
(C) 新產品的上市
(D) 董事會會議

解答　(B)

54. 男子說「聽眾的反應很好」的意思是什麼？

(A) 他希望聽眾給回饋。
(B) 他同意會議一定要改期。
(C) 他希望全體員工都會參加活動。
(D) 他覺得凌先生具備做某些工作的資格。

解答　(D)

55. 女子接下來最有可能會做什麼事？

(A) 跟經理報告
(B) 演講
(C) 打電話
(D) 開會

解答　(C)

Questions 56-58 refer to the following conversation.
第56-58題請參照以下的對話。

M : Crystal, [56] I hear your design company just won an award for being the best new business.

▶ 這題問的是女子的職業，所以要專注於跟職業有關的單字。男子提到「設計公司剛獲得最佳新興企業獎」，由此可推測出女子是設計公司的設計師。(C) 為正確答案。

W : Yes, and since we won the award, I have gotten much busier, [57] so I'm planning to hire an assistant.

▶ 這題問的是對話主題，但是出題順序是第二題，在這種情況下線索會在中間出現。只聽到第一句話的話，可能會選擇 (A) 當正確答案，但是從結果來看，女子因為變忙而想要僱用更多的人，所以 (B) 為正確答案。

M : I know someone, Kenny. He just graduated from

university, and he is looking for a job. If you want to interview him, I can introduce you.

W : That's good news! [58] Could you ask him to send his resume to me?

▶ 這是詢問提議／請求內容的題目，所以要專心聆聽後半段。女子說「請他寄履歷」，所以 (C) 為正確答案。

男：克莉絲特爾，我聽說妳的設計公司剛獲得最佳新興企業獎。

女：對，而且因為我們得獎，我變得更忙了，所以我打算僱用一名助理。

男：我知道一個叫肯尼的人。他剛從大學畢業，正在找工作。如果妳想面試他，我可以介紹給妳。

女：真是好消息！你可以請他寄履歷給我嗎？

單字　award 獎項　hire 僱用　assistant 助理，助手　introduce 介紹　resume 履歷

56. 女子的職業最有可能是什麼？

(A) 店員
(B) 會計師
(C) 設計師
(D) 藝術家

解答　(C)

57. 說話者主要在討論什麼？

(A) 獎項
(B) 職缺
(C) 企業
(D) 新聞報導

解答　(B)

58. 女子想要肯尼寄什麼東西給她？

(A) 獎品
(B) 應徵表格
(C) 個人簡歷
(D) 信件

解答　(C)

Questions 59-61 refer to the following conversation.
第59-61題請參照以下的對話。

W : Hello. This is Sonya Roberts. [59] I ordered an ink cartridge on your online shopping mall a few days ago. [60] And I got an e-mail from your store last night. It said that my order would arrive sometime this morning. But it hasn't arrived yet.

▶ 女子在前半段提到自己在男子工作的購物中心買了墨水匣，所以 (A) 為正確答案。

▶ 女子說從業者那裡收到今天上午會收到包裹的電子

郵件，但是東西還沒到，所以 (C) 為正確答案。

M : Sorry for the inconvenience. Delivery has been backed up lately due to the holiday season. Do you have an order number?

W : My order number is 29390.

M : The deliveryman is on the way, and your order will arrive within hours.

W : Can you tell me the deliveryman's phone number? [61] I'm a bit worried because I have to prepare some materials for tomorrow's meeting.

▶ 女子在前半段提過自己訂的墨水匣還沒到，又補充說明要準備會議用的資料，所以很擔心。由此可以猜測到女子急著要用影印機，所以 (B) 為正確答案。

M : Of course. His number is 086-555-3848.

女：哈囉，我是桑雅・羅伯特茲。我幾天前在你們的線上購物中心訂了墨水匣。然後我昨晚收到你們商店寄來的電子郵件，說我的訂單會在今天早上送來。但是到現在都還沒來。

男：抱歉給您造成的不便。由於現在是假日季節，最近的配送有所延遲。請問您有訂單號碼嗎？

女：我的訂單號碼是29390。

男：送貨員正在路上，您的訂單會在幾個小時內送達。

女：你可以跟我說送貨員的電話號碼嗎？我有點擔心，因為我要替明天的會議準備一些資料。

男：沒問題。他的電話號碼是086-555-3848。

單字　order 訂購　arrive 抵達　yet 還（沒）
inconvenience 不便　delivery 寄送　be backed up 堆積　lately 最近　due to 由於～　holiday season 假日季節
on the way 途中，在去（來）的路上　within 在～以內
deliveryman 送貨員　prepare 準備　material 資料，材料
stationery 文具類　catering 提供飲食　grocery 食品雜貨
item 物品　damaged 毀損的　apply 應用　on sick leave 請病假中　copier 影印機

59. 男子最有可能在哪裡工作？

(A) 文具店
(B) 外燴公司
(C) 食品雜貨店
(D) 搬家公司

解答　(A)

60. 女子提到什麼問題？

(A) 到貨時就毀損的物品。
(B) 店裡的物品太貴。
(C) 寄送延遲。
(D) 折扣不適用。

解答　(C)

61. 女子說「我有點擔心，因為我要替明天的會議準備一些資料」是暗示什麼？

(A) 她會請幾天病假。
(B) 她需要盡快用到影印機。
(C) 有個預訂被漏掉了。
(D) 一些資料沒有送來。

解答　(B)

Questions 62-64 refer to the following conversation and list. 第62-64題請參照以下的對話和清單。

W : Hello. [62] I'd like to reserve a conference room at your hotel to hold an annual training seminar for our new employees. It'll be a full-day event.

▶ 可以從前半段找到女子的公司要舉辦新進員工培訓研討會的線索，所以 (C) 為正確答案。

M : Thank you for choosing our hotel. When will the seminar take place, and how many people will attend it?

W : The event will be held on March 23, and we need a large space which can accommodate up to 150 people. [63] We are also going to have more than 4 presentations, so we need a projector and microphones.

▶ 這題問的是女子的要求事項，所以要從女子的發言中找線索。女子說會在即將到來的活動中進行四次以上的簡報，所以需要投影機和麥克風，改述這些設備說法的 (B) 為正確答案。

M : [64] We recently had our largest conference room remodeled. I recommend that room. The rate is $75 per person, and the room has audiovisual equipment.

W : Great. I'll go with the room.

▶ 男子建議使用最大的會議室，女子對此表示同意。透過表格可以知道能容納最多人的會議室是 Agora，所以 (A) 為正確答案。

女：哈囉，我想預約你們飯店的會議廳，替我們的新進員工舉辦年度培訓研討會。這會是一整天的活動。

男：謝謝您選擇我們的飯店。研討會將在何時舉辦？會有多少人參加呢？

女：活動會在三月二十三日舉行，我們需要一個可以容納多達一百五十人的大空間。我們還會做四次以上的簡報，所以需要投影機和麥克風。

男：我們最近翻修過最大間的會議室，我推薦那間。費用是每人七十五美元，會議室裡有視聽設備。

女：好。我要選那間會議室。

單字　reserve 預約　conference room 會議室　hold 舉辦，舉行　annual 年度的　training 培訓，訓練　seminar 研討會　full-day 整天的　event 活動　take place 發生　attend 出席　space 空間　accommodate 容納　up to 高達　presentation 簡報　projector 投影機　microphone 麥

克風 recently 最近 remodel 改造 recommend 推薦 per person 每人 audiovisual 視聽的 equipment 設備 go with 接受（計畫、提議等） shareholder 股東 press conference 記者會 new recruit 新進員工 award 獎項 ceremony 典禮 direction 方向 sample 樣品 facility 設施

62. 預計舉辦何種活動？

(A) 股東會
(B) 記者會
(C) 新進員工研討會
(D) 頒獎典禮

解答　(C)

63. 女子要求什麼？

(A) 前往飯店的路線
(B) 簡報設備
(C) 產品樣品
(D) 參觀設施

解答　(B)

64. 請看圖表。女子最有可能會選擇哪個會議室？

(A) 集會廳
(B) 黃金廳
(C) 白銀廳
(D) 商務廳

房型	座位
集會廳	180
黃金廳	100
白銀廳	70
商務廳	30

解答　(A)

Questions 65-67 refer to the following conversation and floor 第65-67題請參照以下的對話和樓層圖。

M : Hello. This is Brian Thompson. [65]I'm going to deliver your printer to your office today.

▶ 這是詢問說話者職業的題目，所以要從前半段中找線索。男子說今天會送印表機到辦公室，由此可知(C)為正確答案。

W : Oh, yes. Can you tell me what time you are arriving?

M : I'll be there around 2 p.m.

W : Hmm. [66]I won't be in my office between 1 and 3 p.m. since I have an important meeting with a client. Besides, my office will be locked while I am out.

▶ 這是詢問女子會做什麼事的題目，所以要從女子的發言中找線索。女子提到下午一到三點有重要的會議，所以 (A) 為正確答案。

M : I see. Then where should I leave your item?

W : Can you leave it with my colleague Walter Cayman?

[67]His office is located right next to the meeting room. If you enter, you can see the meeting room in front of you.

▶ 由於自己到時候不在，女子請對方把包裹拿到同事的辦公室。同事沃特·卡曼的辦公室就在會議室隔壁，透過圖表可以知道男子會去 B 辦公室。(C) 為正確答案。

M : Okay. That shouldn't be a problem.

男：您好，我是布萊恩·湯普森。我今天會配送您的印表機到您的辦公室。
女：喔，好。可以跟我說你會幾點到嗎？
男：下午兩點左右會到。
女：嗯，我下午一到三點不在辦公室，因為我今天跟客戶有個重要的會議。而且，我外出的時候辦公室會上鎖。
男：原來如此。那我應該把您的東西放到哪裡？
女：你可以把東西交給我的同事沃特·卡曼嗎？他的辦公室就在會議室隔壁。你進來之後，就會看到會議室在你前方。
男：好，那應該沒問題。

單字　deliver 寄送 arrive 抵達 since 由於～，自～以來 besides 而且 lock 上鎖 leave 留下，把～交給 item 物品 colleague 同事 located 位於～的 right 不偏不倚地 next to 在～的旁邊 in front of 在～的前面，在～的正面 sales 銷售 representative 代表，員工 janitor 管理員 train 訓練 conduct 實施，做 survey 調查 drop by 順路拜訪

65. 男子是誰？

(A) 銷售員
(B) 辦公室員工
(C) 送貨員
(D) 管理員

解答　(C)

66. 女子今天下午會做什麼？

(A) 出席會議
(B) 訓練新員工
(C) 影印
(D) 進行調查

解答　(A)

67. 請看圖表。男子最有可能順路去哪個房間？

(A) 會議室
(B) A辦公室
(C) B辦公室
(D) C辦公室

C 辦公室	入口	A 辦公室
	會議室	B 辦公室

解答　(C)

Questions 68-70 refer to the following conversation and schedule. 第68-70題請參照以下的對話和日程表。

M : [68] I'm scheduled to give a presentation here at 11 a.m. I just came by to check out the video and audio facilities.

W : [69] I'm going to make a presentation right before you. And I just finished rehearsing my presentation. [69] Well, there is a little problem though. The microphone is making some buzzing noises.

▶ 遇到需要運用圖表來解題的題目時，在聆聽對話之前要先看過圖表。男子說自己預計在早上十一點做簡報，女子則說自己會在他之前上台。透過表格可以知道在十一點之前，十點開始的簡報主題是患者看護，所以 (B) 為正確答案。

▶ 從女子說「有問題」的下一句，可以知道麥克風會發出噪音，將這個問題改述的 (C) 為正確答案。

M : That's terrible. It might bother the audience. I think we'd better have it replaced.

W : We haven't got much time left before the workshop starts. Do we have a spare microphone?

M : [70] Let me go downstairs and check if there's another microphone in the equipment locker.

▶ 這是詢問男子要做什麼事的最後一題，所以要從後半段找線索。男子說要下樓確認有沒有其他麥克風，由此可知 (D) 為正確答案。

男：我被排在早上十一點在這裡做簡報。我只是過來確認視聽設備。

女：我就在你前一個做簡報。我剛彩排完我的簡報。嗯，是有個小問題。麥克風一直有嗡嗡作響的噪音。

男：真糟糕。這可能會干擾到聽眾。我覺得我們最好把它換掉。

女：離工作坊開始沒剩多久的時間了。我們有備用的麥克風嗎？

男：我去樓下確認看看設備置物櫃有沒有另一支麥克風。

單字 be scheduled to 預計～ give a presentation 做簡報 come by 順便來一趟 check out 確認 facility 設施 right before 就在～之前 rehearse 彩排 microphone 麥克風 make a noise 發出噪音 buzzing 嗡嗡聲 terrible 糟糕的、壞的 bother 打擾，煩擾 audience 聽眾 replace 替換 spare 備用的 downstairs 往樓下 another 另一個 equipment 設備 patient 患者 safety 安全 care 關心，看護 mental 精神的 diet 飲食 nutrition 營養 unavailable 沒時間的，沒庫存的 out of stock 沒庫存的 device 裝備，裝置 properly 恰當地 satisfied 滿足的 report to 向～報告 submit 繳交 document 文件

68. 請看圖表。女子會討論什麼主題？

(A) 患者安全
(B) 患者看護
(C) 精神健康

(D) 飲食與營養

時間	主題
上午9:00 - 上午9:50	患者安全
上午10:00 - 上午10:50	患者看護
上午11:00 - 上午11:50	精神健康
下午1：00 - 下午1:50	飲食與營養

解答 **(B)**

69. 女子提到什麼問題？

(A) 有些員工沒空。
(B) 有個物品缺貨。
(C) 裝置無法正常運作。
(D) 顧客不滿意。

解答 **(C)**

70. 男子說他接下來會做什麼？

(A) 查看網站
(B) 跟經理報告
(C) 繳交文件
(D) 下樓

解答 **(D)**

PART 3 FINAL TEST - 2

Questions 32-34 refer to the following conversation.
第32-34題請參照以下的對話。

W : Did you hear that Mary is leaving the company? I'm so sad because [32] she's been doing such a great job in our Sales Department.

▶ 這題問的是第三者的職業，所以要仔細聆聽第三者出現的地方。這裡出現的瑪莉是第三個人物，所以用 she 指稱瑪莉的句子是跟她有關的對話，記住這一點的話，解題會更順利。女子的第一句話提到她是銷售部門的員工，男子則稱她為 manager，所以 (A) 為正確答案。

M : [32/33] Because she's such an efficient manager, I'm sure she'll be missed.

▶ 詢問理由的題目，答題線索通常會在第二句或第三句話之中出現。男子說大家會想念瑪莉是因為她是「有效率的經理」，所以 (D) 為正確答案。

W : In fact, we need someone to replace her. [34] Could you take over her position?

▶ 這是提議句，所以要從後半段尋找線索。最後一句話「Could you take over her position?」的意思是「要對方接下她的職位」，所以 (C) 為正確答案。

女：你聽說瑪莉要離職的事了嗎？我很難過，因為她在我們銷售部門的工作表現非常出色。

男：因為她是做事很有效率的經理，我相信大家會很想念她的。

女：其實，我們需要一個人來代替她。你可以接下她的職位嗎？

單字 efficient 有效率的 replace 取代 position 位置 respect 敬重 candidate 候選人 job applicant 求職者

32. 瑪莉是誰？

(A) 銷售經理
(B) 銷售員
(C) 人事經理
(D) 祕書

解答 (A)

33. 根據說話者，為什麼大家會想念瑪莉？

(A) 她被顧客高度推崇。
(B) 她是最棒的銷售員。
(C) 她在公司工作很久了。
(D) 她工作很有效率。

解答 (D)

34. 女子要求男子做什麼？

(A) 進行工作面試
(B) 替某個工作找應徵者
(C) 接下經理的職位
(D) 面試求職者

解答 (C)

Questions 35-37 refer to the following conversation.
第35-37題請參照以下的對話。

W : Excuse me. [35/36] I'm writing an article about the opening of the new park. Would you like to comment?

▶ 這題問的是職業，所以要仔細聆聽前半段。女子的第一句說「正在撰寫報導」，所以可推測她是選項之一的「記者」。因此，第 35 題的正確答案為 (C)。女子說「報導內容跟新公園開幕」有關，所以第 36 題的正確答案為 (C)。

M : Sure, I'm really happy about it. My family has been waiting for it to open for a long time.
W : What impresses you the most about it?
M : [37] I really like the small pond in the park, and I heard that there will be a fountain show in summer.

▶ 這題問的是男子的事，所以要專心聆聽男子的發言。女子問「印象最深刻的是什麼？」男子回答說「很喜歡小池塘」，所以 (D) 為正確答案。

女：不好意思，我正在撰寫新公園開幕的報導。您想

發表一下意見嗎？

男：當然，我對這個消息感到很開心。我的家人從很久以前就一直在期待公園開幕。

女：最令您印象深刻的是什麼？

男：我真的很喜歡公園裡的小池塘，而且我聽說夏天會有水舞秀。

單字 article 報導 park 公園 comment 發表意見，評論 impress 給～極深的印象，使銘記 pond 池塘 fountain 噴水池

35. 女子最有可能是誰？

(A) 外燴業者
(B) 建築師
(C) 記者
(D) 銷售員

解答 (C)

36. 說了關於公園的什麼？

(A) 關閉了。
(B) 翻修過了。
(C) 開放了。
(D) 搬遷了。

解答 (C)

37. 公園的什麼給男子留下深刻的印象？

(A) 洗手間
(B) 遊樂場
(C) 游泳池
(D) 池塘

解答 (D)

Questions 38-40 refer to the following conversation.
第38-40題請參照以下的對話。

W : Hi. [38] Where can I get on a bus to go to the airport? I need to be on the next bus.

▶ 這是詢問地點的題目，答題線索會在前半段出現。(A) 為正確答案。

M : [39] You have to take the number 90 bus. Go across the road, and you will see a bus station with a red roof.

▶ 男子說想搭公車的話，要過馬路，所以 (D) 為正確答案。

W : Do I have to buy a ticket there?
M : No. [40] You can buy one from the bus driver when you get on the bus.

▶ 這是關於未來的問題，所以要仔細聆聽最後面的對話。(C) 為正確答案。

女：嗨，請問我可以從哪裡搭公車到機場？我必須搭到下一班公車。

男：您可以搭90號公車。過馬路之後，您會看到有紅色屋頂的公車站。

女：我需要在那裡買票嗎？

男：不用，您可以在上車的時候跟司機買。

單字　get on a bus 搭公車　go across the road 過馬路　bus station 公車站

38. 女子想去哪裡？

(A) 機場
(B) 公車站
(C) 火車站
(D) 售票亭

解答　(A)

39. 為什麼女子需要過馬路？

(A) 為了出席會議
(B) 為了拜訪某間店
(C) 為了見某人
(D) 為了前往公車站

解答　(D)

40. 誰會賣票？

(A) 銷售員
(B) 空服員
(C) 公車司機
(D) 技師

解答　(C)

Questions 41-43 refer to the following conversation with three speakers. 第41-43題請參照以下三人的對話。

M1 : ⁴¹Did you guys see the memo about the company contest? The owner wants suggestions for a theme for the new advertising campaign.

▶ 這是詢問競賽宗旨的題目，所以可以在提到競賽（contest）的部分找到線索。男子說老闆想要一些關於新廣告宣傳主題的建議，而將這段話改述成 To create a campaign theme 的 (A) 為正確答案。

W: Yes, I saw it. I presume the advertising agency hasn't thought of anything suitable.

M2: Yeah. We need to come up with something more attractive to customers. Why don't you try, Linda?

W: Well, ⁴²I have to finish these sales figures before the audit, so I don't think I will have time to enter.

▶ 這題是詢問女子無法參加的原因，所以要從女子的發言中找線索。女子說要在查帳之前完成銷售數據，所以應該沒時間參加。(D) 為正確答案。

M1 : That's too bad because ⁴³you made a lot of great suggestions for our last campaign.

M2: ⁴³I agree. You have a very creative mind, and the prize is a trip to France, so perhaps you should find time to come up with something.

▶ 這是推論（暗示）題型，要從男子的發言中尋找跟女子有關的暗示。女子說沒時間參加競賽後，第一個男子就說女子在上次的活動中提供了許多好建議，第二個男子也說女子很有創意，兩人都提到女子想出了很多好點子，所以 (C) 為正確答案。

男1：你們看到公司內部競賽的備忘錄了嗎？老闆想要一些關於新廣告宣傳主題的建議。

女：嗯，我看到了。我猜廣告代理商沒有想到任何合適的主題。

男2：對啊，我們要想出一些更吸引客人的。琳達，妳試試吧？

女：嗯，我必須在查帳之前完成這些銷售數據，所以我想我應該沒時間參加。

男1：好可惜，因為妳替我們上次的活動提供了許多好建議。

男2：我同意。妳很有創意，而且獎勵是法國旅遊，或許妳可以找時間想一些點子。

單字　contest 比賽，大賽，競賽　theme 主題　presume 假設，猜測　suitable 合適的　sales figure 銷售數據　audit 查帳，審計　come up with 想到～，提出　customer base 客群　unsure 不確定的，沒有把握的　deadline 期限，截止時間（日期）　voucher 現金券

41. 競賽的目的是什麼？

(A) 製作宣傳主題
(B) 減少支出
(C) 增加客群
(D) 追加招募員工

解答　(A)

42. 為什麼女子不確定要不要參加？

(A) 她要去度假。
(B) 她會換工作。
(C) 她沒有任何經驗。
(D) 她要趕上工作截止日期。

解答　(D)

43. 男子們暗示了關於女子的什麼？

(A) 她是公司裡唯一的行銷專家。
(B) 她以前得過獎。
(C) 她提過很多有創意的點子。
(D) 她想去歐洲旅遊。

解答　(C)

Questions 44-46 refer to the following conversation.
第44-46題請參照以下的對話。

M : Hi. my name is Omar Khan. I have an appointment with Dr. Smith tomorrow at 2 p.m., but [44] I have to reschedule it due to my work. Is it possible to change my appointment to Friday at 2 p.m.?
▶ 這是詢問主題或目的的題目，所以要仔細聆聽前半段。(D) 為正確答案。

W : [45] I'm sorry. Dr. Smith's schedule is already full on Friday. How about coming on Thursday? She can see you on that day.
▶ 跟職業、公司等有關的題目會在前半段出現。詢問職業的題目，出題順序為第二題時，要想到答題線索應該會在對話的中間出現。女子正在安排預約的時間，所以 (C) 為正確答案。

M : Oh, that'll be great. [46] Then I'll be there on Thursday at 2 p.m.
▶ 尋找跟未來有關的計畫或日程相關線索時，要仔細聆聽最後一句話。男子說會在星期四那天過去，所以 (C) 為正確答案。

男：嗨，我是奧瑪・卡恩。我預約了明天下午兩點見史密斯醫生，但是我因為工作的緣故，要重新安排時間。可以把我的預約改到星期五下午兩點嗎？
女：抱歉，史密斯醫生禮拜五的行程都排滿了。星期四來的話呢？她可以在那天跟您見面。
男：喔，那太好了。那我星期四下午兩點過去。

單字 appointment 預約 reschedule 重新安排時間 due to 由於～

44. 這通電話的主旨是什麼？
　(A) 為了付款
　(B) 為了跟醫生講話
　(C) 為了預約
　(D) 為了重新安排預約

解答 (D)

45. 男子最有可能在跟誰對話？
　(A) 祕書
　(B) 銷售員
　(C) 接待員
　(D) 患者

解答 (C)

46. 男子計劃什麼時候見史密斯醫生？
　(A) 星期二
　(B) 星期三
　(C) 星期四
　(D) 星期五

解答 (C)

Questions 47-49 refer to the following conversation.
第47-49題請參照以下的對話。

M : Hello. This is Rick Glenshaw. [47] I'm calling to schedule an appointment with the dentist. Either next Tuesday or next Friday would be the best day for me.
▶ 打電話的目的會在對話前半段的 I'm calling~ 後面出現。男子提到自己打電話是想預約看牙醫的時間，所以 (D) 為正確答案。

W : Okay, I can assist you with that. There are spots next Tuesday between 4 and 6 p.m., but I am afraid we are fully booked next Friday.

M : [48] Tuesday at 4 p.m. fits my schedule.
▶ 男子說星期二下午四點符合自己的時間安排，所以 (B) 為正確答案。

W : Then I'll schedule you for then. [49] Starting next week, you'll be able to make an appointment on our website. Would you like me to tell you how?

M : I have an emergency meeting soon. Can you e-mail me the instructions?
▶ 女子說可以教男子透過網站預約的方式，男子回覆等一下有個緊急會議。由此可知男子等一下就得掛電話了，所以 (C) 為正確答案。

W : Certainly. I'll send them to you by e-mail.

男：哈囉，我是瑞克・葛蘭休。我來電是想預約看牙醫的時間。我想約下週二或下週五。
女：好，我幫您預約。下週二下午四到六點有空檔，但是下週五的預約都滿了。
男：週二下午四點符合我的時間安排。
女：那我替您安排那個時候。從下週起，您可以在我們的網站上預約。需要告訴您方法嗎？
男：我等一下有個緊急會議。妳可以用電子郵件寄說明給我嗎？
女：沒問題。我會用電子郵件寄給您。

單字 schedule 安排時間 appointment 預約 dentist 牙醫 either A or B A或B其中之一 assist 協助 spot 位置，地點 between A and B 在A和B之間 fully 完全地 booked 預約的 fit 符合，適合 starting 從～開始 emergency 緊急 instruction 說明 sign up for 申請 membership 會員資格 arrange 準備，籌備 right away 立刻，馬上 any longer 不再

47. 男子為什麼打電話？
　(A) 為了詢價
　(B) 為了預約飯店
　(C) 為了申請會員資格

(D) 為了安排預約

解答　(D)

48. 男子可能會在什麼時候來訪？

(A) 下週一
(B) 下週二
(C) 下週四
(D) 下週五

解答　(B)

49. 男子說「我等一下有個緊急會議」的意思是什麼？

(A) 他想要馬上看醫生。
(B) 他想聽到更多的資訊。
(C) 他沒辦法繼續説了。
(D) 他覺得很難變更日期。

解答　(C)

Questions 50-52 refer to the following conversation.
第50-52題請參照以下的對話。

W : Hi. [50/51] I bought this shirt here yesterday, but I just found out that one of the buttons has broken.
▶ 這題問的是對話地點，所以要仔細聆聽前半段。女子說了買了襯衫，所以第 50 題的正確答案為 (B)。遇到跟過去有關的題目時，要專注於前半段。第 51 題的正確答案為 (D)。

M : I apologize for the inconvenience. Would you like to exchange it for something else?
W : No, I want to exchange it for the same item.
M : Unfortunately, we don't have the same product at the moment. In that case, [52] why don't you visit our online store?
▶ 這是建議句，所以要仔細聆聽跟建議有關的措辭（Why don't you~?、You could / should~）。男子建議她逛線上網站，所以 (C) 為正確答案。

女：嗨，我昨天在這裡買了這件襯衫，但是我剛才發現有個鈕扣壞了。
男：抱歉給您造成不便。您要換成別的嗎？
女：不，我想換成一樣的。
男：可惜的是，我們目前沒有一樣的商品。這樣的話，您要不要到我們的線上網站看看？

單字　**find out** 發現，得知　**button** 鈕扣　**inconvenience** 不便　**exchange** 交換，互換　**unfortunately** 不幸地，可惜地　**at the moment** 目前，此刻

50. 這則對話的發生地點在哪裡？

(A) 電子產品店
(B) 服飾店

(C) 超市
(D) 辦公室

解答　(B)

51. 女子昨天做了什麼？

(A) 她拜訪了朋友。
(B) 她跟另一個員工講過話。
(C) 她去了博物館。
(D) 她買了襯衫。

解答　(D)

52. 根據對話，男子建議女子做什麼？

(A) 打電話給總公司
(B) 改天再來
(C) 逛線上網站
(D) 去另一間店

解答　(C)

Questions 53-55 refer to the following conversation.
第53-55題請參照以下的對話。

M : Hi. My name is Steve Harper. [53] I am here to interview for the technical support position.
▶ 可以在前半段找到拜訪目的的相關線索。男子說自己是來面試的，所以 (C) 為正確答案。

W : Let me check. Mr. Harper, interviews are going on in the order that the applications were received. [54] You will have your turn in a few minutes.
▶ 前半段提到男子的拜訪目的是面試，而這句話是要告知男子等一下就輪到他面試了。(B) 為正確答案。

M : I am supposed to meet with Ms. Packer in meeting room 5. Is that right?
W : [55] Oh, Ms. Packer is on a trip to conduct some urgent business. Ms. Summers will be meeting you. Please take the elevator to the fifth floor. The meeting room is at the end of the corridor on the right.
▶ 女子跟男子說佩克女士去出差處理急事了，所以由桑默斯女士負責面試。(D) 為正確答案。

男：嗨，我是史帝夫·哈潑。我是來這裡面試技術支援職位的。
女：我確認一下。哈潑先生，面試是按照申請書的受理順序進行。幾分鐘後就會輪到您了。
男：我應該要在五號會議室跟佩克女士見面，對吧？
女：噢，佩克女士去出差處理急事了。桑默斯女士會面試您。請搭電梯到五樓。會議室就在走廊盡頭的右邊。

單字 technical 技術的 support 支援，協助 position 職位 order 順序 application 申請書 turn 次序，輪到（順序） be supposed to 應該要～ on a trip 旅行，出差 conduct 做，實施 urgent 緊急的，急迫的 at the end of 在～的盡頭 corridor 走廊 reschedule 重新安排時間 repairperson 維修員 arrange 安排 transportation 交通工具 product 產品 out of stock 沒庫存的 celebration 慶祝活動 at the moment 目前 be transferred 調職的 on sick leave 請病假中 for a while 暫時，片刻 currently 目前 away 不在，遠離

53. 男子為什麼會在那間公司？

(A) 為了重新安排會議時間
(B) 為了跟維修員講話
(C) 為了面試
(D) 為了安排交通工具

解答 (C)

54. 女子為什麼說「幾分鐘後就會輪到你」？

(A) 某些產品好像沒庫存了。
(B) 男子的面試快開始了。
(C) 慶祝活動即將開始。
(D) 有位重要客戶正在等男子。

解答 (B)

55. 女子說了關於佩克女士的什麼？

(A) 她目前正在開會。
(B) 她已經調到另一個辦公處了。
(C) 她暫時請病假中。
(D) 她目前出差不在。

解答 (D)

Questions 56-58 refer to the following conversation.
第56-58題請參照以下的對話。

M : Hi. ⁵⁶ I'm calling to see if you can help me to find my mobile phone. I was in your restaurant yesterday, and I think I left it there.
▶ 要在對話的前半段專心聆聽來電目的或理由。男子打電話來說自己在找手機，所以 (B) 為正確答案。

W : ⁵⁷ Is it black in color? One of our staff members found a black phone.
▶ 女子問是不是黑色的，男子接著說「對」，所以 (A) 為正確答案。

M : Yes, I think that is mine. Can I go to your restaurant to get it later?

W : ⁵⁸ Since our restaurant is about to close, why don't you

---

come tomorrow?
▶ 這是提議句，所以要專心聆聽跟提議有關的措辭（why don't you~?、You could~）。女子在請對方明天再來之前，提到餐廳快打烊了，所以 (D) 為正確答案。

男：嗨，我來電是想看看你們能不能幫我找手機。我昨天去過你們的餐廳，我想我掉在那裡了。
女：是黑色的嗎？我們有個員工發現了一支黑手機。
男：對，我想那是我的。我晚一點可以去你們餐廳拿嗎？
女：我們餐廳快打烊了，您明天再來吧？

單字 mobile phone 手機 in color ～的顏色 be about to 快要～

56. 男子為什麼打電話？

(A) 為了詢問店家的營業時間
(B) 為了詢問遺失物品的事
(C) 為了跟經理說話
(D) 為了要求退款

解答 (B)

57. 對話指出了關於手機的什麼？

(A) 是黑色的。
(B) 有刮痕。
(C) 在桌上。
(D) 是白色的。

解答 (A)

58. 為什麼女子請男子明天再來？

(A) 員工正在度假。
(B) 餐廳正在施工。
(C) 晚餐還沒準備好。
(D) 餐廳快打烊了。

解答 (D)

Questions 59-61 refer to the following conversation.
第59-61題請參照以下的對話。

M : Hi, Rebecca. ⁵⁹ Do you want to join me to go to an art gallery this coming Saturday? The admission is half price on Saturday this month only.
▶ 這是詢問對話主題的題目，所以要仔細聆聽前半段。兩人正在討論美術館的展覽，所以 (C) 為正確答案。

W : Really? I want to go, ⁶⁰ but I can't. I have an appointment with a client.
▶ 詢問理由的題目，答題線索通常會在中間／後半段

出現，尤其經常在帶有轉折語氣的對比（but）詞彙後面出現。(D) 為正確答案。

M：Oh, that's a pity. [61] I'll bring some brochures and a schedule of the exhibition so that you can go on another day.

▶ 要在對話的最後面專心聆聽關於未來的計畫。男子說會帶一些小冊子回來，所以 (C) 為正確答案。

男：嗨，瑞貝卡。這個星期六妳要跟我一起去美術館嗎？只有這個月的星期六是半價門票。
女：真的嗎？我想去，但是沒辦法。我跟客戶有約。
男：喔，好可惜。我會拿一些小冊子和展覽時間表回來，這樣妳就可以改天再去了。

單字　art gallery 美術館　admission 入場，入場費　half price 半價　appointment 約會　brochure 小冊子　schedule 日程，時間表　exhibition 展覽會

59. 說話者主要在討論什麼？
(A) 培訓課程
(B) 開幕特賣
(C) 展覽會
(D) 國際研討會

解答 (C)

60. 女子為什麼這個星期六沒辦法去？
(A) 她要出差。
(B) 她要搬到另一間辦公室。
(C) 她必須完成某個專案。
(D) 她有其他約會了。

解答 (D)

61. 男子說他會做什麼？
(A) 替女子訂位
(B) 替女子買票
(C) 從美術館拿回一些小冊子
(D) 等到下個禮拜跟女子一起去

解答 (C)

Questions 62-64 refer to the following conversation and price list. 第62-64題請參照以下的對話和價目表。

M：Hello. [62] I came to have the sleeves on this jacket shortened.

▶ 這是要善用圖表才能作答的題目。男子為了修短夾克的袖子而到店裡來。透過圖表可以知道改袖子的費用是二十美元，所以 (D) 為正確答案。

W：Let me take a look... You can pick it up this Friday. I'm way behind in my work these days.

M：Hmm... [63] I have a job interview the day after tomorrow, so I hope the jacket will be ready as soon as possible. I mean... by tomorrow evening at the latest.

▶ 透過男子的發言，可以知道他後天要去面試，所以 (C) 為正確答案。

W：Oh, I see. Then I'll get it done by tomorrow evening. Here's the receipt.

M：Thank you. [64] Can you tell me when you close in the evening?

▶ 這題是問男子的諮詢內容，所以要從男子的發言中尋找線索。男子想知道業者的打烊時間，所以 (B) 為正確答案。

W：We close at 9 p.m. every day. I'll see you then.

男：哈囉，我來請你們修短這件夾克的袖子。
女：讓我看看……您可以星期五過來拿。我這幾天工作進度落後很多。
男：嗯……我後天有個面試，所以我希望可以盡快準備好夾克。我是指……最慢明天晚上。
女：噢，我明白了。那我明天晚上之前改好。收據給您。
男：謝謝。請問你們晚上幾點關門？
女：我們每天晚上九點關門。明天見。

單字　sleeve 袖子　shorten 縮短　pick up 領取，拾起　behind 落後的　these days 最近　the day after tomorrow 後天　be ready 準備好的　as soon as possible 盡快　at the latest 最晚　receipt 收據　close 關（門）　apply for 申請～　attend 出席　conference 會議　inquire 詢問　laundry 洗衣

62. 請看圖表。男子最有可能付多少錢？
(A) 15美元
(B) 16美元
(C) 18美元
(D) 20美元

修改種類	價格
改長度 - 褲子	15美元
改長度 - 裙子	18美元
改袖子 - 夾克	20美元
換拉鍊 - 褲／裙	16美元

解答 (D)

63. 男子說他後天會做什麼？
(A) 申請工作
(B) 出席會議
(C) 去面試
(D) 跟客戶開會

解答 (C)

64. 男子詢問了什麼？

(A) 洗衣價格
(B) 打烊時間
(C) 折扣
(D) 清潔用品

解答 (B)

Questions 65-67 refer to the following conversation and list. 第65-67題請參照以下的對話和清單。

M: Good afternoon. [65] I'd like to book some tickets for Blue Moon starting at 7 tonight. The movie guide said the film is getting glowing reviews.

W: [65] How many tickets would you like?

▶ 這題問的是女子的職業，所以可以從前半段中尋找線索。男子說想買電影票，女子問他需要幾張票，由此可知女子是售票處員工。(B) 為正確答案。

M: Five, please. I'm going to see a movie with my coworkers tonight, and we all want to see it together.

W: Hmm... Let me see. I am sorry, but we only have three seats left for the movie.

M: Oh, I see. [66] Then can you recommend a popular one?

▶ 沒辦法看想看的電影之後，男子請女子推薦電影。這裡的 one 指的是 movie。(A) 為正確答案。

W: How about the movie which Jewel Austin is starring in? It is one of the hottest movies these days. [67] Fortunately, there are 6 seats left for it.

▶ 女子向男子推薦裘爾‧奧斯汀出演的電影，補充說明還剩六個座位。圖表中剩下六個座位的電影是《人在巴黎》，所以 (C) 為正確答案。

- -

男：午安。我想訂幾張晚上七點開場的《藍月》電影票。電影指南說這部電影不斷獲得好評。

女：您要幾張票？

男：五張，麻煩妳。我今晚要跟我的同事們看電影，我們希望大家能坐在一起。

女：嗯……我看看，抱歉，這場電影我們只剩下三個座位。

男：噢，我知道了。那妳可以推薦其他受歡迎的電影嗎？

女：裘爾‧奧斯汀主演的電影怎麼樣？這是最近最熱門的電影之一。幸好還剩下六個座位。

單字　book 預訂　starting 從～開始的　glowing 熱烈讚揚的　review 心得　coworker 同事　together 一起　recommend 推薦　how about ～如何？　star in 主演　hot 熱門的　these days 最近　fortunately 幸運地　favorite 最喜歡的　actress 女演員　box office 售票處　director 導演　critic 評論家

65. 女子最有可能是誰？

(A) 女演員
(B) 售票處員工
(C) 電影導演
(D) 電影評論家

解答 (B)

66. 男子問了女子什麼？

(A) 受歡迎的電影
(B) 下週的電影時刻表
(C) 電視節目
(D) 電影明星

解答 (A)

67. 請看圖表。男子最有可能看哪部電影？

(A) 藍月
(B) 獵人
(C) 人在巴黎
(D) 皇后

電影名稱	剩餘座位
藍月	3
獵人	4
人在巴黎	6
皇后	5

解答 (C)

類型分析 11　公告
Unit 29　公司內部公告

Step 3 實戰演練

Questions 4-6 refer to the following announcement.
第4-6題請參照以下的公告。

Attention, all employees. [4/5]I'd like to remind you that some of the printers in our department will be replaced with new ones this afternoon.

▶ 問候、地點或公告目的會在前半段出現，所以要專心聆聽在問候語（Attention, all employees.）後面出現的內容。公告內容是「印表機會換成新的」，由此可知地點是辦公室。第四題的正確答案為 (A)。

▶ 提到地點的部分也會透露出聽者是誰，所以請記住要在同個部分一起作答詢問地點和對象的題目。從這裡可以得知這是給辦公室員工的公告，所以 (C) 為正確答案。

[6]A maintenance man will come to replace them this afternoon.

▶ 日程和變更事項會在中間出現。遇到詢問時間點（this afternoon）的題目時，要仔細聆聽提到時間點的地方。公告說下午會進行印表機更換作業，所以 (B) 為正確答案。

All employees should step out of the office while the replacement work is going on. If you have any further questions, please call the Maintenance Department.

請所有員工注意。我想提醒各位，今天下午我們部門有一部分印表機會換成新的。下午會有維修人員來換。進行更換作業時，所有員工都要暫時離開辦公室。如果各位有任何問題，請打電話給維修部門。

單字　**attention** 注意，專心　**remind** 提醒　**replace** 替換　**Maintenance Department** 維修部門　**step out** （暫時）離開

4. 聽者在哪裡？

　(A) 辦公室
　(B) 機場
　(C) 超市
　(D) 博物館

解答　(A)

5. 公告對象是誰？

　(A) 技師

　(B) 顧客
　(C) 辦公室員工
　(D) 店經理

解答　(C)

6. 根據公告，什麼會在下午開始？

　(A) 翻修
　(B) 設備的更換
　(C) 檢查
　(D) 修理

解答　(B)

Unit 30　公共場所公告

Step 3 實戰演練

Questions 4-6 refer to the following announcement.
第4-6題請參照以下的公告。

[5]Attention, visitors.

▶ 透過問候語可以知道公告對象是參觀者，也就是訪客，所以正確答案是 (A)。

[4]Our gallery will be closing in 1 hour.

▶ 詢問時間點的題目，答題線索會在前半或後半段出現，在這裡的出題順序是第一題，所以要能推測到線索會在前半段出現。閉館時間是一小時後，所以 (C) 為正確答案。

The coffee shop and restaurant will remain open until 8 p.m. for your convenience. Once again, since the gallery will be closing in 1 hour, [6]all visitors are asked to leave the main lobby.

▶ 這是請求題，所以要在後半段找線索。公告請「各位參觀者從大廳離開」，所以 (A) 為正確答案。

If you checked your personal belongings at the information counter, do not forget to get them back. We hope to see all of you again soon.

參觀者請注意。我們畫廊將在一小時後閉館。為了您的方便，咖啡廳和餐廳會營業到晚上八點。再次提醒各位，畫廊將在一小時後閉館，請各位參觀者從大廳離開。若您在服務台寄放了個人隨身物品，請別忘了取回。我們希望很快能再次見到您。

單字　**gallery** 畫廊　**convenience** 便利，方便　**belongings** 隨身物品

4. 畫廊何時閉館？

　(A) 十分鐘後
　(B) 三十分鐘後
　(C) 一小時後

(D) 兩小時後

解答 (C)

5. 公告對象是誰？

(A) 訪客
(B) 員工
(C) 圖書館員
(D) 藝術家

解答 (A)

6. 聽者被要求做什麼？

(A) 離開大廳
(B) 移動到咖啡廳
(C) 離開餐廳
(D) 在商店買禮物

解答 (A)

Review Test

Questions 1-3 refer to the following announcement.
第1-3題請參照以下的公告。

Good morning, employees. I'd like to announce that we're going to move to our company's new building next Monday. [1] I'm sure that everyone is expecting to see a pleasant environment to work in. [2] The movers will be transporting everything this Friday.

▶ 遇到詢問日程和公告變更事項的題目時，要仔細聆聽前半段或中間的部分。公告提到了愉快的環境，所以第一題的正確答案為 (B)。搬遷時間點是星期一，所以第二題的正確答案為 (D)。

It's a good opportunity for us to throw away unnecessary office supplies. [3] Please make sure you have done this by Thursday.

▶ 遇到詢問要求事項的題目時，要仔細聆聽後半段的「Please~」句子。公告要求聽者清理物品，所以 (C) 為正確答案。

- -

各位員工早安。我想宣布我們將在下週一搬進公司的新大樓。我確信每個人都很期待在愉快的環境中工作。搬家工人會在本週五搬運所有的東西。這是丟掉不需要的辦公用品的好機會。請各位確保在週四之前完成這件事。

單字 **expect to** 期待～ **pleasant environment** 愉快的環境 **opportunity** 機會 **throw away** 清除，丟棄 **unnecessary** 不需要的

1. 根據說話者，新辦公室是怎樣的？

(A) 有設備齊全的會議空間。
(B) 有愉快的環境。
(C) 有美景。
(D) 有寬敞的會議室。

解答 (B)

2. 公司會在何時搬進新大樓？

(A) 星期五
(B) 星期六
(C) 星期日
(D) 星期一

解答 (D)

3. 聽者被要求做什麼？

(A) 訂購辦公用品
(B) 搬走舊家具
(C) 整理辦公用品
(D) 搬自己的文件

解答 (C)

Questions 4-6 refer to the following announcement.
第4-6題請參照以下的公告。

Attention, [4] all passengers on Sky Airline's Flight 302 to Paris.

▶ 問候、地點、介紹等會在前半段出現。參考天際航空班機這段話的話，可以知道 (D) 為正確答案。

[5] Due to unexpected bad weather conditions, all flights have been delayed.

▶ 公告目的會在問候、地點、介紹後面出現。飛機因為天氣惡劣而延後起飛，所以 (A) 為正確答案。

[6] This flight was originally scheduled to depart at 7 a.m., but it has been rescheduled and will now leave at 11 a.m., so it will be delayed by four hours.

▶ 在公告目的後會出現說明。公告說飛機出發時間已延後，所以 (B) 為正確答案。

Thank you for your understanding. We sincerely apologize for this inconvenience. We will provide all passengers with meal coupons which you can use at any of the restaurants at the airport.

- -

飛往巴黎的天際航空三〇二班機的乘客請注意。由於意料之外的惡劣天候狀況，所有班機已延誤。本航班原定上午七點出發，但時間已經過調整，將在延遲四小時後的上午十一點起飛。感謝您的理解。對於造成的不便，我們深感抱歉。我們會提供所有乘客餐券，您可以在機場內的任何餐廳使用。

單字 **passenger** 乘客 **originally** 原本 **departure** 出發

delay 延遲，延誤 inconvenience不便 meal coupon 餐券

4. 這則公告最有可能在哪裡出現？
(A) 飛機
(B) 公車站
(C) 郵輪
(D) 機場

解答 (D)

5. 造成問題的原因是什麼？
(A) 惡劣天候狀況
(B) 機械問題
(C) 先前的班機延誤
(D) 跑道維修

解答 (A)

6. 根據公告，什麼東西被改了？
(A) 抵達時間
(B) 出發時間
(C) 旅遊行程
(D) 餐券

解答 (B)

Questions 7-9 refer to the following announcement.
第7-9題請參照以下的公告。

> Good morning. I want to make an announcement before we start. As you all know, our annual party is tomorrow, [7] but we moved the event to the Upper Star Resort.
> ▶ 遇到詢問日程和變更事項的題目時，要仔細聆聽前半段或中間。派對地點已變更，所以 (D) 為正確答案。
>
> [8] We did that due to a problem with our reservation. However, it will be at the same time from 7 p.m. to 9 p.m.
> ▶ 雖然地點變了，但是派對如期在七點到九點舉行。(B) 為正確答案。
>
> You can check out a rough map of how to get to the new location on our website. I believe many of you have already seen it on the notice board in the lobby. [9] If you have any questions or need transportation, please contact Jeremy at 234-4257.
> ▶ 遇到詢問諮詢內容或聯絡方式的題目時，要仔細聆聽後半段。說話者表示有其他疑問，或關於交通工具的問題時請打電話，所以 (A) 為正確答案。

早安。在我們開始前，我想宣布一件事。正如各位所知道的，明天就是我們的週年派對，但是我們把活動地點改到上星度假村了。我們這麼做是因為預約方面的問題。不過，時間仍是晚上七點到九點。各位可以

在我們的網站上確認前往新地點的簡略地圖。我相信很多人已經在大廳的布告欄看過了。如果有任何問題或需要交通工具的話，請打234-4257聯絡傑洛米。

單字 make an announcement 公布，發表 annual 年度的 reservation 預約 rough map 簡略地圖 notice board 布告欄

7. 關於週年派對的什麼變更了？
(A) 來賓
(B) 日期
(C) 價格
(D) 地點

解答 (D)

8. 派對會在何時開始？
(A) 晚上六點
(B) 晚上七點
(C) 晚上八點
(D) 晚上九點

解答 (B)

9. 員工為什麼需要聯絡傑洛米？
(A) 為了安排交通工具
(B) 為了知道方向
(C) 為了買票
(D) 為了預約位置

解答 (A)

Questions 10-12 refer to the following announcement.
第10-12題請參照以下的公告。

> [10] I want to inform you all about a change in policy regarding working hours.
> ▶ 詢問公告主題的題目，答題線索會在前半段出現。說話者一開始說想通知某件事，並且是跟工作時間有關的政策變更。將 a change in policy regarding working hours 改述為 a new working arrangement 的 (B) 為正確答案。
>
> You recently completed a questionnaire on efficient practices in the office, and the consensus is that you would be more productive if you took a shorter lunchbreak and left earlier in the day. So, umm… [11] Here's the deal. [12] We will try out this suggestion starting next week, when your lunchbreak will be reduced by one hour.
> ▶ 這是詢問說話者隱含的意圖的題目，要從句子的鋪陳中掌握為什麼會使用「here's the deal」這個措辭。說話者說員工表示午餐時間短一點、早點下班，這樣更有生產力，接著說「here's the deal」，告知大家從下週開始會實施這項政策。由此可知，說話者是想跟

員工提議這個做法。在告知某個事實或意見時，可以先說意為「這樣做吧」的「here's the deal」。

Employees will then be able to leave the office half an hour earlier than previously. [12] Please note that these adjustments will come into effect following the weekend.

▶ 中間說到「We will try out this suggestion starting next week」，表示從下個禮拜開始實施。又在後半段說一次這個調整事項會在週末後開始生效。following the weekend 的意思即為 next week（下個禮拜）。

我想通知各位關於工作時數的政策變更。各位最近填寫了關於在辦公室有效率地工作的問卷，你們一致同意午餐時間短一點、早點下班的話，會更有生產力。所以，嗯……我們這麼做吧，我們會從下週開始嘗試這項提議，午餐時間縮短為一個小時，員工就可以比之前早半小時下班。請注意這些調整事項將從本週末之後開始生效。

單字　policy 政策，方針　regarding 關於　questionnaire 問卷　practice 慣例，實踐　consensus 意見一致，共識　try out 試行　adjustment 調整，修改　come into effect 生效，開始實施　following 接下來的　enhance 提升　attract 吸引，引起（注意）　qualified 有資格的，勝任的　take effect 生效，實施

10. 公布了什麼？
　　(A) 重新安排時間的會議
　　(B) 新的工作安排
　　(C) 辦公室搬遷
　　(D) 加薪

解答　(B)

11. 女子說「我們這麼做吧」的意思是什麼？
　　(A) 她正在嘗試提出建議。
　　(B) 她想發一些東西給聽者。
　　(C) 她不同意某些員工的意見。
　　(D) 她正在對聽者表示謝意。

解答　(A)

12. 說話者說變更會在何時生效？
　　(A) 立刻
　　(B) 隔天
　　(C) 下個月
　　(D) 下週

解答　(D)

聽寫訓練

Unit 29 公司內部公告

Q4-6. Attention, all employees. I'd like to remind you that some of the printers in our department will be replaced with new ones this afternoon. A maintenance man will come to replace them this afternoon. All employees should step out of the office while the replacement work is going on. If you have any further questions, please call the Maintenance Department.

Unit 30 公共場所公告

Q4-6. Attention, visitors. Our gallery will be closing in 1 hour. The coffee shop and restaurant will remain open until 8 p.m. for your convenience. Once again, since the gallery will be closing in 1 hour, all visitors are asked to leave the main lobby. If you checked your personal belongings at the information counter, do not forget to get them back. We hope to see all of you again soon.

Review Test

Q1-3. Good morning, employees. I'd like to announce that we're going to move to our company's new building next Monday. I'm sure that everyone is expecting to see a pleasant environment to work in. The movers will be transporting everything this Friday. It's a good opportunity for us to throw away unnecessary office supplies. Please make sure you have done this by Thursday.

Q4-6. Attention, all passengers on Sky Airline's Flight 302 to Paris. Due to unexpected bad weather conditions, all flights have been delayed. This flight was originally scheduled to depart at 7 a.m., but it has been rescheduled and will now leave at 11 a.m., so it will be delayed by four hours. Thank you for your understanding. We sincerely apologize for this inconvenience. We will provide all passengers with meal coupons which you can use at any of the restaurants at the airport.

Q7-9. Good morning. I want to make an announcement before we start. As you all know, our annual party is tomorrow, but we moved the event to the Upper Star Resort. We did that due to a problem with our reservation. However, it will be at the same time from 7 p.m. to 9 p.m. You can check out a rough map of how to get to the new location on our website. I believe many of you have already seen it on the notice board in the lobby. If you have any questions or need transportation, please contact Jeremy at 234-4257.

Q10-12. I want to inform you all about a change in policy regarding working hours. You recently completed a questionnaire on efficient practices in the office, and the consensus is that you would be more productive if you took a shorter lunchbreak and left earlier in the day. So, umm… Here's the deal. We will try out this suggestion starting next week, when your lunchbreak will be reduced by one hour. Employees will then be able to leave the office half an hour earlier than previously. Please note that these adjustments will come into effect following the weekend.

類型分析12　各大主題攻略—訊息
Unit 31　語音訊息

Step 3 實戰演練

Questions 4-6 refer to the following telephone message.
第4-6題請參照以下的電話語音訊息。

Hello. ⁴/⁵ This is Mary Johnson, the sales manager at the Star Dress Boutique.
▶ 來電者的資訊會在訊息開頭出現，所以要仔細聆聽提到名稱、部門、公司種類的部分。第四題、第五題的線索都要在這個地方尋找，第四題的正確答案為 (A)，第五題的正確答案為 (B)。

I'm calling because you sent me the wrong products instead of what I ordered. The shipment you sent me contained shirts, not skirts. I'd appreciate it if you could send the correct order as soon as possible, and I don't want you to make a mistake again. ⁶ We're having a special promotion next weekend.
▶ 關於未來的日程會在後半段出現。說話者表示下週末有促銷活動，所以 (C) 為正確答案。

As for the wrong shipment, I will send it back to you by this weekend.

哈囉，我是星點洋裝精品的銷售經理瑪莉·瓊森。我來電是因為你們寄錯商品給我，而不是寄我訂的東西。你們寄給我的貨物包含襯衫，而不是裙子。如果你們可以盡快寄正確的訂購物品給我，我會很感謝。希望你們不要再失誤了。我們下個週末有特別促銷活動。至於寄錯的貨物，我會在這個週末寄回去。

單字　instead of 代替～　order 訂購　shipment 運輸品，裝載的貨物　contain 包含　correct 正確的　as soon as possible 盡快　make a mistake 失誤

4. 來電者最有可能是誰？
(A) 銷售員
(B) 工程師
(C) 房地產仲介
(D) 供應商

解答 (A)

5. 說話者最有可能在哪裡工作？
(A) 郵局
(B) 服飾店
(C) 銀行
(D) 餐廳

解答 (B)

6. 促銷活動會在何時開始？
(A) 這個週末
(B) 下週
(C) 下週末
(D) 下週一

解答 (C)

Unit 32　自動回覆系統

Step 3 實戰演練

Questions 4-6 refer to the following recorded message.
第4-6題請參照以下的錄音訊息。

Thank you for calling the Victory Zoo. ⁴ Our zoo is internationally famous for our wide variety of animals.
▶ 訊息的前半段是介紹公司的部分，訊息指出動物園有各種不同的動物。(B) 為正確答案。

We're open every day from 10 a.m. to 5 p.m. Entrance tickets can only be booked by phone. ⁵ If you want to make a reservation now, press 1.
▶ 服務導引號碼的相關線索會在「press＋號碼」的地方出現。想預訂的話要按1，所以 (A) 為正確答案。

Cash and credit cards are accepted, and you can pay at the ticket booth near the entrance. ⁶ For more information, please call one of our customer service representatives at 999-6738.
▶ 請求和叮嚀事項會在後半段出現，語音訊息指出想知道更多資訊的話，要打電話。(C) 為正確答案。

感謝您來電維多利動物園。我們的動物園以種類廣泛的動物享譽國際。我們的開放時間為每天早上十點至下午五點。入園門票只能透過電話預訂。如果您現在預訂，請按1。付現和刷卡皆可，您可以在入口附近的售票亭付款。若想了解詳情，請撥打999-6738給我們的客服人員。

單字　internationally 國際地，國際間地　famous 有名的　variety 多元性，各種　book 預訂　reservation 預約　credit card 信用卡　accept 接受

4. 根據訊息，維多利動物園以什麼聞名？
(A) 美味的食物
(B) 多元的動物
(C) 各種各樣的昆蟲
(D) 奇特的植物

解答 (B)

5. 聽者為什麼需要按1？

(A) 為了預訂門票
(B) 為了買票
(C) 為了取消預約
(D) 為了諮詢資訊

解答　(A)

6. 聽者該如何獲得更多資訊？

(A) 按數字鍵1
(B) 查看網站
(C) 撥打提供的電話號碼
(D) 索取手冊

解答　(C)

Review Test

Questions 1-3 refer to the following telephone message.
第1-3題請參照以下的電話語音訊息。

Good morning. This is Linda Rey from Star Realty.
▶ 詢問發訊者、收訊者、職業、行業類別、公司資訊的題目，答題線索會在前半段的問候語中出現。聽到 Realty 就能知道答案是房地產相關的選項。(C) 為正確答案。

I'm calling to let you know that an office which you might be interested in has become available.
▶ 遇到詢問目的、問題、狀況的題目時，要仔細聆聽以「I'm calling~」開頭的句子。來電者表示有個聽者會感興趣的辦公室，所以 (B) 為正確答案。

It's near the bus station, bank, and post office. The rent is $1,000 per month. I'm sure you must be interested in seeing the office. Please get in touch with me as soon as possible, and I'll ask the owner of the building whether you can have a look at it tomorrow or not. You can call me on my mobile phone. Thanks, Mr. Anderson.
▶ 詢問接下來會做什麼事的題目，答題線索會在後半段出現。來電者請聽者打電話，所以可以推測聽者很快就會打電話。(C) 為正確答案。琳達．雷伊是房地產仲介，不是地主，所以 (D) 為錯誤答案。

I hope to hear from you soon.

早安，我是史塔房地產的琳達．雷伊。我來電是想告知您，現在有您可能會感興趣的辦公室。它距離公車站、銀行和郵局很近。租金是每月一千美元。我相信您一定對參觀辦公室很感興趣。請您盡快與我聯繫，我會問問看大樓所有人您明天是否能去看房。您可以打我的手機，謝謝。安德森先生，希望很快就能收到您的消息。

單字　**available** 可得的，可使用的　**bus station** 公

車站　**get in touch with** 跟～聯絡　**owner** 主人，所有者　**whether** 是否～　**mobile phone** 手機

1. 來電者最有可能是誰？

(A) 辦公室承租人
(B) 維修人員
(C) 房地產仲介
(D) 地主

解答　(C)

2. 這則訊息的目的是什麼？

(A) 為了提供辦公室的位置
(B) 為了通知男子辦公室提供出租
(C) 為了通知建設工程的事
(D) 為了宣傳新大樓

解答　(B)

3. 聽者接下來會做什麼？

(A) 簽約
(B) 搬到新的辦公室
(C) 聯絡琳達．雷伊
(D) 打電話給大樓所有者

解答　(C)

Questions 4-6 refer to the following recorded message.
第4-6題請參照以下的錄音訊息。

Thank you for calling the Blackberry Online Store, the best online shopping mall in the U.K.
Blackberry is known for selling unique designs of clothes and accessories.
▶ 公司的介紹會在「Thank you for calling~」或在那之後的句子中出現。語音訊息提到販飾和飾品，由此可知第四題的正確答案為 (B)。而且該網站以獨特的設計聞名，所以第五題的正確答案為 (B)。

Please listen carefully to the following options. Please press 1 to check the current status of a delivery. Press 2 to check the status of an order.
▶ 詢問服務導引內容的題目，答題線索會在「press＋號碼」的地方出現。可以按 1 查詢遞送狀態，所以 (A) 為正確答案。

For all other inquiries, please press 0, and one of our customer service representatives will help you soon.

感謝您來電英國最棒的線上購物中心，黑莓線上商店。黑莓以販售設計獨特的衣服和飾品而聞名。請仔細聆聽以下的選項。若想確認目前的運送狀態，請按1。若想確認訂單狀態，請按2。若有其他疑問，請按0，我們的客服人員會迅速協助您。

4. 聽者打電話給什麼種類的公司？

(A) 家具店
(B) 服飾店
(C) 電腦店
(D) 文具店

解答 (B)

5. 該線上商店以什麼聞名？

(A) 堅固的家具
(B) 獨特的衣服
(C) 現代設計
(D) 簡單的付款系統

解答 (B)

6. 為什麼聽者該按1？

(A) 為了確認運送狀態
(B) 為了知道位置
(C) 為了訂購商品
(D) 為了跟員工說話

解答 (A)

Questions 7-9 refer to the following telephone message.
第7-9題請參照以下的電話語音訊息。

Hello. 7 This is Joy from Joy's Computer Store.
▶ 職業和公司資訊會立刻接在問候語的後面出現。(A) 為正確答案。

8 I'm calling to see if you mind answering some questions regarding our products and services.
▶ 遇到詢問目的、理由、問題的題目時，通常都要仔細聆聽以「I'm calling～」開頭的句子。來電者請聽者寫問卷，所以 (A) 為正確答案。

If you answer this questionnaire, we'll send you a discount coupon which will give you 30% off any future purchase at our store. But you should make haste as you must call us within two days to receive the discount coupon. 9 Just call us at 695-4215 so that we can send you a questionnaire.
▶ 遇到詢問要求或提議內容的題目時，要仔細聆聽後半段的 if 子句或命令句（please～）。來電者說想寫問卷的話，要打電話給他們。問卷跟申請書不一樣，所以 (A) 為錯誤答案。正確答案是 (D)。

您好，我是喬伊電腦店的喬伊。我來電是想問您，是否願意回答幾個關於我們的產品和服務的問題。若您回覆這份問卷，我們會寄折價券給您，之後在我們店

內的任何一筆消費都可以打七折。不過，為了獲得折價券，您要趕緊在兩天內撥打電話給我們。只要撥打695-4215，我們就會寄一份問卷給您。

7. 該商店賣的是什麼？

(A) 電子裝置
(B) 家具
(C) 文具
(D) 書籍

解答 (A)

8. 喬伊為什麼會打電話來？

(A) 為了請求做調查
(B) 為了送免費禮物
(C) 為了討論會員費
(D) 為了提供聽者工作機會

解答 (A)

9. 聽者被要求做什麼？

(A) 寄申請書
(B) 在兩天內拜訪商店
(C) 續訂會員資格
(D) 打電話給店家

解答 (D)

Questions 10-12 refer to the following telephone message. 第10-12題請參照以下的電話語音訊息。

Hello, Mr. Conner. I'm Karen Riley from Apartment B6. I'm calling to let you know that I will be managing the Boston branch starting next month. 10 So I have to move out of this place a few months ahead of schedule. I've arranged for a moving company to pick up my furniture on July 26, and I'll be sure to have the apartment cleaned afterward.
▶ 這題是詢問電話語音訊息的接收對象，可以在前半段找到相關線索。說話者表示要提前搬走，之後的內容也是在詢問退還保證金的事，由此可知說話對象是大樓管理員。(C) 為正確答案。

But… 11 here's the thing. Um… When I signed the contract two years ago, I think there was a clause about a penalty related to the early reimbursement of the security deposit.
▶ 遇到掌握意圖的題目時，要完整地了解句子的鋪陳才行。「Here's the thing」是提某個問題或提議時放在開頭的措辭。女子說完「Here's the thing」之後，說不記得跟保證金有關的條款內容了，由此可知女子想解釋某個問題。(D) 為正確答案。

I don't remember the exact terms, [12] so can you please return my call and explain them to me? Thanks a lot.

▶ 此類詢問說話者的請求事項的題目，線索通常會在最後面的 could / can / would you 的句子中出現。說話者在後半段提到自己不太清楚退還保證金的事，結尾時則請對方回撥說明。由此可知，正確答案為將 explain 改述為 give her information 的 (B)。

您好，康納先生。我是B6公寓的凱倫·萊利。我來電是想告知您，我從下個月開始要管理波士頓分公司。所以我必須提早幾個月搬離這裡。我已經安排搬家公司七月二十六日來取走我的家具，之後我一定會把公寓打掃乾淨。但……問題是，嗯……我兩年前簽約的時候，有一個跟提早退還保證金有關的罰金條款。我不記得確切的條款內容了，可以請您回撥跟我說明嗎？非常謝謝。

單字　ahead of schedule 提前　clause 條款　penalty 罰金　reimbursement 退還　security deposit 保證金

10. 這則訊息的對象最有可能是誰？
(A) 建築師
(B) 人事經理
(C) 大樓管理員
(D) 搬家公司的員工

解答　(C)

11. 女子說「問題是」的意思是什麼？
(A) 她對取消合約感到抱歉。
(B) 她找到她之前在找的東西了。
(C) 她想給男子某個東西。
(D) 她想解釋某個問題。

解答　(D)

12. 說話者請聽者做什麼？
(A) 退還她花的錢
(B) 告知她一些資訊
(C) 幫她打掃公寓
(D) 寫新的合約

解答　(B)

聽寫訓練

Unit 31 語音訊息

Q4-6. Hello. This is Mary Johnson, the sales manager at the Star Dress Boutique. I'm calling because you sent me the wrong products instead of what I ordered. The shipment you sent me contained shirts, not skirts. I'd appreciate it if you could send the correct order as soon as possible, and I don't want you to make a mistake again. We're having a

special promotion next weekend. As for the wrong shipment, I will send it back to you by this weekend.

Unit 32 自動回覆系統

Q4-6. Thank you for calling the Victory Zoo. Our zoo is internationally famous for our wide variety of animals. We're open every day from 10 a.m. to 5 p.m. Entrance tickets can only be booked by phone. If you want to make a reservation now, press 1. Cash and credit cards are accepted, and you can pay at the ticket booth near the entrance. For more information, please call one of our customer service representatives at 999-6738.

Review Test

Q1-3. Good morning. This is Linda Rey from Star Realty. I'm calling to let you know that an office which you might be interested in has become available. It's near the bus station, bank, and post office. The rent is $1,000 per month. I'm sure you must be interested in seeing the office. Please get in touch with me as soon as possible, and I'll ask the owner of the building whether you can have a look at it tomorrow or not. You can call me on my mobile phone. Thanks, Mr. Anderson. I hope to hear from you soon.

Q4-6. Thank you for calling the Blackberry Online Store, the best online shopping mall in the U.K. Blackberry is known for selling unique designs of clothes and accessories. Please listen carefully to the following options. Please press 1 to check the current status of a delivery. Press 2 to check the status of an order. For all other inquiries, please press 0, and one of our customer service representatives will help you soon.

Q7-9. Hello. This is Joy from Joy's Computer Store. I'm calling to see if you mind answering some questions regarding our products and services. If you answer this questionnaire, we'll send you a discount coupon which will give you 30% off any future purchase at our store. But you should make haste as you must call us within two days to receive the discount coupon. Just call us at 695-4215 so that we can send you a questionnaire.

Q10-12. Hello, Mr. Conner. I'm Karen Riley from Apartment B6. I'm calling to let you know that I will be managing the Boston branch starting next month. So I have to move out of this place a few months ahead of schedule. I've arranged for a moving company to pick up my furniture on July 26, and I'll be sure to have the apartment cleaned afterward. But… here's the thing. Um… When I signed the contract two years ago, I think there was a clause about a penalty related to the early reimbursement of the security deposit. I don't remember the exact terms, so can you please return my call and explain them to me? Thanks a lot.

類型分析 13　各大主題攻略—廣播

Unit 33　天氣預報

Step 3 實戰演練

Questions 4-6 refer to the following radio broadcast.

第4-6題請參照以下的電台廣播。

Good morning. There will be no rain for a few days. Through the morning, ⁴the temperature will increase rapidly, there will be scorching hot weather along with humid air.

▶ 請記住天氣報導會在問候和介紹節目後的前半段出現。預報說整個早上都會很熱，所以 (C) 為正確答案。

However, I have some good news for you. The wind will blow on Saturday, and it will be a perfect day for surfing. ⁵But it looks like a big typhoon is coming our way on Sunday. We'll keep you posted.

▶ 未來的天氣經常在 But、However 後面被提到。預報說會颱風，所以 (B) 為正確答案。

⁶Now, let's go to Jane Watson for an update on today's top sports news.

▶ 遇到 next 題型時，要仔細聆聽後半段。天氣播報完之後會播體育新聞，所以 (C) 為正確答案。

早安。未來幾天不會下雨。早晨氣溫會急速上升，天氣酷熱，空氣潮濕。不過，我有些好消息要跟各位分享。週六會颱風，是非常適合衝浪的好日子。但是看起來週日會有個強颱來到。我們會持續跟各位更新消息。那麼接下來由簡恩·華森播報本日的體育頭條新聞。

單字　temperature 溫度 rapidly 快速地 scorching 激烈的，灼熱的 humid air 潮濕的空氣 typhoon 颱風 surf 衝浪

4. 今天天氣會變得怎樣？

(A) 會下雪。
(B) 會變冷。
(C) 會變熱。
(D) 會起霧。

解答　(C)

5. 週日會發生什麼事？

(A) 氣溫會上升。
(B) 會颳強風。
(C) 預計會下雪。
(D) 溫度保持不變。

解答　(B)

6. 聽者接下來有可能會聽到什麼？

(A) 交通報導
(B) 廣告
(C) 體育報導
(D) 商業新聞

解答　(C)

Unit 34　交通廣播

Step 3 實戰演練

Questions 4-6 refer to the following radio broadcast.

第4-6題請參照以下的電台廣播。

Good evening. This is Mary Cooper with your PPB traffic report. ⁴′⁵Many cars are stuck in a traffic jam around the shopping mall and in the downtown area. Even the outer road is full of cars due to people celebrating Christmas Eve.

▶ 尋找塞車原因時，要仔細聆聽問候之後的前半段內容。此處提及塞車原因和塞車道路。第四題的正確答案為 (A)，第五題的正確答案為 (B)。

Drivers may need 30 minutes to go from the outer road to the downtown area. ⁶We recommend avoiding the outer road and taking Highway 22 since traffic is clear on this road.

▶ 出現 recommend 的地方是提出替代方案的句子。第六題的正確答案為 (C)。

Stay tuned for Minn's international business news today.

晚安。我是PPB路況報導的瑪莉·庫柏。許多車輛都被困在購物中心附近和市區的車陣內。由於大家都在慶祝平安夜，連銜接道路都擠滿了車子。駕駛人可能需要花三十分鐘從銜接道路開到市區。我們建議各位避開銜接道路，改走二十二號高速公路，因為這條路的路況很順暢。請繼續收聽米恩的本日國際財經新聞。

單字　stuck in 陷入，困在～ downtown area 市區 outer road 銜接道路 celebrate 紀念，慶祝 avoid 避免

4. 聽者應該預期哪裡會發生延滯？

(A) 銜接道路
(B) 二十二號高速公路
(C) 火車站附近
(D) 郊區

解答　(A)

5. 是什麼造成了延滯？

(A) 交通意外
(B) 平安夜慶祝活動
(C) 繁忙的交通
(D) 出口封閉

解答 (B)

6. 說話者建議做什麼？

(A) 降速駕駛
(B) 收聽最新消息
(C) 改走另一條路
(D) 打電話給警察

解答 (C)

Unit 35 新聞

Step 3 實戰演練

Questions 4-6 refer to the following news report.
第4-6題請參照以下的新聞報導。

Thanks for listening to VNC's morning business report. Early this morning, Vivian Nelson, the president of Design Boutique, ¹announced that her company has launched a new wedding dress with a simple design.

▶ 這題是問新聞的主題，所以要仔細聆聽「announced / said that」的句子，(C) 為正確答案。

²Nelson said that the public will be able to purchase this dress at an affordable price.

▶ 這題跟人物有關，所以要仔細聆聽出現人名的句子。奈爾森女士是公司總裁，表示大眾能以便宜的價格購買婚紗，所以 (B) 為正確答案。

The dress is expected to be sold at many boutiques soon. ³Ms. Nelson also announced that at the end of the year, 20% of the company's total sales will be donated to charity. And now for an update on the morning weather forecast.

▶ 這是 next 題型，所以要專心聽後半段結尾的句子，(B) 為正確答案。

- -

謝謝收聽VNC的晨間財經報導。今天稍早，迪塞恩精品的總裁薇薇安‧奈爾森宣布她的公司已推出一件設計簡潔的新款婚紗。奈爾森說，大眾將能以便宜的價格買到這件婚紗。婚紗預計很快就會在多間精品店販賣。奈爾森女士也宣布會在今年底將二十％的公司總銷售額捐給慈善機構。接下來是最新的晨間天氣預報。

單字 **president** 會長，總裁 **announce** 公布 **launch** 推出 **at an affordable price** 以便宜的價格 **public** 大眾的，一般的 **charity** 慈善機構

4. 這則新聞報導主要跟什麼有關？

(A) 新公司開業
(B) 慈善活動的舉辦
(C) 新產品介紹
(D) 兩間公司的合併

解答 (C)

5. 奈爾森女士提到了什麼？

(A) 將會展示種類多元的婚紗。
(B) 每個人都能以便宜的價格買到婚紗。
(C) 這款婚紗數量有限。
(D) 這款婚紗只適合上流人士。

解答 (B)

6. 根據奈爾森女士，年底最有可能會發生什麼事？

(A) 公司會開一些新的分公司。
(B) 公司會捐錢給慈善組織。
(C) 婚紗的銷售會增加。
(D) 將僱用額外的員工。

解答 (B)

Review Test

Questions 1-3 refer to the following news report.
第1-3題請參照以下的新聞報導。

In local news, ¹the North American Water Resources Corporation is asking area residents to conserve water.

▶ 新聞的前半段可以得知說話者是誰、主題或目的。報導內容跟節約用水有關，所以 (C) 為正確答案。

²The corporation said that our state may have a water shortage soon.

▶ 問候並表明說話者是誰之後，會詳細地敘述問題或是主題和原因。(A) 為正確答案。

³Therefore, the corporation is requesting that people take some easy water-saving steps like taking short showers and turning off the faucet while brushing their teeth.

▶ 叮嚀事項和下個播報順序會在後半段出現。這裡要求大眾節約用水，所以 (D) 為正確答案。

More information can be found on the North American Water Resources Corporation's website.

- -

以下是當地新聞。北美水資源公司呼籲地區居民節約用水。該公司表示我們這州可能即將缺水。因此，該公司要求大眾採取一些簡單的節水措施，像是短時間淋浴和刷牙時關水龍頭。各位可以在北美水資源公司的網站上找到更多資訊。

單字 **Water Resources Corporation** 水資源公司 **area resident** 地區居民 **conserve** 保存，節省 **state** 陳述，州 **water shortage** 缺水 **turn off the faucet** 關水龍頭

1. 這則報導的主要目的為何？

(A) 宣傳新產品

(B) 尋找員工
(C) 請大眾節約用水
(D) 介紹新企業

解答 (C)

2. 根據報導，即將發生什麼事？
(A) 缺水
(B) 水災
(C) 缺電
(D) 財務困難

解答 (A)

3. 聽者接下來有可能會做什麼？
(A) 參訪公司
(B) 回報服務問題
(C) 聯絡公司
(D) 減少耗水量

解答 (D)

Questions 4-6 refer to the following broadcast.
第4-6題請參照以下的廣播。

[¹Unseasonably cold and dry weather will continue through this coming weekend.
▶ 天氣預報的前半段會出現問候、播放時間、節目介紹等。這個廣播是天氣預報，所以 (B) 為正確答案。

²So let us make some important recommendations. The most important thing is to keep your body warm by drinking hot tea.
▶ 目前的天氣和建議會在介紹完節目後出現。說話者說天氣寒冷，所以要多喝熱茶。(A) 為正確答案。

That is especially important in extremely cold weather like we are having this weekend. ³For more information on how to stay healthy in winter, check out our website at www.weatherforecast.com.
▶ 關於接下來的天氣資訊、其他資訊和廣播介紹等會在後半段出現。此處提到網站上有保持健康的方法，所以 (C) 為正確答案。

不合時節的寒冷和乾燥天氣將在接下來的週末持續下去。所以讓我們在此做一些重要的建議。最重要的是藉由喝熱茶保持身體暖和。像是在本週末的嚴寒天氣裡，這一點特別重要。請到我們的網站www.weatherforecast.com確認更多該如何在冬天保持健康的資訊。

單字 **unseasonably** 不合時節地 **suggest** 建議，忠告 **recommendation** 建議，推薦 **extremely** 極度地，非常 **stay healthy** 保持健康

4. 這則廣播的主旨是什麼？
(A) 介紹演員
(B) 播報天氣狀況
(C) 宣布建設作業
(D) 宣傳某間醫院

解答 (B)

5. 說話者建議聽者做什麼？
(A) 喝杯熱茶
(B) 穿上溫暖的夾克
(C) 帶雨傘
(D) 等待下一個天氣資訊

解答 (A)

6. 根據說話者，聽者可以在網站上找到什麼？
(A) 當地新聞報導
(B) 天氣狀況
(C) 健康資訊
(D) 路況報導

解答 (C)

Questions 7-9 refer to the following broadcast.
第7-9題請參照以下的廣播。

Good morning. This is Caroline Mack at WABC. ⁷Starting next Monday, Highway 10 will be closed due to road repairs.
▶ 問候語和節目名稱在交通廣播的前半段出現後，接著會出現路況說明和塞車原因。(C) 為正確答案。

Traffic jams around the airport area will become unavoidable when the roadwork starts.
⁸It is recommended that drivers take Route 27 until the roadwork is completed next month.
▶ 尋找要求事項時，要仔細聆聽以 recommend 開頭的句子。因為塞車的緣故，說話者建議駕駛人改道。(D) 為正確答案。

⁹Please visit our website at www.abcstation.com to check out the news about the construction.
▶ 替代方案和下個廣播的介紹會在後半段出現。說話者請聽眾到網站上確認工程消息。(C) 為正確答案。

早安。我是WABC的卡洛琳·麥克。自下週一起，十號高速公路將因為修路而關閉。道路施工開始時，機場附近的地區難免會塞車。在道路施工於下個月完成之前，建議駕駛人改走二十七號道路。請拜訪我們的網站www.abcstation.com確認工程消息。

單字 **road repair** 修路 **traffic jam** 交通堵塞 **unavoidable** 不可避免的，難免的 **roadwork** 道路施工

7. 這則報導的主要目的為何？

(A) 提供天氣報導
(B) 公布城市節慶
(C) 提供工程資訊
(D) 宣傳新車

解答　(C)

8. 說話者建議做什麼？

(A) 聆聽最新消息
(B) 小心開車
(C) 搭乘大眾交通工具
(D) 改走另一條路

解答　(D)

9. 聽者該如何獲得最新資訊？

(A) 聽廣播
(B) 看電視
(C) 拜訪網站
(D) 撥打電話號碼

解答　(C)

Question 10-12 refers to the following broadcast and chart. 第10-12題請參照以下的廣播和圖表。

For people living in and around the Southeast Coastal areas, [10, 11] thunderstorms are starting to form in the region.

▶ 這題要結合圖表，選出公告發布的時間。前半段提到了雷雨，所以跟天氣預報相符的是星期四。(D) 為正確答案。

[10] Some of them are expected to be severe during the afternoon, bringing very heavy rainfall that may cause localized flash flooding.

▶ 這題是詢問公告目的。從第一句「thunderstorms are starting to form in the region」可以知道這則廣播是在講天氣，要特別注意暴漲的洪水（flash flooding）。(C) 為正確答案。

The State Emergency Service advises that people in the areas should seek shelter, preferably indoors and never under trees. Try to avoid using cell phones in the thunderstorm. Beware of fallen trees and power lines, and [12] avoid driving, walking, or riding through floodwaters.

▶ 建議、要求等通常會在公告的最後面出現。此處跟當地居民建議了很多事，其中跟選項一致的是不要開車，所以 (D) 為正確答案。

For more updated weather forecasts, please continue to tune in to FM 107.7.

在此提醒居住在東南海岸地區附近的居民，此地區的雷雨開始成形。部分雷雨預計會在下午變得劇烈，帶來的大量降雨可能會使局部地區洪水暴漲。州立緊急服務中心建議當地居民尋找避難所，最好待在室內，避免待在樹下。試著避免在大雷雨中使用手機。注意倒塌的樹和電線，以及避免開車、走路或騎車經過洪水處。請繼續收聽FM 107.7更多的最新天氣預報。

單字　thunderstorm 雷雨　be expected to 預計～ severe 嚴重的，劇烈的　rainfall 降雨　localized 局部的 flash flooding 暴漲的洪水　shelter 避難所　beware of 注意　floodwater 洪水

10. 這則公告的目的為何？

(A) 警告大眾注意龍捲風
(B) 建議居民不要在雪天外出
(C) 告誡大眾小心暴漲的洪水
(D) 報導週末的天氣

解答　(C)

每週預報

星期一	星期二	星期三	星期四	星期五	星期六	星期日
18°	25°	26°	21°	18°	22°	27°

11. 請看圖表。此公告是星期幾發布的？

(A) 星期一
(B) 星期二
(C) 星期三
(D) 星期四

解答　(D)

12. 受影響地區的居民被建議不要做什麼？

(A) 待在室內
(B) 撥打911
(C) 遮蓋車輛
(D) 開車經過洪水處

解答　(D)

聽寫訓練

Unit 33　天氣預報

Q4-6. Good morning. There will be no rain for a few days. Through the morning, the temperature will increase rapidly, there will be scorching hot weather along with humid air. However, I have some good news for you. The wind will blow on Saturday, and it will be a perfect day for surfing. But it looks like a big typhoon is coming our way on Sunday. We'll keep you posted. Now, let's go to Jane Watson for an update on today's top sports news.

Unit 34 交通廣播

Q4-6. Good evening. This is Mary Cooper with your PPB traffic report. Many cars are stuck in a traffic jam around the shopping mall and in the downtown area. Even the outer road is full of cars due to people celebrating Christmas Eve. Drivers may need 30 minutes to go from the outer road to the downtown area. We recommend avoiding the outer road and taking Highway 22 since traffic is clear on this road. Stay tuned for Minn's international business news today.

Unit 35 新聞

Q4-6. Thanks for listening to VNC's morning business report. Early this morning, Vivian Nelson, the president of Design Boutique, announced that her company has launched a new wedding dress with a simple design. Nelson said that the public will be able to purchase this dress at an affordable price. The dress is expected to be sold at many boutiques soon. Ms. Nelson also announced that at the end of the year, 20% of the company's total sales will be donated to charity. And now for an update on the morning weather forecast.

Review Test

Q1-3. In local news, the North American Water Resources Corporation is asking area residents to conserve water. The corporation said that our state may have a water shortage soon. Therefore, the corporation is requesting that people take some easy water-saving steps like taking short showers and turning off the faucet while brushing their teeth. More information can be found on the North American Water Resources Corporation's website.

Q4-6. Unseasonably cold and dry weather will continue through this coming weekend. So let us make some important recommendations. The most important thing is to keep your body warm by drinking hot tea. That is especially important in extremely cold weather like we are having this weekend. For more information on how to stay healthy in winter, check out our website at www.weatherforecast.com.

Q7-9. Good morning. This is Caroline Mack at WABC. Starting next Monday, Highway 10 will be closed due to road repairs. Traffic jams around the airport area will become unavoidable when the roadwork starts. It is recommended that drivers take Route 27 until the roadwork is completed next month. Please visit our website at www.abcstation.com to check out the news about the construction.

Q10-12. For people living in and around the Southeast Coastal areas, thunderstorms are starting to form in the region. Some of them are expected to be severe during the afternoon, bringing very heavy rainfall that may cause localized flash flooding. The State Emergency Service advises that people in the areas should seek shelter, preferably indoors and never under trees. Try to avoid using cell phones in the thunderstorm. Beware of fallen trees and power lines, and avoid driving, walking, or riding through floodwaters. For more updated weather forecasts, please continue to tune in to FM 107.7.

類型分析 14　各大主題攻略—介紹、導覽
Unit 36　人物介紹

Step 3 實戰演練

Questions 4-6 refer to the following instruction.
第4-6題請參照以下的介紹。

Thank you for coming to our annual awards ceremony. ⁴I'm pleased to announce this year's best salesperson is Jinny.

▶ 前半段是出現「問候語、自我介紹、聚會目的」的地方。說話者想介紹年度最佳員工，所以 (C) 為正確答案。

⁵She joined the Sales Department nearly three years ago.

▶ 接在目的後面的句子是具體介紹得獎者的部分。金妮在銷售部工作了三年，所以 (D) 為正確答案。

⁶She has worked on many projects, and they were all very successful. Our sales have also increased dramatically.

▶ 中、後半段提到了得獎者的成就，說她執行過很多案子。沒有提過她親自販賣東西，所以 (C) 不是正確答案，(B) 才是正確答案。

And now I would like to invite Jinny to come onto the stage to receive her award. Let's give a big hand for Jinny, who has worked tirelessly to contribute to our company.

感謝各位蒞臨我們的年度頒獎典禮。很高興在此宣布今年的最佳銷售員是金妮。她約莫在三年前加入銷售部門，負責過許多案子，而且都很成功。我們的銷售也有顯著的成長。現在我想邀請金妮上台領獎。讓我們熱烈鼓掌歡迎堅持不懈地為我們公司貢獻的金妮。

單字 **award ceremony** 頒獎典禮 **announce** 宣布 **dramatically** 戲劇性地 **invite** 邀請 **stage** 舞台 **give a big hand** 熱烈鼓掌 **tirelessly** 不知疲倦地，不懈地 **contribute to** 為～貢獻

4. 這個演講的目的是什麼？
(A) 提案
(B) 通知員工開會
(C) 表彰員工
(D) 給予獎金

解答　(C)

5. 金妮在銷售部工作多久了？

(A) 半年
(B) 一年
(C) 兩年
(D) 三年

解答 (D)

6. 根據說話者，金妮做了什麼？

(A) 她拜訪過很多國家。
(B) 她完成了很多案子。
(C) 她賣出了很多產品。
(D) 她簽約了。

解答 (B)

Unit 37 導覽

Step 3 實戰演練

Questions 4-6 refer to the following instruction.
第4-6題請參照以下的介紹。

All right, everyone, now we are at the most remarkable and attractive cathedral in Europe. This cathedral was built nearly a century ago.

▶ 問候、主題或地點的相關線索會在前半段出現，說話者說大教堂於一世紀（一百年前）建造，所以 (B) 為正確答案。

In addition, this place is well-known for being the most beautiful cathedral in the world. You have three hours to have lunch and to enjoy looking around the cathedral.

▶ 特徵、優點或程序等細節會在中間的部分出現，說話者說會有三小時的時間吃飯和逛教堂，所以 (D) 為正確答案。

Remember that our tour bus will be waiting for you right here, and you must return to the airport by this bus. You must be at the airport on time.

▶ 尋找叮嚀／要求事項時，要仔細聆聽後半段的「Please~、If 子句，must ＋原形動詞」，說話者叮嚀大家搭巴士到機場，所以 (C) 為正確答案。

好的，各位，我們現在在歐洲最非凡、最具魅力的大教堂。這座教堂大約在一世紀前建造。此外，這個地方作為全球最知名的美麗大教堂而聞名。各位有三個小時可以享用午餐和參觀大教堂。請記得我們的觀光巴士在這裡等各位，而且各位一定要搭這台巴士回機場。請各位務必準時抵達機場。

單字 **remarkable** 值得注意的，非凡的 **attractive** 有魅力的 **cathedral** 大教堂 **century** 世紀，一百年 **well-known** 有名的，出名的

4. 說了關於大教堂的什麼？

(A) 現在是一座博物館。
(B) 一百年前建造的。
(C) 是全世界最有歷史性的建物。
(D) 位於東南亞。

解答 (B)

5. 遊客會在大教堂待多久？

(A) 三十分鐘
(B) 一小時
(C) 兩小時
(D) 三小時

解答 (D)

6. 大家被要求回到哪裡？

(A) 大教堂
(B) 火車
(C) 機場
(D) 飯店

解答 (C)

Review Test

Questions 1-3 refer to the following instruction.
第1-3題請參照以下的介紹。

Ladies and gentlemen, welcome to the Hospitality Management Conference.

▶ 介紹的發生地點會在前半段出現，此處出現了 conference，所以 (A) 為正確答案。

I'd like to introduce our special guest, the general manger of the Brington Hotel, Michael Rupin.

▶ 前半段的問候話，目的說明結束後，開始介紹來賓，請記住來賓的姓名和身分／職責等總是會連在一起，這裡介紹的是飯店總經理邁可．魯平，因此，第二題的正確答案為 (C)，第三題的正確答案為 (C)。

I'm sure all of you know his recent book on hospitality management, which has sold more than two million copies. Many people are eager to hear about his experiences in the hospitality industry because of his good reputation. Now, everyone, please welcome Mr. Michael Rupin.

各位先生女士，歡迎來到飯店管理大會。我想介紹我們的特別來賓，布靈登飯店的總經理邁可．魯平。相信各位都知道他最近出版的飯店管理書籍已經賣了兩百萬本以上。因為他的良好聲譽，很多人都想聽聽他在飯店業的經驗。現在請所有人歡迎邁可．魯平。

單字 **hospitality management** 飯店管理 **conference** 大會 **reputation** 名聲，聲譽 **hospitality industry** 飯店業，服務業

1. 這個介紹是在哪發生的？

(A) 大會
(B) 頒獎典禮
(C) 員工培訓課程
(D) 當地廣播電台

解答　(A)

2. 這個談話的目的是什麼？

(A) 通知員工開會
(B) 宣傳新書
(C) 介紹演講來賓
(D) 選拔新經理

解答　(C)

3. 邁可・魯平是誰？

(A) 銷售員
(B) 大會籌劃者
(C) 飯店總經理
(D) 會計師

解答　(C)

Questions 4-6 refer to the following instruction.
第4-6題請參照以下的介紹。

Good morning. ⁴I'll be your guide today. First, we will start our tour by looking at some mosques.
▶ 問候語或自我介紹會在前半段出現。說話者表明自己是導遊，所以 (D) 為正確答案。

Please look to the right. You can see a mosque that looks quite different than the other mosques. It is called the B.P. Mosque. It was built by the famous architect Bryan Peter.
⁵He always sought to make a unique design for each of his structures. If anyone wants to know more about this mosque, we will come back here and look around tomorrow.
▶ 觀光地點的介紹和訪問行程會在中間的部分出現。導遊正在解說 B.P. 清真寺的特別設計，所以第五題的正確答案為 (D)。

⁶After that, our next stop on the tour will be another one of Mr. Peter's unique designs.
▶ next 題型的答題線索，會在後半段的最後一句出現。(B) 為正確答案。

早安。我是各位今天的導遊。首先，我們會看一些清真寺來開啟今天的旅程。請看右邊，各位會看到一座跟其他清真寺相當不一樣的清真寺。它叫做B.P.清真寺，由著名建築師布萊恩・彼特所建造。他向來追求替他的每個建築物創造獨特的設計。如果有任何人想更了解這座清真寺的話，我們明天會回來逛這裡。在這之後，這趟旅程的下一站是彼特先生的另一個獨特設計。

單字　mosque（伊斯蘭）清真寺　architect 建築師　structure 建築物，結構物　unique 獨特的

4. 說話者最有可能是誰？

(A) 攝影師
(B) 技師
(C) 建築師
(D) 觀光導遊

解答　(D)

5. 根據談話，B.P.清真寺跟其他清真寺有何不同？

(A) 顏色跟其他清真寺不一樣。
(B) 看起來比其他清真寺老舊。
(C) 比其他清真寺大。
(D) 設計跟其他清真寺不一樣。

解答　(D)

6. 聽者接下來會做什麼？

(A) 去看其他清真寺
(B) 看彼特先生的另一個建築物
(C) 在清真寺短暫休息
(D) 搭觀光巴士回飯店

解答　(B)

Questions 7-9 refer to the following instruction.
第7-9題請參照以下的介紹。

Welcome to our 5th annual employee awards ceremony. ⁷I'm very pleased to announce this year's salesperson of the year, Ms. Stephanie Johns.
▶ 前半段會出現問候語和聚會的目的。說話者宣布了最佳銷售員的得獎者，所以 (D) 為正確答案。

Thanks to her efforts, ⁸our new laptop's total sales increased by 20% this year compared to last year.
▶ 介紹得獎者之後，出現了得獎理由、成就、得獎者的職位或資訊等等。說話者提到新型筆記型電腦，由此可知他們工作的地方是電子產品公司，所以第八題的正確答案為 (A)。

Ms. Johns, would you please come forward to receive your award? ⁹We'd also like you to share your success story with us.
▶ 這是 next 題型，所以要仔細聆聽後半段的最後一句。強斯女士會上台演講，所以 (B) 為正確答案。

Would all of you join me in congratulating Ms. Johns?

歡迎來到我們的第五屆年度員工頒獎典禮。我很高興能宣布今年的最佳銷售員是史蒂芬妮・強斯女士。多虧了她的努力，我們的新型筆記型電腦總銷售額，相較去年成長了二十％。強斯女士，可以請您出來領獎

嗎？也希望您和我們分享您的成功故事。各位可以跟我一起恭喜強斯女士嗎？

單字　salesperson 銷售員　award 獎項　total sales 總銷售額　compared to 跟～相比　success story 成功的故事

7. 這則談話的目的是什麼？
(A) 歡迎新員工
(B) 推出新產品
(C) 宣傳新的筆記型電腦
(D) 宣布得獎者

解答　(D)

8. 他們在什麼種類的公司工作？
(A) 電子產品公司
(B) 建築公司
(C) 貨運公司
(D) 辦公用品店

解答　(A)

9. 聽眾接下來會做什麼？
(A) 他們會等待下一個來賓。
(B) 他們會聽強斯女士的演講。
(C) 他們會參加員工會議。
(D) 他們會跟強斯女士一起吃午餐。

解答　(B)

Questions 10-12 refer to the following speech and schedule. 第10-12題請參照以下的演講和日程表。

Good afternoon and welcome to the 3rd annual press commission awards ceremony. Before the events get underway, I would like to remind you of a slight change in the schedule. [10]Due to a catering problem, our dinner, which was scheduled to be served simultaneously with the distribution of awards, is now scheduled for right after the special performance. You will be able to enjoy a delicious meal while listening to the chairman's speech.
▶ 這題問的是晚餐的上菜時間。說話者告知大家，原本跟頒獎一起上菜的晚餐改成在特別表演後上菜。圖表上的 Chairman's speech 時間是晚上七點半，所以 (C) 為正確答案。

We are very sorry for those of you who are hungry right now. Um... [11]Now, let's move on to our first award of the day which goes to Mary-Kate Thomas, whose journal article on the homeless on our city streets has won a number of awards.
▶ 題目的關鍵字是 Mary-Kate Thomas，而且有兩道題目都以該名字出題。第十一題是問她是因為什麼而得獎，所以請專注於提到 Mary-Kate Thomas 的部分。

說話者提到，關於流浪漢的報導得到了很多獎項，由此可知她是因為新聞報導而得獎。因此，將 journal article 改述為 newspaper article 的 (B) 為正確答案。

[12]I would now like to award Mary-Kate with her financial prize, which she has very kindly agreed to donate to a homeless charity. Let's have a round of applause for Mary-Kate Thomas.
▶ 演講的後半段說要頒發獎金給瑪莉－凱特，又說她答應將這筆錢捐給無家可歸者慈善團體。因此，將 financial prize 改述為 money 的 (A) 為正確答案。

午安，歡迎來到第三屆年度媒體委員會頒獎典禮。在活動開始之前，我想提醒各位日程表的些微變動。由於供餐問題，原本預計跟頒獎一起上菜的晚餐，現在改成在特別表演後上菜。各位可以一邊享用美食，一邊聽委員長的演講。對於現在肚子餓的人，我們感到很抱歉。嗯……現在讓我們繼續頒發今天的第一個獎項，得獎者是瑪莉－凱特・湯瑪斯，她那篇關於市街流浪漢的期刊報導贏得了許多獎項。現在我想頒發獎金給瑪莉－凱特，她很慷慨地答應將這筆錢捐給無家可歸者慈善團體。讓我們以熱烈的掌聲歡迎瑪莉－凱特・湯瑪斯。

單字　press commission 媒體委員會　get underway 開始～，使進行　journal article 期刊報導　homeless 無家可歸者　instrument in 對～重要的　subsequently 隨後　awareness 認知　financial prize 獎金　a round of applause 一陣掌聲　homeless shelter 無家可歸者庇護所　raise fund 募款　publishing house 出版社

10. 請看圖表。晚餐什麼時候會上菜？
(A) 晚上六點
(B) 晚上七點
(C) 晚上七點半
(D) 晚上八點

活動	時間
頒獎	晚上六點
特別表演	晚上七點
委員長演講	晚上七點半
明年計畫	晚上八點

解答　(C)

11. 瑪莉－凱特・湯瑪斯做了什麼而得獎？
(A) 在社區中心做志工活動
(B) 撰寫新聞報導
(C) 替無家可歸者庇護所募款
(D) 宣傳當地出版社

解答　(B)

12. 瑪莉－凱特・湯瑪斯會收到什麼？
(A) 錢
(B) 電影票
(C) 畫作
(D) 獎盃

解答　(A)

Unit 36　人物介紹

Q4-6. Thank you for coming to our annual awards ceremony. I'm pleased to announce this year's best salesperson is Jinny. She joined the Sales Department nearly three years ago. She has worked on many projects, and they were all very successful. Our sales have also increased dramatically. And now I would like to invite Jinny to come onto the stage to receive her award. Let's give a big hand for Jinny, who has worked tirelessly to contribute to our company.

Unit 37　導覽

Q4-6. All right, everyone, now we are at the most remarkable and attractive cathedral in Europe. This cathedral was built nearly a century ago. In addition, this place is well-known for being the most beautiful cathedral in the world. You have three hours to have lunch and to enjoy looking around the cathedral. Remember that our tour bus will be waiting for you right here, and you must return to the airport by this bus. You must be at the airport on time.

Review Test

Q1-3. Ladies and gentlemen, welcome to the Hospitality Management Conference. I'd like to introduce our special guest, the general manager of the Brington Hotel, Michael Rupin. I'm sure all of you know his recent book on hospitality management, which has sold more than two million copies. Many people are eager to hear about his experiences in the hospitality industry because of his good reputation. Now, everyone, please welcome Mr. Michael Rupin.

Q4-6. Good morning. I'll be your guide today. First, we will start our tour by looking at some mosques. Please look to the right. You can see a mosque that looks quite different than the other mosques. It is called the B.P. Mosque. It was built by the famous architect Bryan Peter. He always sought to make a unique design for each of his structures. If anyone wants to know more about this mosque, we will come back here and look around tomorrow. After that, our next stop on the tour will be another one of Mr. Peter's unique designs.

Q7-9. Welcome to our 5th annual employee awards ceremony. I'm very pleased to announce this year's salesperson of the year, Ms. Stephanie Johns. Thanks to her efforts, our new laptop's total sales increased by 20% this year compared to last year. Ms. Johns, would you please come forward to receive your award? We'd also like you to share your success story with us. Would all of you join me in congratulating Ms. Johns?

Q10-12. Good afternoon and welcome to the 3rd annual press commission awards ceremony. Before the events

get underway, I would like to remind you of a slight change in the schedule. Due to a catering problem, our dinner, which was scheduled to be served simultaneously with the distribution of awards, is now scheduled for right after the special performance. You will be able to enjoy a delicious meal while listening to the chairman's speech. We are very sorry for those of you who are hungry right now. Um... Now, let's move on to our first award of the day which goes to Mary-Kate Thomas, whose journal article on the homeless on our city streets has won a number of awards.

I would now like to award Mary-Kate with her financial prize, which she has very kindly agreed to donate to a homeless charity. Let's have a round of applause for Mary-Kate Thomas.

類型分析 15　各大主題攻略—廣告
Unit 38　產品廣告

Step 3 實戰演練

Questions 4-6 refer to the following advertisement.
第4-6題請參照以下的廣告。

---

⁴The UCA Company's new digital camera looks very cute, and it has many functions.

▶ 廣告中的產品或服務內容會在前半段出現。相機是一種電子裝置，所以 (C) 為正確答案。

⁵First, it's easy to use. It has an auto-system, so you only have to set up the camera the way you like it once.

▶ 前半段出現廣告對象和廣告產品以後，會出現產品的特徵和優點。廣告提到相機容易使用，所以 (A) 為正確答案。

It uses Wi-Fi as well, and it can be connected to a personal computer without any wires. This adorble camera is easy for anyone to use.

⁶ For more information, visit our website at www.ucaelectronics.com.

▶ 遇到關於額外資訊的問題時，要仔細聆聽最後一句。廣告說可以拜訪網站獲得更多資訊，所以 (D) 為正確答案。

UCA公司的新數位相機外觀非常可愛，而且具備多種功能。首先，這台相機容易上手。它有一套自動系統，您只需要按照您喜歡的方式設定相機一次即可。它也能使用無線網路，不需要任何的電線即可連接個人電腦。任何人都能輕鬆使用這台可愛的相機。請拜訪我們的網站www.ucaelectronics.com獲得更多資訊。

單字　**function** 功能　**set up** 設定　**connect** 連結，連接　**personal computer** 個人電腦　**without** 沒有～　**wire** 電線　**adorable** 可愛的

4. 是什麼東西的廣告？

(A) 網路系統
(B) 家具
(C) 電子裝置
(D) 廚房用品

解答 (C)

5. 提到了這款新數位相機的什麼優點？

(A) 很容易使用。
(B) 比去年的型號便宜。
(C) 是全世界最小的相機。
(D) 有各式各樣的顏色。

解答 (A)

6. 聽者該如何獲得更多資訊？

(A) 拜訪商店
(B) 寄電子郵件
(C) 撥打特別的電話號碼
(D) 查看網站

解答 (D)

Unit 39　折扣廣告

Step 3 實戰演練

Questions 4-6 refer to the following advertisement.
第4-6題請參照以下的廣告。

Winter is just around the corner. ⁴The summer season has ended, so we are having a summer clearance sale in preparation for the winter season. ⁵We have everything from swimming suits to short-sleeved shirts.

▶ 廣告的物品或服務會在前半段出現。廣告提到正在舉行夏季清倉大拍賣，而且從泳衣到短袖襯衫都有。因此，第四題的正確答案為 (C)，第五題的正確答案為 (D)。

We are offering up to 50% off summer items. Furthermore, ⁶if you spend more than $200, we'll give you a free beach bag.

▶ 為了獲得贈品或享有折扣而必須做的事情在後半段出現。廣告提到消費兩百美元以上就送海灘包，所以 (B) 為正確答案。

Don't hesitate. This offer will only last for a week. Start saving now!

冬季即將到來。夏季已過，所以為了替冬季做準備，我們正在舉行夏季清倉大拍賣。我們的商品應有盡有，從泳衣到短袖襯衫都有。目前提供夏季商品五十%的折扣。此外，如果您消費兩百美元以上，我們會送您免費的海灘包。

不要再猶豫了，折扣活動只有一個星期，現在就開始省錢大作戰吧！

單字 **swimming suit** 泳衣 **short-sleeved** 短袖 **furthermore** 此外，而且

4. 什麼商品在特賣？

(A) 新商品
(B) 冬季衣服
(C) 夏季衣服
(D) 夏季鞋子

解答 (C)

5. 根據廣告，什麼商品有折扣？

(A) 內衣
(B) 滑雪服
(C) 毛衣
(D) 泳衣

解答 (D)

6. 客人要如何獲得免費的海灘包？

(A) 至少買五樣商品
(B) 消費兩百美元以上
(C) 付現金
(D) 持有優惠券

解答 (B)

Review Test

Questions 1-3 refer to the following advertisement.
第1-3題請參照以下的廣告。

---

¹/²Luxury Apartments will be available to rent next month.

▶ 廣告的產品會在前半段出現。廣告中出現了 Apartment，由此可知是不動產的廣告。因此，第一題的正確答案為 (A)。折扣／販售的開始日期會在前半段或中間出現，廣告提到將從下個月開始出租，所以第二題的正確答案為 (A)。

This is an eco-friendly apartment complex. The property is located in the city center, and there are several restaurants nearby.

³All residents of Luxury Apartments will be able to enjoy free facilities such as a gym, a swimming pool, and a tennis court 24 hours a day.

▶ 產品的特徵和優點會在中間或後半段出現。廣告提到體育館、游泳池和網球場都可以免費使用，所以 (B) 為正確答案。

To look around Luxury Apartments, please call 3451-1156.

豪華公寓於下個月起提供出租。這是環保的公寓社區。該房地產位於市中心，而且附近有好幾間餐廳。所有豪華公寓的住戶皆可二十四小時使用免費的設施，例如體育館、游泳池和網球場。若您想參觀豪華公寓，請撥打3451-1156。

單字　eco-friendly 環保的　property 房地產　resident 住戶，居住者　facility 設施　such as 例如　gym 體育館　look around 參觀

1. 廣告的是什麼？

(A) 不動產
(B) 體育用品店
(C) 家具工廠
(D) 油漆商店

解答　(A)

2. 公寓何時可以提供出租？

(A) 下個月
(B) 明年
(C) 下週五
(D) 年底

解答　(A)

3. 對豪華公寓的所有住戶來說，什麼是免費的？

(A) 超市
(B) 健身設施
(C) 遊樂場
(D) 停車場

解答　(B)

Questions 4-6 refer to the following advertisement.
第4-6題請參照以下的廣告。

[4]Are you planning to buy some furniture for the new year? Then TNT Furniture is offering a great chance for you.
▶ 廣告的物品或服務會在前半段出現。廣告提到了 furniture，所以 (D) 為正確答案。

We will be having our grand opening sale soon. The newest styles of furniture will be arriving at our store soon, and we will also provide huge discounts on old styles. [5]But you should come to our store this Saturday to take advantage of the discounts.
▶ 折扣方法、購買價格與方法，以及聯絡資訊等會在中間或後半段出現。此處提到週六拜訪商店的話能獲得折扣，所以 (B) 為正確答案。

You'd better come early since the discounted furniture is limited in number. [6]This sale will only be held on Saturday.
▶ 折扣期間會在前半段或後半段出現，這題的出題順

序是最後一題，所以要預想到折扣期間會在後半段出現。廣告說活動只在週六舉行，所以 (C) 為正確答案。

您打算為新的一年購買一些家具嗎？那麼，TNT家具提供您一個大好的機會。我們即將舉辦開幕特賣。最新款的家具很快就會抵達我們店裡，舊款式也會有大幅的折扣。不過，您想使用此折扣的話，需在本週六來我們店裡。折扣家具數量有限，所以您最好早點來。此折扣活動只在週六舉行。

單字　plan to 計劃～　furniture 家具　grand opening sale 開幕特賣　huge 龐大的　take advantage of 利用～　be held 舉辦，進行

4. 這是什麼種類的商店？

(A) 食品雜貨店
(B) 書店
(C) 電子產品店
(D) 家具店

解答　(D)

5. 根據廣告，客人為什麼該拜訪商店？

(A) 為了獲得免費商品
(B) 為了獲得折扣
(C) 為了跟員工說話
(D) 為了拿修好的家具

解答　(B)

6. 特賣將在何時舉行？

(A) 週一
(B) 週日
(C) 週六
(D) 週五

解答　(C)

Questions 7-9 refer to the following advertisement.
第7-9題請參照以下的廣告。

[7]Olive Bookstore is pleased to announce that we are having a special promotion.
▶ 廣告的商品和公司會在前半段出現。(C) 為正確答案。

This event is being held to celebrate our ten-year anniversary and also to thank our customers. [8]If you buy a bestseller, you will get a 10% discount on it.
▶ 折扣和購買優惠等資訊會在中間／後半段出現。(D) 為正確答案。

[9]To find a list of all the bestsellers we have in our store, please visit our website at www.olivebooks.com. We hope

to see you at Olive Bookstore.

▶ 購買方法、購買方式或購買處的聯絡方式等會在後半段出現。廣告中請客人拜訪書店的網站，所以 (A) 為正確答案。

橄欖書店很高興地宣布我們正在進行特別促銷。此活動的舉辦宗旨是為了慶祝我們的十週年紀念日，以及感謝我們的顧客。若您購買暢銷書，可享有十％折扣。若想尋找我們店裡所有的暢銷書清單，請拜訪我們的網站www.olivebooks.com。期望能在橄欖書店與您見面。

單字　be pleased to 很高興～　announce 宣布　special promotion 特別促銷　anniversary 紀念日

7. 廣告的是什麼種類的商店？

(A) 文具店
(B) 電子產品店
(C) 書店
(D) 辦公用品店

解答　(C)

8. 客人購買暢銷書之後會獲得什麼？

(A) 文具
(B) 禮券
(C) 免費書籍
(D) 折扣

解答　(D)

9. 根據廣告，客人要怎麼找暢銷書清單？

(A) 查看網站
(B) 撥打特別的電話號碼
(C) 拜訪商店
(D) 寄電子郵件

解答　(A)

Questions 10-12 refer to the following advertisement and price table. 第10-12題請參照以下的**廣告**和**價目表**。

¹⁰It's the most special peak season here at Raymond Hotel London!

▶ 這是詢問廣告對象的題目，所以可以在前半段中尋找線索。廣告說現在是飯店的旺季，後面則是在宣傳打折的客房價格，由此可知廣告對象是打算在飯店投宿的客人。因此，選項中的旅客最恰當。(C) 為正確答案。

¹¹To celebrate our renovation, we are providing our guests with all-time special deals.

▶ 這題是問提供特別優惠的原因。廣告提到為了慶祝翻新，目前提供特別優惠，所以正確答案是紀念

remodeling（改造）的 (D)。

Spend your holidays in our newly remodeled suite rooms at a discounted price. This month only, our Executive Suite will be available for the price of the Executive Standard room, and ¹²the Luxury Suite room will be available for the price of our Executive Suite.

▶ 此處提到會以行政套房的價格提供豪華套房，所以在表格中尋找行政套房的價格即可。正確答案為 (C) 的兩百四十五歐元。

Hurry up and make your booking, to take advantage of these special rates!

現在是雷蒙德飯店倫敦店最特別的旺季！為了慶祝我們翻新，我們目前提供客人全時段的特別優惠。以折扣價在我們最新翻修的套房度假吧！我們只在這個月以行政標準房的價格提供行政套房，以行政套房的價格提供豪華套房。若想享有這些特別優惠，就快來訂房吧！

單字　peak season 旺季　renovation 翻新　special deal 特別優惠　discounted price 折扣價　suite 套房　standard room 標準房　available 可使用的　early sell-out 提早賣完的　take advantage of 利用～

10. 這則廣告的對象最有可能是誰？

(A) 公司高層主管
(B) 翻修工人
(C) 旅客
(D) 飯店員工

解答　(C)

11. 為什麼業者提供特別優惠？

(A) 為了慶祝週年紀念
(B) 為了宣傳企業開幕
(C) 為了替翻修募款
(D) 為了慶祝翻新

解答　(D)

12. 請看圖表。這個月的豪華套房價格是多少？

(A) 190歐元
(B) 215歐元
(C) 245歐元
(D) 270歐元

房型	房價
高級房	190歐元
行政標準房	215歐元
行政套房	245歐元
豪華套房	270歐元

解答　(C)

聽寫訓練

Unit 38　產品廣告

Q4-6. The UCA Company's new digital camera looks very cute, and it has many functions. First, it's easy to use. It has an auto-system, so you only have to set up the camera the way you like it once. It uses Wi-Fi as well, and it can be connected to a personal computer without any wires. This adorable camera is easy for anyone to use. For more information, visit our website at www.ucaelectronics.com.

Unit 39　折扣廣告

Q4-6. Winter is just around the corner. The summer season has ended, so we are having a summer clearance sale in preparation for the winter season. We have everything from swimming suits to short-sleeved shirts. We are offering up to 50% off summer items. Furthermore, if you spend more than $200, we'll give you a free beach bag. Don't hesitate. This offer will only last for a week. Start saving now!

Review Test

Q1-3. Luxury Apartments will be available to rent next month. This is an eco-friendly apartment complex. The property is located in the city center, and there are several restaurants nearby. All residents of Luxury Apartments will be able to enjoy free facilities such as a gym, a swimming pool, and a tennis court 24 hours a day. To look around Luxury Apartments, please call 3451-1156.

Q4-6. Are you planning to buy some furniture for the new year? Then TNT Furniture is offering a great chance for you. We will be having our grand opening sale soon. The newest styles of furniture will be arriving at our store soon, and we will also provide huge discounts on old styles. But you should come to our store this Saturday to take advantage of the discounts. You'd better come early since the discounted furniture is limited in number. This sale will only be held on Saturday.

Q7-9. Olive Bookstore is pleased to announce that we are having a special promotion. This event is being held to celebrate our ten-year anniversary and also to thank our customers. If you buy a bestseller, you will get a 10% discount on it. To find a list of all the bestsellers we have in our store, please visit our website at www.olivebooks.com. We hope to see you at Olive Bookstore.

Q10-12. It's the most special peak season here at Raymond Hotel London! To celebrate our renovation, we are providing our guests with all-time special deals. Spend your holidays in our newly remodeled suite rooms at a discounted price. This month only, our Executive Suite will be available for the price of the Executive Standard room, and the Luxury Suite room will be available for the price of our Executive Suite. Hurry up and make your booking, to take advantage of these special rates!

PART 4 FINAL TEST - 1

Questions 71-73 refer to the following instruction.
第71-73題請參照以下的介紹。

> Good morning, everyone. Welcome to our seminar on the international fashion industry. [71] I'm very pleased to introduce our guest speaker today.
>
> ▶ 前半段以「I'm pleased to~、Welcome~、Everyone、To~、Let me introduce~」等開頭的部分，是出現問候語或聚會目的和背景的地方。(B) 為正確答案。
>
> I'm sure all of you know [72] that Ms. Melissa Rin is one of the most famous fashion designers in the global fashion industry. [73] She has worked in the fashion industry for 30 years ever since she became a fashion designer.
>
> ▶ 介紹完講者之後，出現了講者的經歷，所以第七十二題的正確答案為 (A)，第七十三題的正確答案為 (A)。
>
> Ms. Rin's speech today is entitled "International Fashion Design." She will be sharing some of her experiences with us. Everyone, let's give a big hand for Ms. Melissa Rin.
>
> ----
>
> 各位早安。歡迎來到我們的國際時裝產業研討會。我很高興能在此介紹我們今天的演講嘉賓。相信各位都知道梅麗莎·林女士是全球時裝產業最有名的時裝設計師之一。自從她成為時裝設計師之後，她已經在時裝界工作三十年了。林女士今天的演講主題是「國際時裝設計」。她會跟我們分享一些她的經驗。各位，讓我們以熱烈的掌聲歡迎梅麗莎·林女士。

單字　**guest speaker** 演講嘉賓　**fashion industry** 時裝產業　**global** 全球的　**share** 分享，共享

71. 演講的目的是什麼？
(A) 介紹新員工
(B) 介紹演講嘉賓
(C) 頒獎
(D) 任命教授

解答　(B)

72. 誰是梅麗莎·林？
(A) 設計師
(B) 會計師
(C) 電工
(D) 總經理

解答　(A)

73. 林女士在時裝產業工作多久了？

(A) 三十年
(B) 三十年以下
(C) 三十年以上
(D) 三十五年

解答 **(A)**

Questions 74-76 refer to the following announcement.
第74-76題請參照以下的公告。

Good morning. [74]I want to make an announcement about our new regulations regarding business trips.

▶ 公告的前半段會出現問候、地點或公告目的。(C) 為正確答案。

All employees are required to get approval from their supervisors before they plan their business trips. [75]To get approval, employees must send an email with a form that can be downloaded from the company's website.

▶ 日程和（變更的）公告事項會在中間的部分出現。(A) 為正確答案。

It is also important to note that [76]employees are required to get approval at least a week before going on business trips.

▶ 叮嚀、請求事項、詢問或聯絡資訊等會在後半段出現。說話者提到要在出差一週前獲得批准，所以 (A) 為正確答案。

早安。我想宣布關於出差的新規定。所有員工都需要在規劃出差之前，先得到上司的批准。為了獲得批准，請員工務必用電子郵件寄出表格，該表格可以在公司網站下載。員工需要至少在出差前一週獲得批准，這一點也很重要，請謹記在心。

單字 **policy** 政策 **regarding** 關於～ **leave of absence** 休假 **require** 要求 **approval** 批准，許可 **supervisor** 上司，管理者 **get approval from** 獲得～的批准

74. 這則公告的目的是什麼？

(A) 提供員工訓練的資訊
(B) 介紹新員工
(C) 宣布新政策
(D) 請求捐款

解答 **(C)**

75. 員工可以在哪裡獲得表格？

(A) 公司網站
(B) 人事部門
(C) 圖書館
(D) 服務櫃台

解答 **(A)**

76. 員工必須在何時獲得上司的批准？

(A) 出差七天前
(B) 出差六天前
(C) 出差五天前
(D) 出差四天前

解答 **(A)**

Questions 77-79 refer to the following instruction.
第77-79題請參照以下的介紹。

Thanks for attending the meeting. I'd like to talk to you today about our vision. You all know that our CEO thinks very highly of preserving the environment, [77]so we're once again implementing a recycling system.

▶ 前半段介紹了公司的願景是成為環保型公司，要實施回收制度，所以 (C) 為正確答案。

Please recycle not only documents and trash from the office but your personal garbage as well. [78]Now, I know what you guys are probably thinking. We've done this before, and it didn't last long. But this time, I think it'll be different.

▶ 說要實施回收制度說到一半時，說了「Now, I know what you guys are probably thinking」之後，說雖然這是之前嘗試過、沒有維持多久的政策，但是這次會不一樣，說話者想要藉此說服聽者。由此可知，說話者明白聽者對回收政策的想法並不正面。(A) 為正確答案。

[79]If we manage to maintain a high recycling rate until the end of the year, you will all receive a special bonus. I hope this gives you some motivation.

▶ 說話者說明了回收政策的實施，並在後半段說到年底為止都保持高回收率的話，就能獲得特別獎金。因此，把 bonus 改述成 incentive 的 (B) 為正確答案。

感謝各位出席此會議。今天我想跟各位談談我們的願景。各位都知道我們的執行長非常重視環境保護，所以我們打算再次實施回收制度。不僅是辦公室的文件和垃圾，個人垃圾也要回收。我大概知道各位現在在想什麼。我們之前做過這些了，而且維持不久。不過，我覺得這次會不一樣。如果我們一直到年底都保持著高回收率，各位會收到特別的獎金。希望這能給各位一些動力。

單字 **eco-friendly** 環保的 **preserve** 保存 **implement** 實施 **maintain** 維持 **motivation** 動機 **document** 文件 **personal** 個人的 **garbage** 垃圾

77. 公司嘗試做什麼？

(A) 參加環境研討會
(B) 省電
(C) 實施環保計畫
(D) 搬到其他州

78. 說話者說「我大概知道各位現在在想什麼」的意思是什麼？

(A) 他理解聽者的疑惑。

(B) 他對聽者的話感到同意。

(C) 他在開會前跟聽者談過了。

(D) 他預測公司會遇到一些困難。

解答　(A)

81. 綠屋位於哪裡？

(A) 市政廳附近

(B) 購物中心附近

(C) 郵局附近

(D) 大教堂附近

解答　(D)

79. 如果計畫成功，聽者最有可能會收到什麼？

(A) 慶祝晚餐

(B) 特別的獎勵

(C) 額外的休假日

(D) 勵志的演講

解答　(B)

82. 根據廣告，顧客該如何獲得更多資訊？

(A) 查看網站

(B) 寄電子郵件

(C) 拜訪餐廳

(D) 打電話

解答　(D)

Questions 80-82 refer to the following advertisement.

第80-82題請參照以下的**廣告**。

---

[80]Are you looking for tasty food in your neighborhood? [81]Then you will love Green House, which is located on Manchester Street near the Bolt Cathedral.

▶ 廣告的物品、服務或業者的資訊會在前半段出現，所以第八十題的正確答案為 (A)。Green House 位於 Cathedral（大教堂）附近，所以第八十一題的正確答案為 (D)。

We're open daily for lunch and dinner from 12 p.m. to 9 p.m. We have various kinds of food, including international food, that you can't find at other restaurants. And this month only, we are offering a 20% discount on every item on the menu. Please come and enjoy delicious food at affordable prices! [82]For more information, please call 4132-4546.

▶ 購買地點或聯絡資訊會在後半段出現。廣告說可以打電話了解詳情，所以 (D) 為正確答案。

您在找鄰近地區的美食嗎？那麼您會喜歡綠屋的，我們的餐廳位於靠近伯特大教堂的曼徹斯特街。我們每天中午十二點到晚上九點提供午餐和晚餐。我們有各式各樣您在其他餐廳找不到的食物，其中包含國際性食物。我們只在這個月提供菜單上每個品項八折的優惠。請前來以便宜的價格享受美食！欲知更多資訊，請撥打4132-4546。

單字　**various** 各式各樣的，多種的　**delicious food** 美食　**at an affordable price** 以便宜的價格

80. 廣告的是什麼種類的生意？

(A) 餐廳

(B) 書店

Questions 83-85 refer to the following radio broadcast.

第83-85題請參照以下的**電台廣播**。

---

[83]This is the morning weather report.

▶ 前半段提到問候語，介紹了節目。這是天氣報導，所以 (C) 為正確答案。

Today's weather calls for partly cloudy skies and occasional rain. The temperature will decrease to ten degrees by this afternoon. [84]We're also expecting heavy rain this weekend.

▶ 說完目前的天氣和建議後，出現了未來的天氣預報。週末預計會下豪雨，所以 (B) 為正確答案。

There's a 70% chance of rain throughout next week. So you should carry an umbrella until next week. [85]Now stay tuned for today's World Baseball Classic!

▶ 下個節目的介紹會在最後一句出現。接下來會出現跟棒球有關的節目，所以 (D) 為正確答案。

現在是早晨天氣預報。今天天氣局部多雲，偶爾會下雨。下午時氣溫將降到十度。本週末預計會下豪雨。下週每天皆有七十%的機率下雨，所以請隨身攜帶雨傘直到下週。現在請繼續收聽本日的世界棒球經典！

單字　**weather report** 天氣預報　**partly cloudy** 部分多雲的　**occasional** 偶爾的　**heavy rain** 豪雨　**throughout** 從頭到尾，在～期間　**stay tuned** 繼續收聽

83. 這是關於什麼的報導？

(A) 商業

(B) 健康

(C) 天氣

(D) 體育

解答 (C)

84. 本週末預計會怎樣？

(A) 下雪
(B) 下雨
(C) 晴朗
(D) 起霧

解答 (B)

85. 聽者接下來會聽到什麼？

(A) 音樂
(B) 天氣預報
(C) 商業新聞
(D) 體育新聞

解答 (D)

Questions 86-88 refer to the following announcement.
第86-88題請參照以下的公告。

---

[86] Thank you for visiting the Vermont Museum of Art. I'm Jenny Lee and I'll be your guide today.

▶ 這是問說話者的職業，相關線索通常會在前半段出現。透過 Vermont Museum of Art 和 I'll be your guide 可以知道說話者是在美術館工作的導覽員。(A) 為正確答案。

During our tour, we are going to explore more than 500 works of modern art. And here's some good news for you. [87] At 4 p.m. today, our museum is going to put on a free performance on the first floor of the main building. Seating is limited!

▶ 遇到掌握說話者意圖的題目時，要專心聆聽該句子的前後內容。說話者說美術館會提供免費的表演之後，說了「Seating is limited」。由此可知，說話者的意思是由於座位有限，要提前（盡快）到表演現場。(D) 為正確答案。

Come and enjoy music by singer-songwriter Ian Leighton. [88] Lastly, please do not take any pictures of the exhibits.

▶ 說話者清楚說明參觀者不能拍攝展出作品，所以改述這一點 (B) 為正確答案。

感謝各位前來參觀佛蒙特美術館。我是珍妮·李，今天的導覽員。在導覽中，我們會探索五百件以上的現代藝術作品。有個好消息要跟各位說。今天下午四點，我們美術館會在本館一樓提供免費的表演。座位有限！請前來享受創作型歌手伊安·雷頓的音樂。最後，請勿拍攝任何展示作品。

單字 museum 博物館，展覽館 during 在～期間 explore 探索，查看 modern 現代的 put on 上演 performance 表演 main building 本館 seating 座

位 limited 有限的 take a picture 拍照 exhibit 展覽作品 imply 暗指，暗示 present 出示 ID card 身分證 prepare for 準備～ expansion 擴張 underway 進行中的 venue 地點 beforehand 事先 photography 攝影 permitted 允許的 allowed 允許的 join 一起～，參加

86. 說話者最有可能是誰？

(A) 博物館導覽員
(B) 歌手
(C) 藝術家
(D) 電影導演

解答 (A)

87. 說話者說「座位有限」是想暗示什麼？

(A) 大家需要出示附照片的身分證。
(B) 會花一週以上的時間準備活動。
(C) 博物館的擴館計畫正在進行。
(D) 大家必須事先抵達活動地點。

解答 (D)

88. 說話者提到導覽的什麼？

(A) 十人以上的團體享有折扣。
(B) 禁止攝影。
(C) 兒童不能參加。
(D) 不能攜帶大包包。

解答 (B)

Questions 89-91 refer to the following telephone message. 第89-91題請參照以下的電話語音訊息。

Hello. This message is for Mr. Victor. [89] I'm calling from the Marine Resort to confirm your reservation for three nights from September 11 to 13.

▶ 目的或問題的答題線索會在以「I'm calling~」開頭的地方出現。(A) 為正確答案。

The total amount for this reservation is $400, and [90] you are required to pay $200 as a deposit.

▶ 具體的資訊會在中間的部分出現。說話者表示需要支付兩百美元的訂金，所以 (D) 為正確答案。

For your convenience, [91] we will provide transportation for you from the airport to our resort.

▶ 未來的日程會在後半段出現。說話者說會提供交通工具，所以 (D) 為正確答案。

If you need more details about your reservation, please call our reservation desk at 5324-4126.

您好，這是給維克多先生的訊息。海洋度假村致電給您是想確認九月十一日至十三日三晚的預約。該預約的總金額為四百美元，您必須支付兩百美元作

為訂金。為了您的方便，我們提供從機場到度假村的交通工具。如果您需要更多的預約細節，請撥打5324-4126聯繫我們的預約處。

單字　confirm 確認　total amount 總額，總計　require 要求，需要　deposit 保證金，訂金　convenience 便利，方便　transportation 交通工具

89. 這則訊息的主要目的是什麼？

(A) 確認預約
(B) 宣傳度假村
(C) 安排交通工具
(D) 取消預約

解答　(A)

90. 維克多先生應支付多少訂金？

(A) 四百美元
(B) 兩百美元以上
(C) 兩百美元以下
(D) 兩百美元

解答　(D)

91. 根據這則訊息，說話者會提供聽者什麼？

(A) 折扣
(B) 飲料
(C) 免費餐點
(D) 交通工具

解答　(D)

Questions 92-94 refer to the following news report.
第92-94題請參照以下的新聞報導。

This is Allen Scott from WTT Broadcasting, your station for the latest in local news. [92] Construction on the new public museum on Brington Street was completed yesterday.

▶ 新聞的主題會在前半段出現。報導內容與公立博物館有關，所以 (C) 為正確答案。

It was expected to be completed last month, but [93] construction was delayed for a month due to the tremendous amount of snow that fell.

▶ 在問候語和說話者的介紹之後，會出現主題和細節等。報導指出工程因為大雪而延宕，所以 (A) 為正確答案。

[94] So the opening ceremony for the new public museum has been delayed until this Friday.

▶ 關於未來的預測會在後半段出現。延到星期五的意思是開幕典禮會在星期五舉行。(B) 為正確答案。

And now for an update on the weather.

我是傳遞最新當地消息的WTT廣播的艾倫·史考特。布靈頓街上的新公立博物館建設已在昨天竣工。原本預計上個月完工，但是工程因為大雪而延宕一個月。所以新公立博物館的開幕典禮延期至本週五。接下來是最新的天氣預報。

單字　latest 最近的，最新的　construction 工程　public museum 公立博物館　complete 完成，結束　tremendous 極大的　opening ceremony 開幕典禮

92. 這則報導主要跟什麼有關？

(A) 購物中心
(B) 市立公園
(C) 公立博物館
(D) 公立圖書館

解答　(C)

93. 什麼耽擱了工程？

(A) 大雪
(B) 大雨
(C) 資金不足
(D) 人力不足

解答　(A)

94. 根據這則報導，禮拜五會發生什麼事？

(A) 特價銷售
(B) 開幕典禮
(C) 節慶
(D) 維修工程

解答　(B)

Questions 95-97 refer to the following broadcast and map. 第95-97題請參照以下的廣播和地圖。

Good afternoon. [95] This is Dave Voyles with a local traffic update at Perth News.

▶ 可以在前半段尋找詢問主題的題目答題線索。說話者正在介紹播報當地路況的自己，所以 (C) 為正確答案。

[96] There is a delay on Santa Rica Road as a truck turned over in the middle of the road.

▶ 這題要善用圖表才能解題。透過廣播內容可以知道聖瑞卡路發生了車輛翻覆的意外，從圖表來看，位於這條路上的建築物是圖書館。(D) 為正確答案。

It will take about one or two hours to remove the truck from Santa Rica Road, so the road is temporarily closed. [97] To avoid any delays, we advise you to take an alternative route. I'll be back after the break with today's weather forecast.

午安。我是佩斯新聞當地路況報導的大衛‧沃約斯。由於一台卡車在道路中央翻覆，聖瑞卡路目前有所延滯。預計要花一到兩小時才能移除聖瑞卡路上的卡車，所以該道路暫時封閉中。為了避免任何的延滯，我們建議各位改走替代道路。休息之後將為您帶來天氣預報。

單字　local 當地的　traffic 交通的　update 最新消息　delay 延滯　turn over 翻覆　in the middle of 在～的中間　remove 移除　temporarily 暫時地　closed 封閉的　avoid 避免　advise 建議　alternative 其他的，代替的　route 道路　break 休息　weather forecast 天氣預報　public 大眾的，公共的　hearing 公聽會　annual 年度的　condition 情況　financial 財政的　affected 受影響的　accident 意外　community center 社區中心　city hall 市政府　detour 繞道　public transportation 大眾交通工具　participate in 參加～

95. 電台廣播主要是關於什麼？

(A) 公聽會
(B) 年度活動
(C) 當地交通情況
(D) 財政報告

解答　(C)

96. 請看圖表。哪棟建築物最有可能被意外影響？

(A) 社區中心
(B) 銀行
(C) 市政府
(D) 圖書館

解答　(D)

97. 說話者推薦什麼？

(A) 繞道
(B) 使用大眾交通工具
(C) 查看網站
(D) 參加活動

解答　(A)

Questions 98-100 refer to the following excerpt from a meeting and chart.
第98-100題請參照以下的會議摘錄和圖表。

I called this meeting to review the results of the customer satisfaction survey we recently conducted. 98/99We surveyed customers who visited our car rental business during the last 6 months.

And now the results are in. According to the results, we are doing much better than I expected except in one area. As you may know, a competitor is going to move into the neighborhood next month. We should not let them take our clients away from us. 100For this reason, I'd like to discuss how to improve the weakest area with you.

我召開這個會議，是為了檢討我們最近做的顧客滿意度調查。我們調查了過去六個月以來，使用過我們的租車業務的顧客。現在調查結果出爐了。根據結果，除了一個領域以外，我們表現得比我預期的好很多。各位可能已經知道了，有個競爭對手將在下個月搬到這附近。我們不能讓他們搶走我們的客人。基於這個原因，我想跟各位討論怎麼改善最弱的領域。

單字　call 召開（會議）　review 檢討　result 結果　satisfaction 滿意　survey 調查　recently 最近　conduct 實施　car rental 汽車出租　according to 根據～　expect 預期　except 除～之外　area 領域，區域　competitor 競爭者　neighborhood 鄰近地區　take A away from B 從B那裡搶走A　reason 理由　discuss 討論　improve 改善　weak 脆弱的　recently 最近　location 位置，地點　knowledgeable 博學的　quality 品質　vehicle 車輛

98. 說話者在什麼種類的行業工作？

(A) 飯店
(B) 旅行社
(C) 租車公司
(D) 航空公司

解答　(C)

99. 說話者說公司最近做了什麼？

(A) 下單
(B) 搬進新辦公室
(C) 開新分店
(D) 做調查

解答　(D)

100. 請看圖表。說話者想要聽者討論哪個領域的事？

(A) 知識豐富的員工
(B) 地點
(C) 價格
(D) 車輛品質

解答 (C)

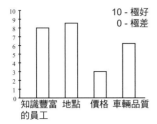

10 - 極好
0 - 極差

知識豐富的員工　地點　價格　車輛品質

PART 4 FINAL TEST - 2

Questions 71-73 refer to the following announcement.
第71-73題請參照以下的公告。

[71]Attention, all passengers on Pacific Airlines Flight 070 bound for Washington.
▶ 公共場所廣播的前半段會出現問候、地點或介紹等。此處提到了飛機，由此可知聽者在機場。(A) 為正確答案。

[72]Your departure time has been delayed due to fog.
▶ 公告目的會在問候、地點或介紹的後面出現。這則廣播的目的，是要通知乘客班機因為濃霧的緣故而延後起飛。用壞天氣來表達濃霧的 (D) 為正確答案。

Flight 070 is now scheduled to leave at 2 p.m. We apologize for the inconvenience, and we are offering everyone a free meal voucher that can be used at any restaurant or cafe in the airport. [73]Please come to Gate 13 to receive a voucher.
▶ 接下來會做的事情在後半段出現。廣播請乘客到十三號登機口，所以 (C) 為正確答案。

Again, Pacific Airlines Flight 070 bound for Washington is now scheduled to depart at 2 p.m.

飛往華盛頓的太平洋航空〇七〇班機的乘客請注意。由於大霧，出發時間已延後。〇七〇班機目前預計於下午兩點起飛。對於造成的不便，我們深感抱歉。我們會提供每個人免費的餐券，可以在機場內的任何餐廳或咖啡廳使用。請到十三號登機口領取餐券。再重複一次，飛往華盛頓的太平洋航空〇七〇班機目前預計於下午兩點起飛。

單字　passenger 乘客　departure time 起飛時間　delay 延遲，延期　fog 濃霧　inconvenience 不便　voucher 現金券

71. 聽者最有可能在哪裡？
(A) 機場
(B) 火車站
(C) 公車站
(D) 港口

解答 (A)

72. 是什麼造成了延誤？
(A) 飛機維修
(B) 跑道的維修作業
(C) 意外
(D) 壞天氣

解答 (D)

73. 聽者接下來會做什麼？
(A) 出示登機證
(B) 登機
(C) 去十三號登機口
(D) 繫安全帶

解答 (C)

Questions 74-76 refer to the following advertisement.
第74-76題請參照以下的廣告。

Are you looking for a company to remodel your house? [74]Bigston Interior Design on Golden Street can help you do that.
▶ 廣告的物品、服務或公司等等會在前半段出現。廣告目的是介紹公司，所以 (B) 為正確答案。

[75]Bigston is well-known for its experienced interior designers who can satisfy your needs.
▶ 關於公司的說明在中間的部分出現。該公司以經驗豐富的室內設計師聞名，所以 (A) 為正確答案。

We also have a variety of floor tiles and wallpaper and a diverse amount of furniture and lamps to fill your home. [76]For more information, or if you want to speak with one of our designers, please call 3695-4254.
▶ 購買地點或聯絡資訊會在後半段出現。廣告說聽者可以打電話跟員工討論，所以 (D) 為正確答案。

您正在找改造自家房子的公司嗎？黃金街上的畢格斯登室內設計可以幫您。畢格斯登以經驗豐富的室內設計師聞名，能夠滿足您的需求。我們也有各種地磚、壁紙和大量的家具、燈具能夠填滿您的房子。欲知更多資訊，或是想跟我們的設計師討論，請撥打3695-4254。

單字　remodel 改造，翻修　interior design 室內設計　be well-known for 以～聞名的　need 需要，需求　a variety of 各式各樣的　wallpaper 壁紙　diverse 多變化的

74. 這則廣告的目的是什麼？
(A) 提到某個週年折扣
(B) 介紹公司
(C) 邀請客人參加活動
(D) 宣布新公司的開業

解答　(B)

75. 該公司以什麼聞名？

(A) 有經驗的員工
(B) 產品的高品質
(C) 便宜的價格
(D) 該城市裡成立最久的設計公司

解答　(A)

76. 根據廣告，為什麼聽者要打電話給該公司？

(A) 為了預約會面
(B) 為了收到手冊
(C) 為了預約
(D) 為了跟員工說話

解答　(D)

Questions 77-79 refer to the following announcement.
第77-79題請參照以下的公告。

Good morning, everyone. [77] I'm Sarah from the Human Resources Department.

▶ 發布公告的人或公告對象會在前半段出現。來自人事部的人正在跟辦公室員工說話，所以 (A) 為正確答案。

Since you are now a member of our staff, [78] we will go on a tour around our headquarters today.

▶ 除了公告對象以外，目的、日程或地點等也會在前半段出現。(C) 為正確答案。

[79] If you have any question during the tour, don't hesitate to ask me.

▶ 叮嚀和請求事項的相關線索，會在後半段的 if 子句或命令句中出現。說話者鼓勵大家提問，所以 (C) 為正確答案。

Now, I'm going to show you the Sales Department, where all of you will be working soon. After that, we will go to the main lobby to take a short break. So all of you, please follow me.

各位早安。我是人事部的莎拉。由於各位現在是我們的員工之一了，我們今天會參觀總公司。參觀期間如果有任何問題，不用猶豫，儘管問我。現在我要帶各位參觀銷售部，不久之後各位就會在此工作。之後我們會到大廳短暫休息。請各位跟我來。

單字　Human Resources Department 人事部
headquarters 總公司　during 在～期間　hesitate 猶豫
Sales Department 銷售部

77. 說話者是誰？

(A) 辦公室員工

(B) 銷售員
(C) 律師
(D) 外國觀光客

解答　(A)

78. 這個談話最有可能在哪裡發生？

(A) 餐廳
(B) 機場
(C) 公司
(D) 購物中心

解答　(C)

79. 聽者有問題的話，應該要做什麼？

(A) 寄電子郵件
(B) 去服務櫃檯
(C) 跟員工談話
(D) 等到參觀結束

解答　(C)

Questions 80-82 refer to the following announcement.
第80-82題請參照以下的公告。

[80] Attention, Grand Department Store shoppers.

▶ 遇到詢問廣播地點的題目時，可以從前半段尋找線索。廣播清楚地提到 Grand Department Store shoppers 這個線索，所以 (C) 為正確答案。

We are having our big anniversary sale this Friday, March 7, through Sunday, March 9. On Friday, you will enjoy steep discounts on spring clothing. On Saturday, bring your used pots and pans, and you will receive various discounts on cooking utensils. Lastly, on Sunday, you will get a wide variety of famous electronic products at a reduced price.
[81] We also remind that we will be closing 1 hour late at 9 p.m. during our anniversary sale.

▶ 廣播提到折扣期間會延後一小時於晚上九點打烊，所以 (B) 為正確答案。

Thank you for shopping at Grand Department Store.
[82] This could be the best chance you've ever had.

▶ 遇到掌握說話者意圖的題目時，要特別注意該句子的前後內容。整個廣播的主要內容都是折扣活動，所以 this 指的是 the anniversary sale。這句的意思是，這會是顧客所體驗過的折扣活動中最棒的一個，由此可推測出這次的折扣活動規模是最大的。(D) 為正確答案。

葛蘭德百貨公司的購物者請注意。從本週五三月七日到週日三月九日，我們將舉辦週年慶大折扣。星期五時，您可以享有春季服飾的大幅折扣。星期六時，若帶二手的鍋碗瓢盆來，您可以享有廚具的各種折扣。

最後，在星期日時，各式各樣的知名電子產品都會降價。同時提醒您在週年慶折扣期間，我們將延後一小時於晚上九點打烊。感謝您在葛蘭德百貨公司購物。這可能會是您目前為止有過的最佳機會。

單字 **attention** 注意 **anniversary** 紀念日 **sale** 折扣，販賣 **through** 透過～，到～為止 **steep** 陡峭的，急遽的 **clothing** 服飾 **bring** 帶來 **pots and pans** 鍋碗瓢盆 **various** 各式各樣的 **cooking utensils** 廚具 **lastly** 最後 **a wide variety of** 各式各樣的 **electronic** 電子的 **reduced** 減少的 **remind** 提醒，使記起 **during** 在～期間 **throw away** 丟棄 **bulk** 大量的 **purchase** 購買 **applicable to** 可以應用於～的 **performance** 表演

80. 公告地點是哪裡？

(A) 禮品店
(B) 書店
(C) 購物中心
(D) 超市

解答 (C)

81. 店家折扣期間會在幾點打烊？

(A) 晚上八點半
(B) 晚上九點
(C) 晚上九點半
(D) 晚上十點

解答 (B)

82. 說話者說「這可能會是您目前為止有過的最佳機會」的意思是什麼？

(A) 大家可以享有大量購物的折扣。
(B) 折扣適用於家具。
(C) 大家可以享受免費的表演。
(D) 即將有規模最大的折扣活動。

解答 (D)

Questions 83-85 refer to the following advertisement.
第83-85題請參照以下的廣告。

Are you planning to upgrade your air-conditioning system for summer? Then Richmond Air Conditioning is for you. [83] We take pride in our professional and friendly staff, and they are ready to help you.

▶ 這是詢問為什麼要選擇該業者的題目，所以要從提到業者優點的部分尋找線索。廣告提到員工專業和親切，所以 (B) 為正確答案。

[84] To make sure your air conditioner is working properly, call us at 555-3949 and arrange for a free consultation offered only this month. Our experts will visit your home to inspect your system and will explain what needs to be done.

▶ 廣告內容為只有本月可以使用免費的到府諮詢服務，檢查自家的冷氣機，所以 (A) 為正確答案。

[85] Are you still hesitating?

▶ 遇到掌握說話者意圖的題目時，要掌握住該句子的前後文。中間要聽者聯絡業者，接受免費的諮詢，所以「您還在猶豫嗎」的意思是：「您還在猶豫聯絡業者這件事嗎」。由此可知說話者的意圖是鼓勵聽者聯絡業者。(C) 為正確答案。

Then just visit our website to check out some comments from our many satisfied users.

您打算升級空調系統以因應夏天嗎？那麼，理查蒙德冷氣機就是為您打造的。我們對我們專業和親切的員工引以為榮，而且他們已經準備好要協助您了。為了確保您的冷氣機正常運作，請撥打555-3949來安排只在本月提供的免費諮詢。我們的專家會到貴府檢查系統，以及說明需要做的事。您還在猶豫嗎？那就拜訪我們的網站，確認我們眾多滿意的用戶評價吧。

單字 **upgrade** 升級 **air-conditioning system** 空調系統 **take pride in** 對～引以為榮 **professional** 專業的 **friendly** 友善的，親切的 **ready** 準備好的 **make sure** 確保 **work** 運作 **properly** 正確地 **arrange** 安排 **consultation** 諮詢 **expert** 專家 **inspect** 檢查 **explain** 說明 **hesitate** 猶豫 **check out** 確認 **location** 地點 **around the clock** 二十四小時，日以繼夜的 **region** 區域 **checkup** 檢查 **next-day** 隔天的 **generous** 慷慨的，大方的 **complimentary** 免費的 **installation** 安裝 **ask for** 要求 **technical** 技術的 **benefit** 好處 **encourage** 鼓勵 **contact** 聯絡 **audience** 聽眾，觀眾 **patronage** 惠顧，資助

83. 根據說話者，為什麼聽者應該選擇這家業者？

(A) 有很多分店。
(B) 有專業的員工。
(C) 二十四小時營業。
(D) 提供該區域最低的價格。

解答 (B)

84. 本月提供什麼特別優惠？

(A) 免費的檢查服務
(B) 隔日寄送的服務
(C) 大方的折扣
(D) 免費安裝

解答 (A)

85. 女子為什麼會說「您還在猶豫嗎」？

(A) 為了向聽者請求技術性協助
(B) 為了提供更多的折扣和好處
(C) 為了鼓勵聽者聯絡業者
(D) 為了感謝聽者的光顧

解答 (C)

Questions 86-88 refer to the following telephone message. 第86-88題請參照以下的電話語音訊息。

Hello, Ms. Rilly. [86]This is Kenny from technical support.
▶ 問候語、發訊者、收訊者、行業類別、職業或公司等資訊會在前半段出現。這是來自技術支援組的電話，所以 (A) 為正確答案。

I just received your email about your computer problems. Actually, several employees in your department have already inquired about a similar problem.
I think [87]there must be something wrong with the new program which I installed.
▶ 問題或情況說明會在訊息的前面／中間出現。這題的出題順序是第二題，所以要預想到答題線索會在中間的部分出現。電腦程式發生了錯誤，所以 (D) 為正確答案。

But you don't have to worry about it. I'll be in your office in twenty minutes. [88]Please be sure you reboot your computer before I reach your office.
▶ 請求題的答題線索，會在後半段的 if 子句或命令句中出現。肯尼要理利女士重新啟動電腦，所以 (D) 為正確答案。

您好，萊利女士。我是技術支援組的肯尼。我剛剛收到您關於電腦問題的電子郵件。其實，貴部門有好幾名員工已經諮詢過類似的問題。我覺得我安裝的新程式應該是哪裡出錯了。不過您不用擔心。我會在二十分鐘內到您的辦公室。請在我到您的辦公室之前重新啟動電腦。

單字 technical support 技術支援 several 幾個的 inquire 諮詢 similar 類似的 install 安裝 reboot 重新啟動，重新運作

86. 說話者在哪裡工作？
(A) 技術支援組
(B) 人事部門
(C) 銷售部門
(D) 行銷部門

解答 (A)

87. 發生什麼事了？
(A) 新員工開始工作。
(B) 文件被偷了。
(C) 一些舊家具被搬走了。
(D) 電腦程式出現錯誤。

解答 (D)

88. 萊利女士被要求做什麼？
(A) 跟其他員工談話
(B) 簽約
(C) 影印文件
(D) 重啟電腦

解答 (D)

Questions 89-91 refer to the following instruction.
第89-91題請參照以下的介紹。

[89/90]I'm very pleased to introduce Mr. James, the new chef at our restaurant.
▶ 歡迎的問候語和主角的介紹會在前半段出現，這個部分就是說明目的的句子。說話者介紹了新主廚詹姆斯，所以第八十九題的正確答案為 (C)，第九十題的正確答案為 (B)。

Most recently, he worked for 10 years at a five-star hotel in New York, and before that, he studied for five years in Paris to learn about international food. I believe that his experience will help us to attract a wide range of customers. [91]We will be having a party to welcome him on Friday. Everyone on the staff is required to attend the party.
▶ 請求或叮嚀事項會在後半段出現。說話者說禮拜五要辦歡迎派對，所以 (A) 為正確答案。

我很高興地介紹我們餐廳的新主廚，詹姆斯先生。他最近在紐約的五星級飯店工作了十年，在這之前，他為了學習國際美食的知識，在巴黎讀了五年的書。我相信他的經驗能幫我們吸引廣泛的客人。我們會在星期五舉辦派對歡迎他。全體員工都要出席派對。

單字 chef 主廚，廚師 five-star hotel 五星級飯店 experience 經驗，經歷 attract 吸引 a wide range of 廣泛的，多樣的

89. 談話的目的是什麼？
(A) 頒獎
(B) 宣傳餐廳
(C) 介紹新員工
(D) 討論新政策

解答 (C)

90. 詹姆斯先生是誰？
(A) 學生
(B) 廚師
(C) 建築師
(D) 技師

解答 (B)

91. 星期五會舉辦什麼？
(A) 歡迎派對
(B) 退休派對
(C) 慶祝公司成立的派對
(D) 開幕典禮

解答 (A)

Questions 92-94 refer to the following excerpt from a meeting and ratings.

第92-94題請參照以下的會議摘錄和評分。

Welcome to our monthly staff meeting. Today, I'd like you to read the article in Fine Cuisine I just distributed. [92] You'll see that the article gave our restaurant five stars in two areas.

▶ 遇到詢問說話者工作地點的題目時，要從前半段尋找線索。說話者明確地提到 our restaurant，所以 (C) 為正確答案。

It's not that surprising that we got a poor rating in the location area.

[93] But I am very disappointed to see that we received a poor mark in the other area, where we got only 2 stars. In order to maintain our successful business, we are going to invest more in the area from now on.

▶ 說話者說預計在獲得兩科星的領域做更多的投資。圖表中得到兩顆星的領域是 Atmosphere，所以 (D) 為正確答案。

[94] So I want you to give some ideas on how to improve our sales in this meeting.

▶ 說話者要求聽者提出改善餐廳銷售的點子，所以將 give some ideas 改述成 make some suggestions 的 (A) 為正確答案。

歡迎來到我們的每月員工會議。今天請各位閱讀我剛才發的《精緻佳餚》裡的文章。各位可以看到，這篇文章針對兩個領域給了我們餐廳五顆星。在地點這個領域收到糟糕的評價並不令人意外。但是看到我們在另一個領域的分數很差，這讓我非常失望，我們只得到兩顆星。為了保持成功的生意，我們從現在起會對這個領域進行更多的投資。所以我希望各位能在本會議上提出如何改善銷售的點子。

單字　monthly 每月的　article 文章　distribute 分發　area 領域，區域　surprising 驚人的　poor 糟糕的，貧乏的　rating 評價　location 位置　disappointed 失望的　mark 分數　the other 其他　in order to 為了～　maintain 保持　successful 成功的　invest 投資　from now on 從現在起　improve 改善　sales 銷售　make a suggestion 提議　complete 完成　paperwork 文書作業　review 檢閱

92. 說話者在哪裡工作？

(A) 博物館
(B) 美容院
(C) 餐廳
(D) 牙醫診所

解答 (C)

93. 請看圖表。說話者想多投資哪個領域？

(A) 顧客服務
(B) 清潔
(C) 地點
(D) 氣氛

評價

顧客服務 ★★★★★
清潔 ★★★★★
地點 ★
氣氛 ★★

解答 (D)

94. 說話者要求聽者做什麼？

(A) 提出建議
(B) 完成文書作業
(C) 看簡報
(D) 檢閱文件

解答 (A)

Questions 95-97 refer to the following telephone message and seating chart.

第95-97題請參照以下的電話語音訊息和座位表。

Hi, Mr. Hiro. This is Roy Harper.

[95] I'm calling about our upcoming marketing seminar. I just booked a meeting room at the Ritz Hotel.

▶ 遇到詢問來電目的的題目時，要從前半段尋找線索。說話者說已經替行銷研討會訂好會議廳了，所以 (B) 為正確答案。

I reserved the business package, which includes a buffet lunch.

[96] It's 30 dollars per person, but they said they will give a 30% discount on rooms for all overnight guests who participate in the event.

▶ 這題問的是飯店提議要做的事。飯店方面表示會給參加活動的過夜客人提供七折的房價，所以 (C) 為正確答案。

As you said, I asked them to set up a round table with 9 chairs put around it.

[97] In addition, they said they will prepare some free coffee and tea right next to the entrance.

▶ 題目中提到的 refreshments（茶點）是改述了 coffee 和 tea 的詞彙。這裡提到免費的飲料會擺在會議廳入口旁邊，透過圖表可以知道 Location A 會是擺放茶點桌的位置，所以 (A) 為正確答案。

Please let me know if there are any problems with this reservation.

嗨，西羅先生。我是羅伊‧哈波。我來電是想討論即將到來的行銷座談會。我剛在瑞茲飯店訂了會議廳。

我訂的是包含自助午餐的商業方案。每人三十美元，不過他說會給參加活動的過夜客人七折的房價。我按照你說的，要求他們擺設一張圓桌配九張椅子。此外，他們說會在入口旁邊準備免費的咖啡和茶。如果有任何關於這個預約的問題，請再跟我說。

單字　upcoming 即將到來的　book 預訂　reserve 預約　reservation 預約　per person 每個人　overnight 過夜的　participate in 參加～　set up 擺設　in addition 此外　prepare 準備　next to 在～旁邊　entrance 入口　venue 地點　seating 座位，席位　arrangement 籌備，安排　refund 退款　penalty 罰金　valet 代客泊車　room rate 房價　refreshments 茶點　place 放置

95. 說話者來電說了什麼？

(A) 行程的變更
(B) 活動地點
(C) 新公司政策
(D) 座位安排

解答　(B)

96. 飯店提出要做什麼？

(A) 沒有罰金的退款
(B) 提供免費的代客泊車服務
(C) 提供房價的折扣
(D) 替訂房升級

解答　(C)

97. 請看圖表。茶點桌子會被擺在哪裡？

(A) A位置
(B) B位置
(C) C位置
(D) D位置

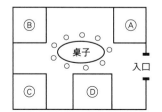

解答　(A)

Questions from 98-100 refer to the following telephone message and chart.

第98-100題請參照以下的電話語音訊息和圖表。

Hello. This is Daphne Berliner from Politico magazine. [98] I'm calling to request an interview with Rebecca Lee.
▶ 來電目的的相關線索，通常會在前半段出現。來電者說來電是想進行採訪，所以 (C) 為正確答案。

I'm currently working on a story about [99] the new hydroelectric power station being built in the White Water River Valley basin.
▶ 說話者說最近在寫跟建設工程有關的報導，所以 (D) 為正確答案。

The project is rather controversial, so [100] I would like to ask

the lead engineer a few questions and hear what she has to say about the situation.
▶ 這題要邊看圖表，邊尋找李女士工作的地點。說話者表示有些問題想問李女士，想知道總工程師的說法，由此可知李女士的工作部門是工程。圖表中的工程部門位於三樓，所以 (B) 為正確答案。

Could you have her call me at 555-9843? I would be grateful if she would agree to speak with me. Thank you.

哈囉。我是《政治》雜誌的達芬·博利納。我來電是想邀請瑞貝卡·李進行採訪。我目前正在撰寫建造於白水河谷流域的水力發電廠的相關報導。這個工程相當有爭議性，所以我想跟總工程師請教幾個問題，以及聽聽看她對這個狀況的說法。可以請您讓她撥打555-9843聯絡我嗎？若她同意跟我談談的話，我會很感激的。謝謝。

單字　request an interview 要求採訪　hydroelectric power station 水力發電廠　basin 流域，盆地　controversial 有爭議的

98. 說話者為什麼來電？

(A) 為了索取文件
(B) 為了規劃會議
(C) 為了安排採訪
(D) 為了重新調整會面時間

解答　(C)

99. 說話者提到了什麼事件？

(A) 即將到來的選舉
(B) 有爭議性的新聞報導
(C) 年度大會
(D) 建設工程

解答　(D)

100. 請看圖表。李女士最有可能在哪裡工作？

(A) 二樓
(B) 三樓
(C) 四樓
(D) 五樓

組織表	
部門	樓層
研發	二樓
工程	三樓
會計	四樓
行銷	五樓

解答　(B)